ATLANTICA:
Stories from the Maritimes and Newfoundland

D1559011

ATLANTICA

Stories from the Maritimes and Newfoundland

Edited by LESLEY CHOYCE

GOOSE LANE

Cover painting: *Couple on Beach* by Alex Colville, 1957, © National Gallery
of Canada, Ottawa, purchased 1959. Reproduced by permission of the artist.
Photo © National Gallery of Canada, Ottawa.
Book design by Julie Scriver.
Printed in Canada by AGMV Marquis.
10 9 8 7 6 5 4 3 2 1

Canadian Cataloguing in Publication Data

Atlantica: stories from the Maritimes and Newfoundland

ISBN 0-86492-309-0

1. Short stories, Canadian (English) — Atlantic Provinces.   2. Canadian fiction
(English) — 20th century. I. Choyce, Lesley, 1951-

PS8329.5.A85A85 2001   C813'.01089715   C2001-901737-5
PR9198.2.A852A85 2001

Published with the financial support of the Canada Council for the Arts,
the Government of Canada through the Book Publishing Industry Development
Program, and the New Brunswick Culture and Sports Secretariat.

Goose Lane Editions
469 King Street
Fredericton, New Brunswick
CANADA E3B 1E5

Contents

Introduction

Atlantica is a region of the imagination, a literary nation unto itself that includes the provinces of Newfoundland, New Brunswick, Prince Edward Island and Nova Scotia, but it is not exclusive to physical geography. It is an ever-changing territory populated with citizens both real and fictional. Like any nation, it is a place of dreams and disappointments, all chronicled by writers who seek to get at the truth through the stories they write. At their best, writers reveal Atlantica to be a complex place of great fortune and great conflict. The greatest fortunes, perhaps, are created by those who work with music and literature and art and those everyday words spoken on the streets. The greatest conflicts are always those formed within the human heart itself.

An anthology of stories from the Atlantic Region must speak with many voices, not a single voice. *Atlantica* is, by its nature, diverse and informed by individuals, not groups; the politics are all personal, the stories all intimate. No one writer speaks for the entire region or even for a province. Every writer speaks from a personal knowledge of his or her world, real and imagined, past or present. For obvious reasons, most of the stories in *Atlantica* are set in Atlantic Canada, although, as always, writers tend to choose whatever array of characters and geography that suits their needs.

The late twentieth and early twenty-first century has been a golden age for Atlantic literature, with fiction that is rich and diverse. No one can say Atlantic literature is shackled to a single theme or issue. One Toronto critic of an Atlantic writer recently said that her novel "did not ring true," that it did not portray the "way it really is" on the Atlantic East Coast. The critic suggested that the book lacked the "gritty rural poverty and despair" that dominates the region. I wouldn't deny for a second that some semblance of "gritty rural poverty" exists within the perimeters of our Atlantica. But I would also insist that the stories told by those who live urban lives, the stories from the suburbs and from the middle class, are equally authentic. There are stories to be told from the malls as well as the wharves.

Atlantic Canadians have a strong literary tradition to build upon: the fiction of Thomas H. Raddall, Lucy Maud Montgomery, Ernest Buckler, Alden Nowlan and Percy Janes, to name just a few. We are by nature an independent, self-reliant people, often argumentative when it comes to standing up for our rights and the rights of our neighbours. In the 1920s, H.S. Congdon was a leading exponent of a Maritime Rights movement designed to improve the lot of Maritimers by achieving maximum political independence from the rest of Canada. He blamed Upper Canadians and Prime Minister Mackenzie King for trying to "have these provinces destroyed." In 1957, downtrodden Maritimers, now joined by Newfoundlanders, still felt victimized by what historian W.S. MacNutt called the "economic conquest" of the region by Central Canada. MacNutt predicted a potential "Atlantic Revolution."

Few voices are lifted in these early years of the new century for an Atlantic Revolution or secession from the rest of Canada, but many of us still feel deeply that we live in a place apart. We are different from the rest of Canada, and our lives are radically distinct from those of the Americans as well. Our stories reflect that distinction. Some of us are descended from generations of Atlantic Canadian stock; others have only recently immigrated. But we all know that *who* we are has something to do with *where* we are.

Recently I was driving along the Atlantic coast and stopped in a village where a man came up to talk to me on the street. I asked him about the town. One of the first things he bragged about was that no one in his town ever locked their doors and that most people always left their keys in their cars. He was divulging this fact to a complete stranger because it was important to him. It meant, not only that people in the community still trusted each other completely, but that they also retained considerable faith in human nature in general.

Although *Atlantica* is long overdue, it has three sustaining predecessors: *Best Maritime Stories* (Formac, 1988), edited by George Peabody, *The Atlantic Anthology* (Ragweed, 1984), edited by Fred Cogswell and *Stories from Atlantic Canada* (Macmillan, 1973), edited by Kent Thompson. All presented a range of enduring talent and were created by editors with a love for the literature of the region. There are a dozen or more writers I would like to have included if there were room. To capture a sense of the developing writers, dip into the pages of periodicals like *The Fiddlehead*, *The Antigonish Review*, *Tickle Ace*, or *The Pottersfield Portfolio*; to get a sense of fiction writers who are on the verge of publishing their first full-length book, read Ian Colford's anthology, *Water Studies* (Pottersfield Press, 1998).

Atlantica includes strong works of fiction by some of our most talented writers, though to call them our "best" writers would be to commit what is a cardinal sin in our region — pretentiousness. Most of the writers in *Atlantica* might be described as "mid-career" and actively writing. This anthology appears at a time when one of our own has achieved great international fame — Alistair MacLeod was awarded the IMPAC Dublin Literary Award, the world's richest literary prize for a single work of fiction, for his powerful novel, *No Great Mischief* (McClelland and Stewart, 1999). MacLeod remains an inspiration to all writers with his tenacity, diligence, hard work and ability to capture in story the rich mix of beauty and sorrow of our lives.

All of the stories herein display a love for the craft of writing and a caring for audience. Missing, perhaps, is any trace of the smug, hip cynicism to be found in some fashionable fiction. Nonetheless, the style and the narratives are provocative and contemporary. Any anthology of this nature is an attempt to say, "Here is where we are now." Carol Bruneau, Lynn Coady, David Adams Richards and Wayne Johnston recreate the opulence that is the contemporary vocabulary and syntax of Atlantic Canada. While embracing techno-jargon and the pop culture lexicon, we have also retained the elegance of the language of our heritage — the poetry of words related to the sea and sailing, the dialect infusion of regional and ethnic language, and the attitudinal slang that evolves from living in a region fiercely independent of the mainstream culture of North America.

At the heart of fiction is conflict: a character with a problem, an issue to be resolved. I'm pleased to say that in the Republic of Atlantica, there are no easy answers. Instead of cliché and stereotype, you will find humour, wisdom, compassion and insight — writers grappling with the essentials of living. While an editor can stand back and suggest such lofty things, most fiction writers will scoff at the notion and tell you that their goal was just to tell a good story. Even so, what happens in the story may not be as important as the way the story is told. In the literary Republic of Atlantica, story remains essential. We cultivate our eccentricities and cherish the way we weave our lives into anecdote, narrative, legend and myth. When speaking the details of our day-to-day occupations fails to lift us from our mortality, we burst into fiction and discover that there are no boundaries to the multi-dimensional region we call home.

LESLEY CHOYCE
Lawrencetown Beach, Nova Scotia
Atlantica
September 1, 2001

Clearances

ALISTAIR MacLEOD

In the early morning he was awakened by the dog's pulling at the Condon's woollen blanket, which was the top covering upon his bed. The blanket was now a sort of yellow-beige although at one time, he thought, it must have been white. The blanket was made from the wool of the sheep he and his wife used to keep and it was now over half a century old. When they used to shear the sheep in the spring they would set aside some of the best fleeces and send them to Condon's Woollen Mill in Charlottetown; and after some months, it seemed miraculously, the box of blankets would arrive. In the corner of each blanket would be a label which read, "William Condon and Sons, Charlottetown, Prince Edward Island," and the Condon's Latin motto, which was *Clementia in Potentia*.

Once, when they were much older, their married son, John, and his wife had taken them on a trip to Prince Edward Island. It was in July and they left Cape Breton on a Friday and came back on Sunday afternoon. This was in the time before the Anne of Green Gables craze and they did not really know what people were supposed to visit on Prince Edward Island, so on Saturday morning they went to look at Condon's Woollen Mill because it was the name that was most familiar to them. And there it sat. He remembered that they had put on their good clothes although they did not know why, and that he had placed his hat upon his knee because of the perspiration that gathered on his hatband and on his brow. They did not get out of their car but merely looked at the woollen mill through the haze of the July heat. Perhaps they had expected to see Mr. Condon or one of his sons busily converting wool into blankets, but they saw nothing. Later his wife was to tell her friends, "We visited

Condon's Woollen Mill on Prince Edward Island," as if they had visited a religious shrine or a monument of historical significance and, he thought, she was probably right.

Sometimes in the early passion of their love they would throw the blanket back over his shoulder toward the foot of the bed, or sometimes it would land on the floor by the bed's side. Later, when their ardour had cooled, he would retrieve it and spread it carefully over his wife's shoulders and his own. His wife always slept on the side of the bed closest to the wall, while he slept on the outside in a protective manner. He was always the last person to go to bed and the first to rise. It was the sleeping pattern followed by his own parents and his grandparents as well.

The blanket had been on them when his wife died; died without a sound or a shudder. He had been talking to her for a while in the early morning darkness. He had on his heavy woollen Stanfield's underwear and she her winter nightgown, and the bed was warm from their mutual heat. At first he had thought she was playing a trick on him by refusing to answer or that she was still sleeping, but then in an instant of full wakefulness he recognized the absence of her regular breathing and reached his hand, in the winter darkness, towards her quiet face. It was cool to his touch because of its exposure to the winter air, but when he grasped her hand which lay beneath the blankets it was still warm and seemed to close around his own. He got up, and, trying not to panic, phoned his married children who lived nearby. At first they seemed sceptical in their early morning grogginess, asking him if he was "sure." Perhaps she was only sleeping more soundly than usual? He noticed the whiteness of his knuckles as he grasped the telephone receiver too tightly, trying to get a grip, not only on the receiver, but on the whole frightening situation. Trying to control his voice and remain calm in delivering a message he did not want to deliver and they did not wish to receive. Finally they seemed convinced, but then he noticed the panic rising in their own voices even as he attempted to control it in his own. He found himself trying to recapture the soothing tone of his early fatherhood, speaking to his married, middle-aged children in a manner he might have used thirty or forty years ago in the face of some childhood disaster. With the coming of the VCR and the microwave and the computer and digital recording and so much more, both he and his wife felt that *they* were becoming the children and he sometimes recognized in his children's voices that adult tone of impatience that might have been his at an earlier time. Sometimes he thought the tone bordered on condescension. But now the roles were suddenly reversed once again. "We will have to do the best we can," he heard himself saying. "I will phone the ambulance and the doctor and the clergyman. It is still early in the morning and most of the world is not yet awake. We will contact the authorities before making any long-distance calls. No, there is no reason to come over here right away. I am fine for a while."

He went back to the bed and pulled the Condon's woollen blanket over her face, but before he did so, he laid his cheek against what he thought of as the stilled beating of her heart.

The previous summer she had been given a variety of multi-coloured pills by the doctor, but they had caused dizziness and drowsiness and a variety of skin eruptions, and she had said, "I wanted to feel better, not worse." One summer's day she opened the screen door and flung all of the pills into the yard. The flock of hens, who always responded to the table scraps flying from the door, raced towards the bounty. Later, five of the most aggressive hens were found dead. "If they did that to the hens," she had said, "what would they do to me?" He had agreed, somewhat reluctantly, to join her in a pact of secrecy. "You don't tell children everything," she had said. "You know that."

It was now ten years later and, of course, he did not think all of these thoughts as the dog pulled at the blanket. Still, they would all come to him later, as they had every day since her death.

He still lived in the house his grandfather had built. It was a large wooden house modelled after the others of its time. It had always appeared quite splendid from the outside but the inside, particularly the upstairs, had remained unfinished for years. For him and his wife it had been their project "to finish it" over the decades of their marriage. They had worked at converting the vast upstairs expanse into individual rooms, drywalling one room and wallpapering another whenever money was available. By the time they had finished the upstairs rooms, the children for whom the rooms had been intended had already begun to leave home; their older daughters going first, as had their aunts, to Boston or Toronto. Now there was only himself and his dog, and when he visited the upstairs rooms they seemed like a museum that he had had a hand in creating.

When he was a child, the vast upstairs contained only one room with a door, where his grandfather slept. The rest had been roughly sectioned into a girls' side and a much smaller boys' side, as he was the only boy.

The sections were separated by a series of worn blankets strung on wires. His parents had slept downstairs in the room he occupied now.

As his parents' only son he had gone into the fishing boat with his father when he was eleven or twelve. His grandfather would go with them, sitting on an overturned bait bucket, chewing and spitting tobacco and rising frequently to attempt urination over the boat's side. The old man, he realized now, probably suffered from prostate trouble but had never in all his life been to a doctor. His grandfather seemed always to understand the weather and the tides and where the fish were, as if operating by private radar. They fished for lobster and haddock and herring and hake. In the summer they set their hereditary salmon net.

They conducted almost all of their lives in Gaelic, as had the previous generations for over one hundred years. But in the years between the two world wars they realized, when selling their cattle or lambs or their catches of fish, that they were disadvantaged by language. He remembered his grandfather growing red in the face beneath his white whiskers as he attempted to deal with the English-speaking buyers. Sending Gaelic words out and receiving English words back; most of the words falling somewhere into the valley of noncomprehension that yawned between them. Across the river the French-speaking Acadians seemed the same, as did the Mi'kmaq to the east. All of them trapped in the beautiful prisons of the languages they loved. "We will have to do better than this," said his grandfather testily. "We will have to learn English. We will have to go forward."

He himself had enlisted in the Second World War to escape what seemed like poverty and, perhaps, as well to seek adventure. Of the latter he found too much and had promised and prayed in the trenches of the dying young that if he were saved he would return home never to leave again. He had prayed in Gaelic, looking across the flames to the German trenches. Prayed in Gaelic because it was more reflexively natural and he felt he could make himself more clearly understood to God in the prayers of his earliest language. It seemed his prayers had been answered and in the subsequent years he was able to repress the most horrific of the memories, choosing to recall only one remarkable week of respite.

In that week, he was on furlough in London and, armed with scraps of paper bearing place names and addresses, he took the train to Glasgow. From Glasgow he took another train and then another. As he switched trains and journeyed farther to the north and to the west, he was aware of the soft sounds of Gaelic around him. At first he was surprised, hearing the language only as what seemed like subliminal whispers, but as the train stopped and started in the small rural stations the Gaelic-speaking population began to intensify and the soft language to dominate. At one station a shepherd got on with his dog. "*Greas ort* (Hurry up)," he said to the dog, and then, "*Dean suidhe* (Sit down)." "*S'e thu fhein a tha tapaidh* (It is yourself that's smart)," he added as the dog sat beside him and looked with interest at the passing moors and mountains.

Sitting there in his Canadian uniform he was aware of his difference and his similarity. Quietly, he took from his pocket the scribbled addresses and bits of information. Haltingly he said to the shepherd "*Ciamar a tha sibh*? (How are you?) *Nach eil e latha breagha a th'ann*? (Isn't it a nice day?)"

Instantly the train coach fell silent and all eyes turned towards him. "*Glé mhath. S'e gu dearbh. Tha e blath agus grianach.* (Very well. Yes, it's sunny and warm)," said the shepherd, and then eyeing his epaulette said in measured English, "You are from Canada? You are from the Clearances?" He uttered both statements in the form of questions and pronounced the word "Clearances" as if it were a place instead of a matter of historical eviction.

"Yes," he replied, "I guess so."

Beyond the train's windows the empty moors stretched to the base of the mist-shrouded mountains. The tumbling white-watered streams cascaded down the mountains' sides and a lonely eagle circled over the stone foundations of a vanished people.

"Long time ago," he said to the shepherd, "since we left for Canada."

"Probably lucky," said the shepherd. "Nothing much here any more."

They were quiet for a time. Each of them alone with his own thoughts.

"Tell me, though," said the shepherd, "is it possible that in Canada you can own and keep your land?"

"Yes," he said, "it is."

"Fancy that," replied the shepherd. He was an older man who reminded him of his father.

During the remainder of the week, he tried to do it all. Aided by the information on the scraps of paper and his new-found friends and friends of friends, he went on boats up the inland lochs and across the straits to the offshore islands which he found inhabited mainly by wind and crying seabirds. He found the crumbled gravestones, some bearing his name, beneath the waist-high bracken. Where once people had lived in their hundreds and their thousands, there now stretched only the un-populated emptiness of the vast estates with their sheep-covered hills or the islands which had become bird sanctuaries or shooting ranges for the well-to-do. He saw himself as the descendant of victims of history and changing economic times, betrayed, perhaps, by politics and poverty as well.

In the evenings around the hospitable whisky bottle he tried to explain the landscape of Cape Breton.

"How would you plant crops amidst all the trees?" inquired his shy hosts.

"Oh, the trees had to be cleared first," he explained. "I guess beginning with my great-great-grandfather. They cut the trees and cleared the land of stones."

"After the war will you go back to these cleared lands?" they asked.

"Yes," he said, "I will go back if I get the chance."

In the late afternoons and early evenings he looked across the western ocean, beyond the point of Ardnamurchan, and tried to visualize Cape Breton and his family at their tasks.

"After the clearances," said his friend the shepherd, "there were not many people left. Most of them were gone to Canada or America or Australia. Most of our young men now are in the war or in Glasgow, some in the south of England. But I am here," he added rolling a stem of heather between his fingers, "working for an estate and looking after sheep that are not my own. But the dog is mine."

It was late in the afternoon of his final day and he stood with the shepherd and his ever-watchful dog observing the distant grazing sheep.

He had loved the beautiful dog and his fellows, admired their highly developed intelligence and their eagerness to please. "I will show you how to breed them," said the shepherd. "They will be with you until the end."

After the war he returned with the determined gratitude of those who had survived. With his father's help he cleared yet another field which extended to the ocean's edge. They invested in better cattle and sheep. His friend, the shepherd, sent him a detailed breeding chart for the development of border collies. He sent for pups and, as they matured, endeavoured to keep them in pens during the breeding season so that they might maintain their specialness. His wife shared all of his enthusiasms and never complained, even when as newlyweds they moved into his father's house. His widowed father was respectful of their privacy and gave them the bedroom he had once shared with his wife and journeyed to the upstairs bedroom which his own father had inhabited as an older man.

"Things will get better," said his father. "We are going forward. Maybe next year we will get a bigger boat."

Sometimes in the evenings he would look across the ocean, imagining he could see the point of Ardnamurchan and beyond. Sometimes he would try to explain the Highland landscape to his father and his wife, though never mentioning his experiences in the trenches.

On this day when he emerged from his bed, he looked out the window at the rooftops of the houses he had helped build for his two sons in what seemed like another lifetime. He had merely given them the land and had not bothered to draw up deeds to decide if and where his property ended and theirs began. They had all been enthusiastic about the younger men's approaching marriages; all of them interested in "going forward" and doing the best they could. He had not thought of boundaries or borders until his second son's death eight years ago. His strong athletic son breaking his neck in a fall from his rooftop while trying to clean his chimney. It had seemed so bizarre and unexpected as he, like most parents, had not expected to outlive his children. There was no will, nor title to the deceased man's house, as none of them had, originally, thought such documentation to be important. In a fit of delayed guilt he had drawn up a deed so that his daughter-in-law might have title to her house and to a block of surrounding land. As he had not anticipated his son's death, neither had he anticipated that his daughter-in-law would fall in love with someone else and move to Halifax, selling her property to a surly summer couple who erected a seven-foot privacy fence and kept a sullen pit bull who paced restlessly behind it. He had not been in the house he helped to build since the changing of the land.

He looked in the direction of his son John's house and felt like calling him up and asking him to visit but felt that it was too early and that the younger man, perhaps, needed to stay in bed. He felt great sympathy for John, whom he saw now as a harried middle-aged man. He had helped him finance a large boat in order to be competitive, but the fish quotas had changed and now the boat sat idle, unable to be of use and unable to be sold. For the past two seasons, John had been in Leamington, Ontario, fishing with the Portuguese fishermen he had once known off the coast of Newfoundland; fishing Lake Erie for pickerel and bass, perch and smelt; sleeping in a small room on Erie Street with a pull-out couch and a hot plate. The crying gulls followed the boats of Lake Erie too, John said, but they were a different species.

He felt sorrow for John and his family, watching the older children become, he thought, more unruly and their mother more tight-lipped and worn down. He tried to be involved without being intrusive, well aware that a father-in-law was not a husband. John was currently home to celebrate his wife's birthday, having driven 1,500 miles without pausing to sleep.

He spoke to the dog in Gaelic as he proceeded to put on his clothes. "*S'e thu fhein a tha tapaidh* (It is yourself that's smart)," he said. He had always spoken to the dog and his predecessors in Gaelic, thinking it somehow preserved a link with his own and his animal's ancestral past. He knew that people were amused and impressed by his "bilingual dog," as they persisted in calling him. He looked now at the dog's eagerness and felt a twinge of sadness for the unused potential the dog represented. He was, he felt, somewhat like John's unused expensive boat, except that he was vitally and intensely alive. He felt somehow that he had denied the dog his heritage by no longer keeping sheep or livestock of any kind, with the exception of a few scattered hens.

Many of the neighbouring farms no longer maintained fences, and the keeping of livestock had become almost impossible. Sometimes the dog would fall into a herding position behind the annoyed hens or even younger grandchildren, stimulated by what he was born to do. He was aware also of the dog's sexual frustration, aware that he was eager to breed and eager to herd and eager to please, always looking at him with his hopeful brown eyes, constantly seeking direction. Sometimes the dog accompanied him in the passenger seat of his pickup truck, looking out the window at the passing landscape, his excitement quickening if he happened to view livestock on the distant hills.

The dog had been with him when he had backed out of the Co-op parking lot into the fender of an approaching car. While assessing the damage he had overheard someone say, "He is too old to be driving. He's always preoccupied. The dog would be a better driver." He had gone for a driver's test and passed it with flying colours. "I wish I had your reflexes," said the examiner.

He and the dog had just gone outside to the morning sun when the pickup truck drove into the yard. Although he was temporarily surprised, he recognized the young driver as one of a series of "clear-cutters" who yearned for the spruce trees that had gradually reclaimed the field he had once cleared as a younger man. He was torn between sympathy for the young clear-cutters, who were ambitious and attempting to make a living, and annoyance at their rapaciousness. They would option a parcel of land and cut everything in sight, taking the valuable logs and pulp and leaving a desolation of stumpage and slashed limbs and inferior wood behind. They worked rapidly with their heavy power equipment, sometimes leaving behind trenches the height of a man. They would pay owners such as himself a percentage of the cordage.

The young man identified himself through a Gaelic patronymic, adding helpfully, "I'm your cousin."

He was annoyed by the young man's brashness, recalling that he had a particular reputation for leaving disaster behind him and not being overly forthright in his cordage payments.

"I may as well log off your wood," he said. "It will be good for you and good for me. May as well log it off before the damn tourists get everything."

The tourists were a sore point with some people. They had begun to flood into what they saw as prime recreation area, marvelling at the pristine water and the unpolluted air. Many of them were from the New England area and an increasing number from Europe. They slept late and often complained about the whine of the clear-cutters' saws. In the summer the clear-cutters often began their work at four in the morning in order to avoid the extremes of the summer's heat. Some of the tourists had taken pictures of the carnage left behind by the clear-cutters and had them published in environmental magazines.

"I'm just trying to make a living," said the young man. "This isn't my recreational area. This is my home. Yours too." He felt a wave of sympathy for the young man, recognizing familiar echoes within his speech.

"What about it?" continued his visitor. "Soon the tourists and the government will have everything. Look what happened to the fishing. Look at your salmon nets. Look at the park to the north. We'll all be living in a wilderness area before we know it."

He was surprised that the young man knew about his salmon nets. For generations they had set the delicate, beautiful nets, and they had been a promise for his sons. They had fished under the threat that the government would eliminate such customs as theirs because it was thought to be more beneficial if their few salmon entered the mainland rivers for the benefit of the summer anglers. And the rumours had proven, eventually, to be true.

He winced also at the thought of "the park." Located farther north, it seemed to travel like a slow-moving glacier, claiming more and more land to be used as hiking trails and wilderness areas, while the families in its path worried about eviction notices.

"People like you and me," said the young man, "are no match for the government and the tourists."

"I'll think about it," he said, trying to be polite in the face of growing frustration.

"Think all you like," said the young man. "Thinking doesn't change facts. Here's my card," he said, offering a white rectangle which he drew from his shirt pocket.

"Never mind the card," he said. "I'll know where to find you."

The truck left in what seemed like a hail of small rocks.

He had wanted to say something like, "When I was your age. I was in the trenches," but it seemed like something an old man might say, and, perhaps, it would not matter very much.

He was still deep in troubled thought and looking at the ground when he became aware of John's approach. He had walked quietly across the field that separated their houses.

"Hello," he said with a start when John appeared suddenly before him. "He wants to buy the wood," he added by way of explaining his recent visitor.

"Yes," said his son, "I recognized the truck."

They were silent for a while, moving the pebbles of the driveway with their shoes, uncomfortable with their private and communal thoughts to the extent that they were almost relieved when the bright new car came rapidly but quietly up the driveway. Both of them recognized the casually dressed real estate salesman, although they did not know the more formally dressed couple in the back seat.

"Hi," said the salesman, stepping out of the car and extending his hand in what seemed like a single motion. "These people are looking for land with ocean frontage," he said. "We have driven forty miles and seen nothing they like as well as yours. They are from Germany," he said, dropping his voice, "but they speak perfect English."

"Oh, it's not for sale," he heard himself say.

"You shouldn't say that until you know what they're willing to pay," said the real estate agent. "They say there is no land like this for sale anywhere in Europe."

He found himself amazed for the second time in the still-early day. He recognized that the real estate agent operated on commission, but was not really certain why that should annoy him.

The German couple emerged from the car. They shook hands very formally. "Nice day," said the man, while his wife smiled pleasantly. "Very nice land," he continued. "Runs down to the ocean?"

"Yes," he said, "runs down to the ocean."

The couple smiled and then walked a few yards away and began to converse in German.

John tapped him on the shoulder and beckoned to him. They, in turn, moved a few yards away, and it took a few seconds before he realized John was talking to him in Gaelic. "You could ask them if they want the wood," he said. "If you were to sell, maybe you could sell the wood first and then the land later."

He was startled by what seemed like a family betrayal. They continued to speak uncomfortably in Gaelic while a short distance away the couple continued to converse in German. The real estate agent stood listlessly between them while the July sun contributed to the perspiration forming on his brow. He looked slightly irritated at being banished to what seemed like a state of unilingual loneliness.

"Ask them if they're interested in the wood," said John, moving toward the real estate agent and speaking in English. He explained his issue in low tones and the real estate agent conveyed the information to the couple, who spoke enthusiastically to one another in German.

The real estate agent came back, seemingly impressed by his role as interpretive negotiator. "They don't care about the wood," he said. "They say it just blocks the view of the ocean. You can do what you want with it. They wouldn't take possession until next spring and you can do anything you want with it until then. They will offer a very good price."

The German gentleman approached and smiled. "Very nice land," he repeated. Then he added, "Not very many people around here."

"No," he heard himself say, "not any more. A lot of them gone to the States. A lot of the younger people gone to Halifax or southern Ontario."

"Oh yes," said the man. "Nice and quiet."

He was aware of the presence of John beside him.

"I'll have to think about it," he said.

"Sure," said the real estate agent and handed him his card, "but the sooner the better."

The Germans smiled and shook his hand. "Very nice land," the man repeated. "Hope to hear from you soon."

They got into the car and waved as they departed.

"Not telling you what to do," said John, "but I've spent almost my whole life here, too. You always said, 'We have to go forward' and 'Things will get better.' Maybe if this worked out I could stay here with my wife and children for a while." He stood uncertainly for a moment, uncomfortable in his father's presence. Finally, he said, "Well, I have to go now. Goodbye. *Sin e ged tha* (That's the way it is)."

"Yes," he said, "goodbye. *Sin e ged tha.*"

"It is going to be hot today," he said to himself, "as hot as that day we visited Condon's Woollen Mill." But then he remembered that Condon's Woollen Mill no longer existed.

He and the dog walked down to his little fishing shanty. He opened the door and took down the beautiful salmon nets from the pegs where they were hung. He went to rub the cork buoys between his fingers, but they crumbled at his touch. He came back out and closed the door. He looked at the land once cleared by his great-great-grandfather and at the field once cleared by himself. The spruce trees had been there and had been cleared and now they were back again. They went and came something like the tide, he thought, although he knew his analogy was incorrect. He looked toward the sea; somewhere out there, miles beyond his vision, he imagined the point of Ardnamurchan and the land which lay beyond. He was at the edge of one continent, he thought, facing the invisible edge of another. He saw himself as a man in a historical documentary, probably, he thought, filmed in black and white.

He felt the dog grow tense beside him and emit a low growl. He turned to see the neighbour's pit bull advancing towards them. The large beast wore a collar covered with pointed studs and moved with deliberate measured steps. Its huge jaws were clenched firmly and strings of saliva hung, like beaded curtains, from its bloated, purple lips.

He glanced at his own dog and saw the black and white fur rising determinedly on its neck. "Both of us are overmatched here," he thought, but he heard his voice say softly in Gaelic, "*S'e thu fhein a tha tapaidh* (It is yourself that's smart)."

He looked up at the sun. It had reached its zenith and was about to decline. He looked down at his dog as it trembled beside him. "Neither of us was born for this," he thought, and then, from a great distance, across the ocean and across the years, he heard the voice of his friend the shepherd. He lowered his right hand until his fingertips touched the bristling hair on the dog's neck. A small gesture to give each other courage. And then they both took a step forward at the same time. As the blood roared in his ears, he heard the voice again, "They will be with you until the end."

The Train Family

JOAN CLARK

Years ago, after I moved from the East to the West Coast, I started dreaming about railway tracks. I didn't have this dream while I was on the tracks, travelling, but only after I had been here a while, after I had bought a townhouse and my children and I had settled ourselves in Victoria. In other words, the dream began when I had reached the end of the line and was looking back from where I'd come.

In my dream I'm in the middle of the country, on the prairies, sleeping in the lower berth with my daughters. While I'm asleep, I'm dreaming the tracks are being taken up as soon as we pass over them. There are workmen in heavy jackets and peaked caps outside in the dark. They're picking up the railway ties, carrying them off to build houses, barns, fences. I see iron rails, loose and disjointed as dinosaur bones, sliding into gullies and ditches. The earth closes over, grows miles of rough prairie grass. You understand I was dreaming about dreaming, that the panic came when I wanted to wake up and couldn't, when I wanted to get off the train to stop the workmen but was immobilized in my berth.

Stan and I have talked about this dream. He says it shows my contrariness, that just when I finally get myself going forward, I want to turn around and go back. He says this jokingly, fondly. It's meant to tease me about being a homebody, of not wanting to spend half my life on the road with him. I tell him the dream has to do with what I left behind. Ever since I drifted out of childhood, one way and another I've been trying to get back. I see childhood as the wellspring of pure being, a source of unbridled self-centredness and joy.

It's true men have been taking up the tracks in places like Catalina,

Port Mouton, Blissfield, you can pick them off across the country. I sometimes wonder what the railway has done with the defunct passenger cars: the dining cars, the club cars, the cabooses. I like to imagine them as being regrouped in a place of their own. Caboosetown. No Petro-Canada or Midas Muffler here. It's strictly residential and pedestrian, the paths named after places where the train no longer goes. I see window boxes, picket fences, shutters. Even when they are on the end of the train, cabooses look as if they were meant to be cottages. In Caboosetown, wheels are out of sight, hidden behind latticework, hollyhocks, shrubbery. Maybe this is a retirement colony, one of those busily humming communities with an active Golden Age club. There are a lot of pastel colours, hearts and flowers, angels stencilled on the walls. One of the passenger cars is a movie theatre. The dining car is, of course, a restaurant. The mayor and the minister use the club car for ceremonies, weddings, burials. Though no one is travelling anywhere that you can see, they are unwilling to give up their rites of passage.

———

When I was thirteen and living in Sydney Mines, Cape Breton, I had a train family. This was during the time when my father was trying to make a go of his rope-making business and there was a lot of uncertainty about money. There were four children in my imaginary family, a boy and a girl, a boy and a girl, in that order. There was a mother and a father. They lived in a caboose. I wasn't in the family. I was their manager. These people were faceless. They had no personalities. They were cardboard figures. Age and sex were important only because of the clothes they wore. I ordered their clothes. I can't remember ordering food; apparently this family never ate. I ordered clothes for two seasons, spring / summer, fall / winter. Sometimes I gave in and allowed a small indulgence: an Easter hat, a corduroy weskit in forest green, a magenta shorty coat. Mostly I was strict with my purchases and stuck to the basics, underwear and pyjamas for everyone, skirts and blouses for the girls, pants and shirts for the boys. The mother wore a cotton-print housedress, the father a windbreaker and trousers in cotton drill. I didn't have a job picked out for the father. He wasn't a coal miner, I knew that much. I wanted to keep his clothes clean. He wasn't a doctor or a dentist. They made more money than I had to spend. Probably I saw him as a telegraph operator, a ticket agent, some job connected with the railway.

At first I parked the caboose in a vacant lot next to the graveyard, above Greener's Cliff. When winter came, I worried about the wind sweeping off the ice in the Gulf of St. Lawrence. I moved the caboose out of town and into the woods, where the family would have enough fuel for their stove and there was shelter from the weather. I had never been inside a caboose and imagined it larger than it was. I saw space for two bedrooms curtained off, girls on one side, boys on the other. The mother and father slept in the living room on a dropback davenport. Each bedroom had a double bed and a chest of drawers: one drawer each for inner wear; one drawer for outer wear. The clothing and furniture were ordered from Eaton's catalogue. I spent a lot of time making lists. When a new catalogue came out, I abandoned my old lists and made up new ones. I was bewitched by newness, by yards of unsullied paper stamped with patches of gaudy colour. The hypnotic instructions drew me in: *move softly in supple rayons, weather the winter in style, spot a winner.* I mooned over the captions in the girls' wear section: *top honours, lively twosome, chipper checks.* I was wooed by matching outfits: a cherry red tam and red mitts, a velveteen hood and velveteen muff, twin sweater sets.

I wanted a matching living-room set. It wasn't as friendly as odds and ends of furniture, but it was more hopeful. A living-room set invited people to sit down together and have serious conversation. It put order and decorum into their lives. I wanted my family to have a wine velour chesterfield with two matching chairs, a walnut coffee table and walnut end tables, all of which I could buy for $183.55. If I bought this set, I would have to get rid of the davenport to make room for the chesterfield. There was something indecent about expecting parents to share a narrow chesterfield. There was no other place inside the caboose for them to sleep. They would have to go. I orphaned the children and revised the budget. The children didn't miss their parents, but I did. They thrived on adversity, but the responsibility of supporting the family on my own put too big a strain on me. I needed a father to bring home the bacon, to balance the budget. There was no question of the mother going out to work. She had to put the wash through the wringer on Mondays. She had to darn socks and scrub the floor.

I took away the matching set and reinstated the parents along with the davenport. Now the family had to make do with leatherette hassocks and an unfinished drop-leaf table with the legs sawn off. In struggling with these decisions, it never occurred to me to shop in the town stores. The management of my family had to be carried out in secrecy, in the privacy of my bedroom. Besides, even in a poor town like Sydney Mines, stores provided more choices than I could handle. As my train family became older and the children outgrew their clothes, more money was required to keep them dressed. I had to have more than a cretonne curtain separating the girls from the boys. I worried how I would manage these changes. I picked at my food, bit my fingernails, lost sleep. I thought about moving my family into a house I passed on my way to school, but it didn't suit. The house was too grand, too prosperous-looking. I was afraid that, if I moved my family into so large a house, my budget would get out of hand. I looked around town for something more modest, a bungalow, a four-room cottage. There were plenty of those in town, but I rejected them all. The truth was I couldn't imagine my family living anywhere but inside the caboose.

——————

My father wasn't at all like the father in the train family. My father didn't like working for anyone else. He ran his own show. He started his rope-making business, his spice-bottling plant, got into real estate, kept a second-hand store, whatever he could do to keep himself employed and support a family. I don't think my father was suited to supporting a family. It put too big a strain on him. He wanted too much for us. I don't think he was suited to business. He had been brought up in a business family in Cape Breton, entrepreneurial Scots stock, people who talked about figures in two colours, red and black, who linked pride with being self-employed, being beholden to no one, marching to your own tune.

My father kept a ledger for his accounts. It was a heavy book with a grey cloth cover, steel rivets on the spine. Inside were alphabetized dividers with green leather tabs embossed in gold. My father carried this ledger with him wherever he went. He kept it in a brown zippered briefcase my mother gave him one Christmas. When business wasn't going well, my father would sit at the dining-room table with the ledger and overhaul his accounting system. He would make new categories, label more pages, move figures from one column to another, so that what had once been a debit would now become a credit. After working for hours at the table, he would stand up and pace the floor, chain-smoking, gesturing with his hands as he explained the new system to my mother, who sat on the chesterfield listening, nodding occasionally. He used words like depreciation, promissory note, accounts receivable. I didn't know what most of these words meant. I wasn't interested in them, but I understood that once again my father had managed to move money from one place to another and, in so doing, had created more than he had before. I knew that he was feeling pleased in the same way my mother did after she rearranged the furniture in the living room. I understood the power of this, that by transforming the room, she had transformed herself. She had made a fresh start, given herself another chance.

Somewhere along the line my mother had chosen to sit on the chesterfield and listen to my father. She could do this because she could see her life stretching ahead of her on the tracks in a way my father couldn't. My mother could have left my father, left all that anxiety and worry about money, gone back to being employed as a nurse, lived on real money. She didn't mind working for someone else. Maybe she was waiting until my sister and I left home. Maybe she left it too long. Maybe she decided leaving would require too much physical and emotional strain, that it would take more energy than she had, that it wasn't worth the effort. My mother wasn't ambitious. She didn't make sweeping gestures. She didn't have a grand design for herself, not like my father, who often spoke of becoming a millionaire. My mother reached a point where she sat back and took my father as he was. This humbled my father, made him grateful. If she thought he was foolhardy or mistaken, she never let on. I think my father had an oversupply of ambition, more than was good for him. His ambition hyped him up, made him uneasy and fretful, difficult to live with.

Stan says he gave up ambition when he resigned from the nine-to-five rat race. Stan lives with me, though it's probably more accurate to say he camps here when he's not somewhere else. Stan is a nomad. A one-time computer man, he speaks of himself as programmed to go forward. He got into computers early, when he owned an advertising agency in the

States. Like me, Stan married young. He spent twenty-five years working ten hours a day to support a wife and five kids. He made hundreds of thousands of dollars, which went out faster than they came in. He says that, when he moved to Canada, he cut up his credit cards, cashed in his stocks, and left the money market for good. Now he does carpentry and key-cutting to support himself.

Recently Stan remodelled a house in Nanaimo, extending the dining room into the garage to make an atrium. Now that he has enough money to keep himself going for three months, he's gone back on the road, this time to Alaska. Stan says he doesn't need a home base. Not me. I need some place to come back to. I've been on two long trips with Stan: one driving to Arkansas and on to Mexico, the other across Canada as far as Newfoundland. Stan is the perfect traveller. He'll eat anything, stop anywhere, go down any road. When we're travelling, I depend on him to make arrangements, solve problems. He knows how to repair tires, make a fire from damp wood, cook bannock over a primus stove. He enjoys luxury, small indulgences. For the Alaskan trip he installed a skylight in the van roof, added a detachable screened porch with a folding table and chairs, built in a compact-disc player. I watched him do all this knowing he was assuming I would come along.

Three weeks ago, I was invited to give a one-woman show in Halifax, in the gallery at The Mount. This is something I've been waiting for. I've been in a dozen group shows, but I've never had a show of my own. The lead time is a scant five months, which means I'm probably a substitute for someone else. I told Stan I wouldn't be going to Alaska, I would be staying home to work. "Bring your buckets of papier-mâché and your paints with you," Stan said. "You can work in the porch while I cook supper and poke around." I told him he'd missed the point, that I didn't want to work on the road. I wanted to be left alone. I wanted to give my full attention to my work, not what was left over. Stan offered to cut the trip from three months to two. I refused the offer. Stan told me I'd been unfair, leading him along, saying I might go. He said I should have told him earlier that I wouldn't be coming so he could have made other arrangements. He packed his clothes, both summer and winter, carried his wood-carving tools and his CDs out to the van. Before he closed the door behind him, he said he might not be back. I didn't watch him go. I didn't wave from the window. I kept my head down, feet rooted to the floor. Stan drove away. I unplugged the phone, went downstairs to the basement, and got to work.

———

Some critics call me a sculptural primitive, others a primitive sculpturalist. They don't know what to do with my work, where to put me. There has been some argument as to whether I'm an artist at all, whether what I do is closer to being craft than an art form. I think of my work as theatre, entertainment. I compose stage sets, think in scenes. I call these scenes set pieces. Some of my set pieces are open. My park-bench series was like that. Grass trailed off at the edges; there were no walls or fences. In the series I'm making for the Halifax show, the set pieces are closed. The scenes take place inside rooms, boxes, cars. *Cow Pad* is a scatological set, an apartment for cows. Everything in the pad is round and brown: rugs, stools, tables, pictures, plates. The wallpaper design looks like Danish pastry. *Loony Bin* is a large box filled with pairs of loons. Some are singing duets, some are in straitjackets, some are in bizarre sexual positions. There is something less serious about an artist who recycles newspaper, perhaps because the materials are cheap. As an art form, papier-mâché is labour intensive. It doesn't require expensive equipment, doesn't need firing, it simply dries out. It takes paint well, is easily turned to caricature and decoration.

I work on a table made from a discarded door, one window over from the washer and dryer. My tools are often kitchen utensils: paring knife, spoon, fork, skewer, basting brush. Most of these tools are used to make patterns, which I paint over in bold colours so they look like fabric designs. This gives my work the kind of folksiness associated with Grandma Moses or a sampler stitched with Home Sweet Home.

For the past week I've been working on a set piece entitled *The Train Family*. This is a circus family of animals who live in a caboose, open at the top. I have already made the figures, painted a caboose a fire-engine red, and printed Barnum & Bailey on both sides in canary yellow. There are four children in this family. The eldest boy is a brown monkey with a hula-hoop, the eldest girl a seal balancing a ball on the end of her nose. The other boy and girl are a poker-playing rhinoceros and a hippo. It takes most of a day to paint these figures. Each article of clothing has its own design. Afterwards there will be the walls and floor to paint, and a matching set of furniture.

I am contented doing this. It is all I want. It is all I need, for the time being. The days pass, a week, then two. When I'm not working in the basement, I drive out to Kost's orchard to check my beehives or I go for a long walk in Beacon Hill Park. In the evenings I bake bread. I read. I visit Em, talk to my children on the phone.

The father in my train family is an elephant. Like Stan, his torso is heavy and thick, his legs short. I have chosen an elephant because he looks bulky and comfortable, the same as Stan. I paint on blue-striped overalls, a railwayman's cap, put the elephant in the caboose window, reading a map. I try not to think what Stan had in mind when he said he would have made other arrangements for the trip. Did he mean asking one of his children along, another woman?

I'm tall for a woman, taller than Stan. The mother in this family is a giraffe, a somnambulant, slow-moving animal who towers over the others in the caboose as she stands on tripod legs, staring backwards, looking down the tracks. As a final touch, I give her a telescope.

At last *The Train Family* is finished and I give it two coats of Varathane. Before I cover it with plastic and store it on a shelf, I spin it around on a lazy Susan, eyeing it critically, checking the view from all directions. I'm pleased and not pleased. It will sell, I know that much, but it's too literal to suit me. There is something conventional and plodding about it. Perhaps there's too much of myself in it. Uneasiness sets in, as it always does after I'm finished something and haven't begun another. This has to do with energy draining away, being transferred to an inert lump of paper and paint. It has to do with seeing the result of my efforts in front of me, diminished, circumscribed. I liked *The Train Family* better when it was inside my head.

Stan could be anywhere between here and Fairbanks. He could have decided to go somewhere else, gone in another direction. There have been no postcards or letters. I know he will eventually return, if only to pick up his wine-making equipment, his Elvis records, his carpentry tools. Now, when I go downstairs to work, I plug in the phone, as a concession.

I think about the last time I was in Toronto visiting my sister. I think about a man and a woman I saw come out of a large brick building and walk along Maitland Street. They were wearing plastic raincoats, belts loose at the back. He was on the outside with his arm around her waist. The other hand held an umbrella over their heads. She had her arm crooked on his shoulder which was a natural way to embrace, given the difference in their heights. She was a good six inches taller than he and had her head tilted sideways to accommodate the umbrella. They looked about the same age, in their mid-thirties. They may have been no more than good friends, but I saw them as lovers. They had that relaxed companionableness and gratitude of people who have recently made love. I saw an aura around them, a soft, intimate light they carried with them outside. I saw a room in a first-floor apartment, a painted radiator. A Hide-A-Bed folded out, blankets on the floor. I saw a man and a woman walking around the room naked, in no hurry to put on their clothes, free from vanity and regret. These are the moments I would miss.

In our years together I have pushed Stan and myself into four or five of these separations, not all of them having to do with travel. I can't remember the details of Stan's other departures, but I could probably have made adjustments, been less perverse. This time I could have gone with Stan as far as Fairbanks or Anchorage and flown back, or done it the other way around. Instead I dug in my heels, proclaimed independence, was careless with my lover and friend. After years of managing a family, I covet aloneness. What some people might call loneliness, I call solitude. I think of my enforced solitude as an air-raid drill, an emergency plan. From time to time I am compelled to go underground and test my survival equipment for what lies ahead. I am always surprised to find it still works. There is something exhilarating about this discovery. I emerge from my bunker rejoicing, grateful for my aliveness, my sense of well-being. Which is why, given the chance, I will probably risk love and do it again.

The Boot

WAYNE JOHNSTON

I am a Newfoundlander. Although up to the age of forty-six I would have been voted by those who knew me to be the man least likely to warrant a biography, one has been written.

My mother believed my birthdate, Christmas Eve, 1900, predestined me for greatness. One day before Christ's birthday. One week before the new century. I was the first of thirteen children, the last of whom was also born on Christmas Eve, when I was twenty-five years old. "Thirteen," my father said, "a luckless number for a luckless brood."

No one called my father Charlie. Everyone called him Smallwood, which he hated because, I think, it reminded him that he was a certain someone's son, not self-created.

After accomplishing the rare feat of graduating from high school, my father set out for Boston with high hopes, but came back destitute. He had then worked for a time at the family boot-and-shoe factory, "working under the old mans' boot," he said, referring to my grandfather and the giant black boot with the name Smallwood written on it, which hung suspended from an iron bar that was bored into the cliffs about ten feet above the water at the entrance to the Narrows, so placed by my grandfather to advertise to illiterate fishermen the existence of Smallwood's Boots, a store and factory on Water Street, where a smaller but otherwise identical boot hung suspended from a pole above the wooden sidewalk.

My father hated every minute he spent beneath the Boot, partly because he had to work under his father, who had predicted he would come back to St. John's from Boston with "his tail between his legs," and partly because he believed business to be the least dignified way on earth to make a living. He found a job that at least allowed him the illusion of self-sufficiency, that of lumber surveyor, his daily task being to walk about the decks of ships docked in the harbour and tote up the amount of wood on board. He walked about the cargo holds, tapping on the cords of wood with what he called his toting pole, which was also so-called because he tied his lunch and other sundries to it and in the morning set out for the waterfront with it on his shoulder. It was a stick of bamboo of even width that he often carried with him even when not toting anything, using it as an oversized walking stick, though, because of his mane of hair and bushy beard, it gave him the look of some staff-wielding prophet.

He spent most of his meagre wages on bottles of cheap West Indian rum, which he bought from foreign sailors on the dock. When drunk, he wandered about the house, cursing and mocking the name of Smallwood. He had been told by someone, or had read somewhere, that the name was from the Anglo-Saxon and meant something like "treeless" or "place where no trees grow."

"It wouldn't have been a bad name for Newfoundland," he said.

He could be flamboyantly eloquent when drunk, especially when the subject of his speeches was himself and the flagrant unfairness of his fate. "I should have stayed in Boston," he said. "What in God's name was it that made me leave that land of plenty to come back to this God-forsaken city, where my livelihood depends on a man famous for nothing but having hung a giant black boot at the entrance to the Narrows?"

We often went to the boot-and-shoe store on Water Street. My grandfather, David Smallwood, was a short, bright-eyed man who always wore a tailcoat at the shop and had a beard so long he had to pull it out of the way to see his pocket watch. He had a scraping, servile way with customers that made me feel a little sorry for him. He was, I suppose, born to keep shop. I could not see my father running about, shoehorn in hand, as my grandfather did, fetching boots for people to try on, kneeling down and holding people's feet while he fitted them for shoes. (My father said the old man's hands always smelled of other people's socks. My mother said his wallet smelled of other people's money.) As a customer walked up and down, trying out a pair of shoes or boots, my grandfather would walk beside him, turning when he turned, stopping when he stopped, in a kind of deferential mimicry, eagerly looking now at the customer's face, now at his feet.

The one thing we were never in need of was boots and shoes, for we got them from Smallwood's for next to nothing. It was easy, in our neighbourhood, to spot the Smallwood children; we were the ones wearing the shabby clothes and the absurdly incongruous new footwear, conspicuously gleaming boots and shoes for which we took no end of teasing, especially as we were all fitted for them at the same time.

My father did not avail himself of the special family discount, but instead went for years wearing the same boots and shoes and, when he absolutely needed new ones, bought them full price at a rival store called Hammond's. It is an image that stays with me, his worn tattered shoes, his patched and repatched knee boots, set aside from ours in the hall, in a token gesture of protest. We were always well-heeled, he was always roughshod; it set him apart from us in a way we children found funny, though my mother said it was disgraceful.

To my father, the Boot was like the hag; he would have boot-ridden dreams that when recounted in the light of day seemed ridiculous, but that often kept him up at night, afraid to go to sleep. He would tell me about them, tell me how he had dreamed about the Narrows boot swaying in the wind on the iron bar like some ominously silent, boot-shaped bell. At other times, it was a boot-shaped headstone.

When one day my mother told him there was "more booze than boots" in those dreams of his, he laughed and went around repeating it all afternoon as if in tribute to her wit. That night, however, he stayed up late and announced that having run out of "the usual combustibles," he was about to burn the boots.

"Go ahead," my mother said, thinking to call his bluff, "there's plenty more where they came from." And so he went ahead and did it, built himself a roaring blaze and kept it going all night long with boots, each time announcing which pair it was he was consigning to the flames. "I'm burning Joe's knee boots now," he said. "Now I'm burning Sadie's shoes, the ones with the brass buckles."

"I'm telling Mr. Smallwood," my mother said, once the smell of burning leather made its way upstairs.

All that remained of our footwear in the morning was a heap of charred soles in the fireplace. He had even burned our slippers, which we left by the stove so they would be warm when we came down for breakfast in the morning. The only boots he had spared were his own, in which he had left for work by the time my mother got up. Luckily, my mother kept her slippers beneath her bed. Slipper-clad in mid-

December, she walked all the way to the store on Water Street. A great bundle of boots and shoes and slippers were delivered to the door that night. My father came home late, penitently close to sober. He took Sadie on his lap and told her he was sorry he had burned her little boots, which got her crying, though she had spent the day quite happily, if house-bound and barefoot, as glad as the rest of us to get a day off from school no matter what the circumstances. He sat all evening on the sofa with a chastened, sheepish air about him, staring into the fire.

My mother was always predicting his imminent disappearance. She had never known a drinker not to run, sooner or later. He would up and leave us someday, she was certain, she said; it would not be long now, she had seen men like him before, he was showing all the signs.

"One of these mornings you'll walk out that door and that will be the last we'll ever see of Charlie Smallwood."

"Maybe I will," my father said, which got us youngsters bawling.

"I won't be pining for you when you're gone," my mother said.

After we went to bed, he would start singing "It's a Long Way to Tipperary" and every other song of departure he could think of.

"I'm leaving, Minnie May, do you hear me? First thing in the morning."

"I hear you," my mother said. "Tipperary, first thing in the morning."

"Twilight and evening bell / and after that the dark / And may there be no sadness of farewell / When I embark."

"There won't be," she said.

When he wasn't drinking, he sat about the house in chastened silence, now and then vowing that he would never drink again. "I've had my last drink, boy," he said to me. "I've learned my lesson. You'll never see Charlie Smallwood take another drink, no sir." He would concoct grandiose money-making schemes and enthral us with stories of how rich we would be someday because of him. He went out briefly on the steps and looked wistfully at the sky above the city as if he had just returned home after years away, as if he knew his sobriety would not last, for he was too far gone to stop for good. The suspense when he was sober was unbearable, for I knew that he would go back to drinking and the only question was when. Truthfully, the house did not seem right when he was sober, nor did he seem to know what to do with himself, but would wander around as though in imitation of sobriety, as if not entirely sure what it was that sober people did.

We were forever changing houses, forever being turfed out of the ones we were renting and moving on to even shabbier establishments. All I remember of the houses we lived in is a succession of attics and basements, for these, whether empty or cluttered with objects discarded by strangers, all seemed unique, whereas the houses themselves all seemed the same once the furniture was put in place, our furniture, which went with us from house to house like parts of our essential selves.

I came home from school one day to find the entire contents of our house on Gower Street piled atop two horse-drawn carts at the reins of which were men I had never seen before. My father was at the reins of a third, in which there were hampers of clothing and the smaller bits of furniture. My mother and the younger children had found what room they could among the clutter. It was the first I knew that we were moving, and I thought I had caught them in the act of leaving me behind. It was all my mother could do to convince me that they had not been about to leave without me, but on the contrary, had been waiting for me and would have waited forever if they had to. "You're my little lad," she whispered to me so the others wouldn't hear. "You're my little lad, you know I wouldn't leave you."

We set out, our little procession of three carts, the horses' hooves clopping on the pavement. I had no idea where we were going, and we drove for so long I began to wonder if we had a destination or if my father was merely looking for a place to pitch the tent my mother had often predicted we would wind up in someday. They sat side by side, my parents, not speaking, though I could tell she was mortified at the spectacle we made, pretending not to notice the stares of strangers as we rode along, a dispossessed, disfavoured family with all its belongings on display.

For some reason, the rule was that the longer we spent in transit, the worse our new house and neighbourhood would be. This day's seemingly unending journey convinced me we had hit rock-bottom and, socially speaking at any rate, I was right. "Where are we going?" I said. They didn't answer. I played a game with myself. I would pick a house I liked the look of up ahead and tell myself we were going there, and when we passed it by, I would pick another house and concentrate on it, as if I could thereby influence our fate. But we passed so many houses that looked promising that I sat down with my back against the cart and closed my eyes.

After a while, I felt the cart begin to climb a slight gradient and stood up to find that we were on the bridge crossing the Waterford River, not far above where it flowed into the harbour. We were headed as far from the favoured part of town as it was possible to go, to the south side, the "Brow" of which my mother often spoke as though it lay in outer darkness. It was the least desirable, most scorned of all the city's neighbourhoods; the home, even those brought up like me had been led to believe, of people one step up from savages, the dregs, the scruff of society, a kind of company town whose single industry was crime. A Pariahville of ironically elevated bottom-dwellers.

We drove along the base of a cliff so steep and high the cart was almost always in the shade, then began to make our way up the winding road that climbed the cliff. Our house, bigger and better maintained than the one we had left, affordable to us because the reputation of the neighbourhood kept prices down, was at the very top, in a saddle-like depression of the ridge on the height of the Brow so that, from the front, you could see St. John's and from the back the open Atlantic. From its front windows, the view of the city we had been deemed unworthy to live in was affrontingly spectacular. You could see all the way from Mundy Pond to Signal Hill, and below the Hill, the Narrows and the cliff-face and the Smallwood boot.

I mention this house over all the others because, perversely, as if to spite the city that had spit them out, my parents wound up buying it. My father called it a double-decker because there was a deck on front and back, which would allow us, he said, to escape whichever of the two prevailing winds was blowing, the onshore east wind, which blew when it was stormy or foggy, and the west wind, which in winter made the sunny days so cold. The east wind would not have been a problem had the house been built in the lee of the Brow, but whoever had chosen the site had preferred the double view to being sheltered from the wind. My mother expressed doubts that a house so situated could withstand the kind of wind we got from time to time, but my father said the fact that the house was twenty years old was proof enough for him that it could.

We had not been living there a week when there was an onshore storm with winds well above hurricane force. As I lay in bed, I felt the whole house shift on its foundation. I imagined it toppling end over end down the Brow and landing upright in the harbour, bobbing about among the ships until someone climbed aboard and found us dead. When a gust subsided, the house would slowly right itself, creaking like a ship whose hull was rolling. Once, the house lurched more than usual and there was the sound of creaking boards. My parents came running from their room and got us out of bed (there was a boys' room and a girls' room, two in one, three in the other) and into our coats and boots, then told us to go back to sleep on the kitchen floor. It was my father who fell asleep, however, for he had gone to bed drunk, and we who kept vigil, wondering how we would survive outside if we had to leave the house.

The larger of the two decks, the one that faced the city, was built out over a steep slope and supported by stilts that forever needed shoring up. The other deck faced the ocean. My father, when he was drinking, whatever the time of year, would pace back and forth through the house from deck to deck after I had gone to bed, sometimes forgetting to shut one door, so that, when he opened the other, the wind tore unimpeded through the house, through the funnel of the corridor that ran from deck to deck, eerily howling and causing all the closed doors in the house (closed by my mother in case this very thing might happen) to rattle loudly in their frames.

My father would go out on the front deck at night and alternately extol and curse the city across the harbour, one minute bemoaning our exile from it and the next bidding it good riddance, one minute declaring it too good for us and the next declaring us too good for it. He had found the ideal stage for his soliloquies of rage and lamentation, for the nearest house on either side of ours was two hundred feet away, out of earshot of even Charlie Smallwood's booming voice. He declaimed from the front deck as though the whole city below and across the way were listening, as though the lights along the Southside Road were footlights and the dark mass of the city the unseen gallery hanging on his every word.

Down below, St. John's looked like the night sky, the lights that marked the neighbourhoods like constellations of stars. There was Buckmaster's Circle, Rawlin's Cross, the Upper Battery, the Lower Battery, Amherst Heights, Waterford Heights, Barter's Hill and Carter's Hill, the Hill of Chips, Monkstown, Cookstown, Rabbittown, all with their distinctive patterns of lights. We had, at one time or another, lived in almost all these neighbourhoods; it was our history down there, spelled out in lights. My father pointed them out to me once in reverse order, counting down to Amherst Heights.

He would roar in triumph when the lights were put out in some house across the way, as if he had done it himself, as if, in the face of his blustering eloquence, the people who occupied the house had admitted their defeat and gone to bed.

As she lay in bed one night, my mother provided a subversive commentary like some parody of exhortation, his mocking congregation of one, undercutting him, deflating him, audibly piping up whenever he paused for breath or gave in to sobbing self-pity and loudly blew his nose into his handkerchief.

"I am a Newfoundlander, but not St. John's born, no, not St. John's born," he said.

"You're a bayman and you always will be," my mother said.

"We're not good enough, it seems," my father said. "We are baymen, a brood of baymen among a sea of townies."

"Shut up and go to sleep," my mother said. "Even baymen have to sleep."

"This is what I must endure," he said. "To be spoken to in this manner by a shameless Huguenot named Minnie May."

On the front deck, he ranted and raved against mankind; his enemies; the Smallwoods; his father; his brother, Fred; my mother. But on the other deck, which faced the sea, the object of his wrath was more obscure. God, Fate, the Boot, the Sea, himself. He started out like he might go on for hours but soon stood staring mutely out to sea, the sea he couldn't see but knew was there, as if the sheer featurelessness of the darkness he faced had stifled him. Stuck for words, he looked up at the sky as if in search of inspiration, planning to let loose his fury on the moon or on the stars, but the sky was almost always dark.

"They should have called it Old Lost Land, not Newfoundland but Old Lost Land," he roared, with a flourish of his hand as though to encompass the whole of the island, then held his arms out to the sky like some ham actor beseeching God's forgiveness.

The Tarot Reader

CAROL BRUNEAU

It's like being married to a spider, I think, watching Michael get into his jogging suit. Curled on my side with the duvet pulled up, I watch him work the black spandex over his knees, his hips, tucking his parts into place. (He never wears underwear with it — that would ruin the effect.) I watch him push his arms in, then his shoulders, like a kid wriggling into a snowsuit, except lithe, almost sinister, his arms and legs shiny black sticks. The villain in a cartoon show. Except that my husband's a good guy — a miracle-worker to his patients, a cardiologist. A heart man.

"See you tonight, Barbara." He bends over my pillow, gives my cheek a quick peck. His lips feel cold though he's just out of the shower. He hovers beside me for a second like a machine idling, silent. Same routine as always, every morning of our seven-year marriage: Michael slipping out at dawn for a five-mile jog before heading to school, now the hospital.

In the days before children he used to run with the dog; I'd wake to the sound of her clicking down the hall, tail thumping the floor to go out, then silence. After a while I'd get up and eat breakfast, glance at the paper before going to work. I had a job in a lab at the university; it paid the rent while Michael studied. Slicing a grapefruit, I'd have to remind myself to save him the other half — that's how much we saw of each other. But in a way it kept things interesting, until the kids came along. Just hang in there, I'd tell myself then: one more year — year after year. Hang in till he's done his residency, and all the waiting will pay off. That's how we managed, though God knows now I wonder if my head was screwed on straight.

He missed our daughter's birth because of exams; the entire pregnancy with our son he was on call. "It'll get better," Michael would whisper, getting up for his jog, when Tyler was colicky and I would fall into bed after walking the baby all night and comforting Amy from nightmares. "It'll get better" — but if it has, it's only as far as the money.

The kids never see him. Till lately it hurt, competing with strangers for his attention. More and more, though, it's like a pain near a filling that just goes away. A habit that fades to relief.

———

"Barbara?" He nudges my shoulder and, as I open my eyes, drives his fingers into the gloves matching his suit. Fingers most at home gloved, I think.

"Yes, *darling*?" It sounds like a slur, though that's not my intention. Michael sighs.

"Got a bypass at four so don't hold dinner. I'll grab something on the way home." It's meant as a concession.

"Oh. Yeah, okay."

Then he's off, a shadow slipping out the front door. I picture him sprinting down the sidewalk past driveways, the contours of his bum neat and taut as his thighs, not an extra ounce anywhere.

"Not bad," his friends say, "for a guy who's forty. When the rest of us, ha-ha, are into relaxed-fit jeans." And they're right. Except for the grey hairs you'd never guess Michael's age as he runs along the street, arms pumping like pistons. Legs scissoring like the pieces in Tyler's Meccano set.

No, I take that back — that implies something humble, endearing. I prefer to imagine Michael in white rubber gloves wielding instruments over an open chest, the roiling red mess of somebody's heart.

I burrow under the covers waiting for the kids to stir, a reason to get up. It's March break, so Amy's off school. I'd stay in bed all day if I could, if there were someone else to make breakfast for her and Tyler, someone to dress and play with them, ferry them around on errands. Of course Michael and I can afford help now. But then where would that leave me?

Marry a doctor, my mother always coached, back when I was at university. Even then her advice was embarrassing, but I fell for it just the same. Finding a guy like Michael, his future gleaming, was like winning the 6/49, gift-wrapped. Nobody said I'd end up like part of the packaging, a doctor's wife. My life, a glossy, perfect bow.

The kids start cooing and chirping from their beds and for a second I picture Michael again. Jogging in the park, his Nikes on the frozen pine needles. Nobody around but other joggers, professionals like him, and people walking dogs — big glossy purebreds, never beagles or mutts, not at this hour. Michael's breath fogs the air beneath the branches. He doesn't slow down. He just nods to these people he sees each morning, nods without smiling, like a Doberman in his spandex suit.

If he misses anyone, I bet it's Beulah, our ancient drooling Lab. Only time I've ever seen him cry, when we had to have her put down. He'd have gone right out and bought a pup, but Tyler just born, and of course there was the expense. "Kids need a dog, and once you got it house-trained, Barb, it'd make great company — you could start taking it for runs!" His less than subtle suggestion I could shed a few pounds, my baby weight. I finally put my foot down: no pets, not until the children are grown. And no early-morning jogs — not for me.

You see, I'm no runner. Not once in our lives together have I gone running with Michael, not even before the kids were born. But I've seen him, sprinting past the shops on Spring Garden Road, giving people a terse little nod. Former patients, some of them. They beam and nudge their wives, and watch him disappear. *A young fella who practises what he preaches*, they say. *Some good shape, that Dr. Easton.*

I get the same from the other wives. *He's incredibly fit*, they cluck, checking to see if I'm wearing the latest from Mills' window; warming slightly if I'm not.

What's your excuse? their eyes say. *He's the one under stress.*

Yeah, stress. So much stress that he hasn't touched me in weeks. But like the long hours, the wrecked weekends, it matters less and less — I've known for a long time that I made a mistake. I suspected it soon after the wedding, when Michael got accepted to med school. And later, when he decided to go on and specialize.

How was I to know? This was a guy who brought his dog to class when we first met, when people still did that. It was fourth-year biology. Beulah was a big golden Lab who slept at Michael's feet. Instead of a collar, she had a red bandanna tied around her neck, cowboy-style. It was Beulah caught my eye first, though I've never been a dog person — I tolerated her lying on his futon and, later, slobbering on the kitchen floor.

The kids come in and start bouncing on the bed, their hair tangled and eyes full of sleep. I pull them under the covers, smell their warmth through flannelette, their icy feet on my shins. I hug them until they squirm and wiggle away, pulling off the duvet. I lie there among the twisted sheets a few minutes longer, concocting lists, lists of things to do, to give the day shape. Dry-cleaning to pick up and groceries, always groceries. Errands, a trip to the mall. Either that or stay home, building toy railroads and making Play-Doh pies.

I dress quickly and make the bed, fluff the shams, adjust the balloon shades. The list in my head grows: pick up Michael's tweed jacket, buy salad things and maybe something nice to eat later (tomorrow?) with Michael once the kids are asleep, a bottle of sparkling wine. At least he still has the occasional glass, though he tells everyone else to stop drinking.

———

Late that afternoon we stumble out of the supermarket into the mall. Tyler is asleep in the stroller, his round blond head lolling like a flower. Amy drags along, kicking at the wheels. I bend to straighten his head, and when I look up there's a woman with yellow hair staring at me. She's sitting at a table with a cardboard sign propped on the dusty cloth. *TAROT. $10.* She smiles hopefully as Amy flops down by the table, whining that she's tired.

"This way," I coax, but Amy clings to the plastic chair.

"It's okay," says the woman, fluffing her bright hair.

Goldilocks, I think. A middle-aged Goldilocks in stretchy blue pants.

"Want yer cards read," she says, "while you're waitin'?"

The only thing unusual about her is her jewellery, heavy turquoise rings on every finger. Apart from that she looks like the women you see going into the Bi-Way, riffling through the lingerie.

"This way and we'll get a treat," I say a little louder as the woman lights a cigarette and props it on the foil ashtray. Amy sinks deeper into the chair.

"Treat yourself!" the woman says. "Can't hurt."

Clenching the cigarette between her lips, she brushes flecks of dandruff from her blue sweater as shoppers pass in droves. There are swarms of teenagers with babies, and women my age, with frizzy perms and wide behinds, men in ball caps trailing after them. Not a soul I'd recognize.

"Not today, thanks." I smile, trying to pry Amy off the seat.

"Tough age," the woman says, her watery eyes grazing the crowd. "I know. I had five. It's okay — she can stay put till someone comes. A customer," she adds coolly.

Feeling guilty, I reach into my purse and slip her a ten. I can't believe I'm doing this: *Mrs. Easton getting her fortune told. In the Spryfield Mall, yet.* Something worse creeps in as I pull Amy, wide-eyed and grumpy, onto my lap: what if she tells Daddy about the woman with the funny rings? He'll have a bird, an absolute bird.

"Well." The woman smiles at Amy and starts unwinding the tasselled scarf from her deck of cards. Her fingers flutter through the deck, light as flies despite the jewellery. Glancing down, she arranges the cards in paths over the black tablecloth. I look at her frothy hair, the pink scalp showing through, her lips grey under the peach lipstick.

"It's late. We really have to be getting" — I shift Amy on my knee. "The kids are starving and I — "

"It don't take long." The woman frowns and shakes her head. "You mustn't let *them* dictate, dear." To Amy she says, "You're all right, aren'tcha honey? Let yer mum have a little break now."

Then, gazing at the card in her palm, she looks at me and snorts.

"You a secretary or somethin'? Good at rubbin' things out, I can see. Ya must be handy with the white-out." She turns over another card. "Keep erasin' an' there'll be nothin' left!"

I look at her, embarrassed. What the hell am I doing here? I have no idea what she's talking about. She gazes at me, her eyes slits now, lined like a tabby cat's.

"So dear, what is it you wanna know?" she sniffs.

"Five minutes and we'll get a treat," I whisper to Amy, my eyes on the cards in front of me.

"Nothing new in your love life, not for the next six months anyways." The woman sighs, sliding the cards over the cloth like bumper cars. She lays one face-down at the top of each path, her hands moving so fast I barely glimpse the pictures on them.

Tell me something I don't know, I almost say.

"Ahh. Your husband is a successful man. A lawyer, maybe," she says, squeezing her eyes shut as if to wring something out. "Excuse me, not a lawyer. A *dentist*! The kinds that does braces!"

I shrug, jostle Amy on my knee.

"Oh yes," the woman coos and starts to cough, covering her mouth with the back of her hand. "Sometimes a person's gotta blot out a few things. You know, like whitin' out typos."

She waits for me to nod. When I don't, she draws another card and flashes it at me. It looks like Narcissus in a loincloth, leaning over a pool.

"The father figure," she says knowingly, taking a deep breath and fidgeting with her waistband. "Your husband is an excellent provider, isn't he?" She speaks in a voice that would melt rock.

"Yes, yes. The perfect husband," I agree hastily, setting Amy on her feet. "Look, it's been *really* interesting — "

The woman seems startled.

"But we haven't got to the good stuff yet," she says, suddenly annoyed. "I promise I won't tell ya anything bad, if that's what you're scared of."

I'm standing now, smoothing the creases from my wool slacks. A catty smile creeps over her face.

"Ohhhh," she sighs. "He's tall and dark. A little on the heavy side. But not fat. No dear, not at all what ya'd call *fat*. Oh yes, yer husband's a handsome one, but you gotta watch what ya feed him now. You'll see." Her voice trails off. "The rest of yer life will be fine, just *lovely*." Abruptly she begins wrapping the cards back up in the scarf and digging through her purse for something. As I start to move away, Amy hanging off the stroller, she passes me a black card with a phone number and *Faye's Fortunes* in gold letters. "No appointment necessary," she calls. "Thanks now and have a nice day."

Out in the parking lot it's almost dark, bright beads of snow falling beneath the floodlights. Tyler wakes up as I slide him into his car seat. He starts to scream, Amy crying over and over that she's starving. I've kept them out much too late.

Trudging up the front steps, juggling Tyler and a bag of groceries, I hear the phone ringing inside.

"Maybe it's Daddy saying he'll be home early after all," I say, jiggling the key. The phone keeps ringing — most people know to let it ring more than ten times. Still, there's a queer aimlessness to it, the sound bouncing brightly through the cold, dark house. I get the door open and the kids flop down in the hallway crying, their noses running. If I had half a brain I'd hire help — someone to have dinner waiting, to straighten the boots in the entry, *to keep house*.

The phone is still ringing but I take my time getting it. Nobody calls this time of day — suicide hour, with small children — nobody but tele-researchers and people selling vacuum cleaners. I stop and hang up my jacket, taking care to brush the wet flecks off the lapels. Then I make my way to the kitchen, the comfort of gleaming tiles, and grab the receiver.

"Yes?" I'm too tired to say hello.

"Mrs. Easton?" It's a man, no one I recognize, but with a voice like Michael's, cool and businesslike.

"Can I help you?"

"Mrs. Easton, I don't mean to alarm you but . . . "

"*Yes?* What is it? Who's calling — ?" I'm exhausted now, kids dragging at my knees, trying to pull me to the floor.

"It's Dr. Easton, I have to tell you he's collapsed . . . "

I wait, holding my breath.

"A colleague of his, coronary . . . happened in the OR. . . . We're running tests. . . . I think you should come as soon as poss —"

"*Michael? What's happened?*"

"Two hours ago, myocardial infarc — We've been trying to reach you . . . it would be best if . . . "

"The patient," I mumble stupidly. "What about his patient?" I'm crouching, the children clinging to me, the mess from Tyler's nose on my neck.

"What?" The voice impatient, incredulous. Then a pause. "It's not the patient we're concerned about. I think you'd better come right away."

Stunned, slow as stones underwater, I watch myself hang up, my hand trembling. Amy and Tyler rolling around at me feet, kicking their wet boots in the air. I squat down, hugging myself tight to keep from shaking. Inside there's a cold, bleached feeling, as though all the blood has drained out. I don't know what to tell the kids — how to say we have to go out again, how to get them back in the car.

At the hospital a nurse offers to watch the kids in the reception area outside intensive care. She takes off their mitts and presses Gummi Bears into their fists. A man I've seen somewhere before emerges through the swinging doors, beckoning. His smile cool, impassive. Dr. Lismore, one of Michael's superiors. His fingers feel dry as leaves when he removes his glove to take my hand.

I don't know my husband at first. His eyes are closed, his face ashen, flat and grey as sand. The lines around his mouth gone. Oxygen whistles through a tube in his nose, fluids drip through others in his wrists, his groin. His chest is wired like a circuit board. His stillness deeper than sleep, but for the faint lift and fall, the slow, steady beep of a monitor, the fine green line snaking across the screen.

My stomach lurches, hollow. I'm shivering, it's so cold in here. Deathly silence enveloped in the noisy bustle — the drone of voices, phones ringing; the harsh buzz of fans, oxygen; equipment bleating. An image flashes of Michael's face, once: smooth, rosy, slick with rain.

"Shh," I hear myself whisper, reaching for his hand. Laying my cheek against its vague warmth, against the icy sheet. "Shh." My face is wet. His fingers move, ever so slightly, in mine.

Someone touches my shoulder, leads me outside. The doctor is waiting, his voice soft but firm. "First twenty-four hours, critical . . . blockage . . . but given Mike's shape . . . minimal damage."

Warning? Reassuring? Whatever his words, they pass right over me, scarcely sink in. As though something inside has taken flight, leaving only the cold white space under my heart.

Homarus Americanus

MAUREEN HULL

Becca steps off the bus, stands back from the huffing diesel fumes and hangs over her toes to unkink her spine. The driver is tossing bags and bundles to the ground; she pulls hers out from the pile and walks through the back door of the depot to find Annie. They stop for a flat of beer and cigarettes on the way home.

"For Ned," says Annie. She pulls off the main road to a twenty-kilometre gravelled curve and slide that fetches up at a two-storey white piazzaed house.

"I didn't realize the house was this big." Becca has seen pictures.

"Big and drafty," says Annie.

In the three years since Annie moved down the coast, Becca has seen her twice, both times in the city. Annie'd tried to explain, Becca'd tried to understand why her bright older sister dropped out of law school to go fishing.

"Come for a visit," she said. "Come and see how I live. It suits me. Odd, but there it is. Serendipity saved me from a life of power, success and financial reward."

Becca's parents think Annie needs de-programming. They've financed this trip, rather niggardly, thinks Becca-the-starving-student. She is to suss out the situation. They are out of patience, waiting for Annie to come back, chastened, to rejoin the real world.

Becca hauls her bag from the truck and stands, looking around. The house has a bit of a lean, the paint is flaking here and there. Tomato seedlings are drinking sunshine in flats on the piazza. A fat tabby on the rail twitches her tail back and forth, trying to provoke the elderly Lab snoozing below. *Dirty-double-dare you*, she purrs; he sighs and pushes his nose deeper into his paws.

The property, on a point on the north side of a small bay, touches the sea on three sides, from the sparkling wavelets in the inner cove to the green glassy slide over the reef by the entrance to the deep blue roll that thunders all the way to Ireland.

Becca quotes her father: "The end of the civilized world as we know it." She is going to be a failure as a spy, but she's known that from the beginning. She doesn't understand Annie's choices, but Annie is a hero. Annie, unlike Becca, seems to know what she wants.

The house is clean but disorderly. Fishing clothes are hung everywhere to dry. Rubber boots take up an entire corner. Plants sprawl and bloom. Becca is introduced to Ned, who came to fish for Tom a few years back and stayed.

"He's family, now."

He has a room off the kitchen, and to please Annie, he smokes outside. Becca has met Tom, in the city, the previous winter.

"You'll be coming with us in the boat." They take it for granted.

"Will it be rough? I'd like to come, but not if it's rough."

"Get seasick?" Ned is sympathetic.

"I don't know. I don't want to find out."

"I used to get sick, when I was young. Puked between every trawl for years."

Becca is aghast. "Why did you go fishing, then?"

"Had no choice, my girl."

By nine everyone else is in bed asleep. Becca reads, quietly turning pages. She wishes she could sleep, her alarm is set for quarter to four, but her body is not convinced she is going to do this foolish thing and it will not shut down. When the alarm trips, she struggles up, feeling as if she's been slugged. Annie has laid out a pile of clothing for her: wool sweaters, long johns, wool socks, even a hat.

"It's cold out on the water in May. You'd be surprised."

The sun bleeds a fine rose line at the horizon, underpaints the cloudbank, then flares up, a bloated peony at the edge of the eastern sea. The water below Becca's enthralled gaze is overlaid with burgundy-blue plumes.

"Look, Annie! Look at the colours!"

"I tried to photograph them at first." Annie smiles. "I still try to paint them. Whenever I get close, I quit in frustration. They look like I've been doing acid. Every colour, every shade imaginable is out here, but it takes a fisherman or a sailor to recognize what I try to do. I've seen the sun rise on a grey flat morning and lie all around the boat like gold coins on a brushed aluminum plate. When I paint it, it looks ridiculous. Everybody knows what the ocean looks like — aquamarine waves with white caps and a little spume for effect. A blue pool with a pretty sunrise leaking across one end. Nothing like that." She points to the purple plumes which have become bloody red entrails scrolling across a wrinkled grey sheet as the sun purges itself of rose-red and turns a brilliant orange.

To the port side is the point, a long, low black smudge with a green eye winking at the wharf's end. Farther down the coast, rising from the pulp mill, is a yellowish-brown cloud. Its visible thickness parallels the depth of the land beneath it as it stretches away to the south. It is a vile sight, an ugly yellow piss stain on a watercolour morning.

Ned gives Becca a job and ongoing commentary.

"Stay away from the rope. Them coils can jump up and twist around your feet, and before you know it, you're overboard. If you're lucky, you smash your head on the way down so you ain't conscious when you start to drown. The traps, see, pull you to the bottom, and we'd never get you back up in time. You'd best stand over here." He hands her a bander and shows her how to pick up and hold a lobster with one hand and band it with the other.

"Them big crushers, now, they'll take a man's finger off." He holds up a crab, carapace smashed, legs dangling, raw meat oozing from its wounds, to show what a big lobster can do if not properly banded. "Lobsters is cannibals."

Tom is using fresh mackerel for bait. Some are small enough to go in the bait bags whole, but most need to be cut in half. Ned is chopping them up with a hatchet, their livers, stomachs and gonads squirting viscous fluids across the cutting board and through the air. The mackerel are mother-of-pearl, abalone, shimmering nacreous tints in pink and green, violet, turquoise and silver. The black markings on their skins spill messages along their flanks. Why cut up chickens, thinks Becca, why read entrails, messy, hot and stinking, why not read mackerel skins? *ROY*, she reads, *ONO*, says the next. How has civilization missed this, she thinks — mackerel are the soothsayers, mackerel are oracles from our watery origins. *LOW*, says one and then the mackerel with the message for her — *JOY*, it proclaims. It's written on a fish, it's real, it's achievable. *AIM*, very good, she approves. *ROD* — who the hell is Rod? She paws through the bait tray, blood and guts flying, she is looking for the one that says *BECCA*.

Ned is chatting again.

"Lobsters ain't just green and red. Look close, you'll see all colours. All except purple. See the blue here, and the green, there's yellow and white and orange. Brown and black, too. Usually more of one or two but most have a little of all them colours. I've got one I'll show you at home, black as midnight unless you shine a bright light hard on 'er. And blue. Got two blue, a market and a canner. Beauties. Got one mostly like vanilla pudding. Pretty near all white. Man offered me a hundred for that one, I told 'im, stick a few more zeros on. You've seen the bright orange ones, like they been new painted, and then there's the regular orangey-green ones. I figure somewheres there's a yellow one. See the colour here under this elbow? That's yellow as butter. Somewheres there's one mostly all this colour. But I never seen it, not yet anyways.

"What you don't want to do, see, is cook 'em. My Jesus, no. Put them in hot water and they turn red, then you ain't got your blue lobster no more, have you? What you do is you bury it in an anthill, see? A big lively anthill, and then you leave 'er there awhile. Oh, I dunno, check it every now and again. The ants clean out all the meat, and it don't get bleached cause the sun can't get at it. When it's ready you take it home and wash it three, four times, and when it's dry you dip it in some Varathane. Couple coats keeps it real good."

"Want to pick a few traps?" Annie calls over. "Watch your feet around the rope."

Gingerly, Becca steps up to the washboard. The traps are lively with creatures. The lobsters are put aside to be measured and banded, the rest go back to the sea. Annie is cartwheeling them over the side. Most are rock crabs, tenacious little buggers that strip the bait and fight your efforts to dislodge them. There are sculpins, poisonous spines erect, bug eyes glaring, whiplashing about in an attempt to impale you. The flatfish slap across the trap floor in a frenzy or hold themselves rigid as kites in a stiff wind. They vibrate and suck air through their tiny mis-shapen mouths. Rockfish are the neurotics of the sea; they thrash and silently wail, wriggle and coil themselves around your arm, squirm and slither until they've braided themselves into the trap walls. One rockfish is a panic attack, two is mass hysteria, three is a ward in nineteenth-century Bedlam.

As she waits for the next trap Becca leans over the edge, watching the crabs flail their way back to the bottom. The sun is behind her, the rays strike the back of her head and seem to radiate from her reflection in all directions. She is wearing a halo, she is a medieval saint. She spreads her arms beatifically over the waves.

"Bless you," she murmurs to all the little souls tumbling below her.

"Heads up." Annie slings another trap along the washboard to be picked and baited.

Now the sun is a quarter way up the sky and has burned off most of the fog. The wind stirs, riffling the water to chops and jags and angles. The sun caroms off tips and edges — diamond fields surround the boat. Annie goes forward and returns wearing sunglasses. She hands Tom a pair and gives one to Becca.

"Put these on and don't stare at the water. It'll give you a hellish headache."

"What about Ned?"

"It don't bother me none. I can't work in 'em. The spray gets all over."

"He'd rather fry his retinas." Annie shakes her head, disapproving.

His answer is to wing a crab past her left ear. Becca notices, though, that the myriad wrinkles around his eyes are drawn close and folded together like a drawstring purse, leaving only a thin slit through which he squints at the world.

The wind is still rising. The boat lifts and falls beneath her. It's getting harder to keep her balance. At Tom's command she goes back in the corner to band and measure lobster, to stay out from underfoot, away from the treacherous rope and flying traps.

Annie and Ned roll and dip from trawl to trawl, picking, baiting, hauling the traps up and shoving them off, all the while maintaining balance and speed, staying out of each other's way. Their feet constantly move around and away from the lethal, snaking coils of rope; they are a pair of dancers from a leftist People's Troupe, performing a washboard *pas de deux*.

But now Becca has a problem.

"I have to pee, guys."

"The head's down below, up near the bow. The green door with oil gear hanging on it. Don't crack your head when the boat rolls."

The green door? She'd thought it was a storage cupboard for life jackets. She'll never get in there with all her clothes on. She struggles out of her jacket and oil pants. The ceiling isn't more than four and a half feet from the floor — deck, she corrects herself. She lowers her jeans and backs in. The bowl is a foot off the floor, her knees are up around her ears. She closes the door, turning her feet sideways so it will shut. At least she can't lose her balance and tumble off. She is a jammed-in sardine. The marine architect responsible for this, she decides, is skinny, short, and perverse. The toilet flushes with a hand pump conveniently located to the rear and just out of reach. She opens the door, gets up, whacks her head and staggers out. By the time she's back on deck, twenty minutes have passed.

"How do you stand it?" she asks Annie.

"I drink as little as possible and try to avoid it altogether. The last boat we had didn't have a head. If you think this is bad, imagine perching on a plastic bucket in a pitching sea. The guys just drop the front of their oil pants and piss over the side. That son-of-a-bitch-Freud wasn't all wrong. I suffer from penis envy every time I'm fishing and have to pee."

At eight-thirty, Tom yells, "Lunch!" and shuts the engine off as Annie ties the buoy line to the stern. Becca is ravenous. For the second time that day she eats. Two sandwiches, three squares, a banana, a scant mouthful of coffee.

"It's barely breakfast time." She's surprised at her appetite.

After lunch the wind blows steady, coming first from the south, gradually shifting to the west. Becca stays in her corner, measuring and banding, filling empty bait bags, rocking and rolling and feeling relieved and a little proud of her placid and well-behaved stomach.

"Not seasick, are you?" Ned is watching.

"Of course not," she says grandly.

"Good girl."

Maybe I'll get a tattoo, she thinks. An anchor on my thigh. Discreet but sexy. She beings to hum "Make and Break Harbour." She loses track of time. The sky clouds over and they sail in and out of ragged patches of fog being slowly blown to the east. Years are passing, she thinks she's drifted into a paranormal ocean and will spend eternity in an ill-fitting rubber suit with bits of old bait in her hair.

Then they are finished, and Tom is turning the boat to sail back to land where, amazingly, the sun still shines and it's barely eleven o'clock in the morning. The trip back is fast and lively. The spray breaks against the side of the cabin and shoots a peal of water droplets along the washboard. Whisk, whoosh. When Becca stands so that the sun is behind her, each spray strings a rainbow, a brief flashing prism, a three-foot-long miracle. She counts, "Fifty-nine, sixty, sixty-one. I will have fantastic luck. This is like a thousand cranes, but better. I will be offered a great summer job for big bucks. My plants will be in bloom when I get back. I will meet a wonderful man who will adore me." She knows this is nonsense but the magic of armloads, boatloads of rainbows makes her giddy. "One hundred and three, one hundred and four, one hundred and five . . . "

The process of selling the fish, buying fresh bait, cleaning and tying up the boat takes longer than Becca expects. Tom and Annie are most particular about getting every little bit of old bait washed off and out of the scuppers.

"If you think it smells bad now, imagine what a couple of weeks of June weather does to old bait stuck in the bilge."

Becca walks the length of the wharf at a pitch and stagger. Attuned to the dip and return of the deck, her legs will not adjust to the implacable solidity of dry land — her feet slam down with spine-jarring finality or paw the air a few inches above ground. It's past noon when they enter the house, shedding boots, damp sweaters and jackets with soggy sleeves. After a quick wash and a few mouthfuls of whatever is quickest to hand, Ned goes off to his room, Tom and Annie go upstairs to nap. Becca is too tired to eat.

"I think I'll just lie on the couch for a bit," she mumbles. There is barely time to pull an afghan to her shoulders before she spirals into a deep black hole.

When consciousness returns, with the jerk of a buoy smacking the surface of the sea, she can't remember who or where she is. Her muscles aren't taking incoming calls and her mind has the uncomplicated focus of a snail working its way through a head of lettuce. She is distracted by the sunlight on the opposite wall, bemused by the shape of the spider plant hanging at the end of the couch. Slowly she gathers herself together, begins a dialogue with her arms and legs.

Annie is in the kitchen making salad.

"Have a beer. A few friends from down the road are coming for supper. We work hard all week and the weather's not often as good as it was today, so on Saturday we like to party a little. It's the only night of the week we can stay up late, at least until the season's over."

Tom comes in from the back yard and rummages in the fridge. He opens a beer and hands it to Annie, raises a questioning arc of brow to Becca.

"I'm fine, thanks." She hoists her bottle.

He snaps the cap off a second beer, takes a long swallow and then stands behind Annie to slowly knead the muscles over and under her shoulder blades. She closes her eyes and leans into it, hands poised above the salad bowl. After a few minutes, he drifts back outdoors to check the cooker.

Annie is busy at the salad again, ripping lettuce and humming, her face serene as sunlight on the cove at slack tide. Becca thinks of her own fumbling, angry need to possess / create love and is ashamed of a flash of sour jealousy.

Three days ago she and Peter went out to dinner, an artificial anniversary, an attempt to pump some blood into their flagging affection for one another. The affair was an awkward contrivance that disintegrated into a clenched quarrel over whose shopping list of wants and needs was not being met. She manages to reduce her graceless emotion to a permissible, wistful envy.

Possibly the worst way to eat lobster is in a restaurant with a split carcass piled with de-shelled, chopped meat drowning in a thick pool of sauce, overpriced wine, smarmy waiters and a room full of strangers sitting too close to your table, chewing, slurping and discussing, too loudly, things you'd rather not hear.

The dinner, she tells Annie, was not a success.

"That's no way to eat lobster," says Annie firmly. "Listen. To eat lobster you need: a sunny yard, a picnic table or two and a lot of newspapers, good friends — say, three to a dozen, three or four lobster and a bottle of wine (or a half-dozen beer) per person. One huge salad in chunks (to be eaten by hand) with a simple oil and vinegar dressing, bread — fresh, crusty, sliced if you prefer, torn in chunks is better for sopping up the melted butter and lobster juice.

"Cook the lobster — you know how to do that, of course. Melt a pound of butter, spread the table with newspapers. Open the papers wide and layer them thick. Put the salad in a couple of big bowls and the butter in a couple of small ones. Put them, with the bread, around the outer edges of the table. Dump the cooked, rinsed lobster in the middle. Open a few beer, pour the wine, begin. The wine should be white, any old favourite that has enough backbone to stand up to the fish. If you pour it into wineglasses, sooner or later it will get knocked over. Don't let convention get in the way of common sense; serve the wine in a good chunk of a glass.

"If you shell lobster in a restaurant they give you clever tools and a stupid bib. You don't need that stuff. Wear an old shirt. Gather up all the kitchen shears, hammers and forks you can find. If you're short on hammers, a clean rock works well.

"Lobster, presented properly, is a feast for all the senses. The tastes are obvious but there is so much more. The aroma of hot lobster dipped in butter, the exclamation of the vinaigrette, the bouquet of the wine, the yeasty exhalation of the beer. The colours, incandescent orange and red, rampant glistening greens, bowls of melted sunlight. The crunch of salad greens, the snick of bottle caps, the crack and smash of carapace yielding up its tender secrets. Taste the wine, don't sip, for pity's sake. Take a mouthful. Roll it around, bathe your taste buds, let your tongue wriggle and squirm in ecstasy. Feel the heat of the sun on your back, the icy flow of beer, the slow, languorous sidle of your tongue tracing a butter dribble's path from elbow to wrist. Eat a little too much."

Becca follows Annie's instructions, particularly the part about eating too much. The sleepy afternoon birds background the blissful sighs, moans, gentle grunts of a crowd that has abandoned language as a medium too thin and cerebral to express their pleasure.

"It's a grand life, if you don't weaken," sighs Ned.

Afterward, Annie dumps the implements into the bowls and leaves them on the counter. Tom tosses the shells onto the compost pile while Ned folds the newspapers with the mess inside and puts that on the compost pile, too. A few of the more particular guests rinse their faces, hands and arms with the garden hose. Becca goes to the house to look for a bigger pair of pants. When she comes out, the drinks are fresh and the group is ambling, lazily, down the paths of old, familiar topics: fishing, politics, music. She pours herself more wine, sits back to sip and listen. Eventually the conversation devolves to a rehash of the Meaning of Everything. With the insouciance of regulars they poke and prod the carcass, ever hopeful of finding some juicy knuckle not yet chewed.

Annie comes over to sit beside her.

"How are you, now?" she asks, brushing Becca's hair back from her forehead.

Becca smiles, ruefully. "Full. Too full, and a little bit smashed. Is your life always this idyllic?"

"Sometimes. Usually not."

"You seem to belong here. On the boat. In this house. At the end of the civilized world."

"Most of the time I feel centred. Here and now, Becca. Here and now is the only place to be."

Above and to Becca's left a hummingbird is draining a bleeding-heart bush. His chest glints, his wings veil the air around him. In the middle of the butter and lobster haze, the ruby flitting among emerald leaves, the lace of lazy voices, crisp swallow of wine, cool breeze on her skin, there is a focus — an elegantly balanced harmony, a perfection of time and space that is the essence of being. She can almost feel it, shimmering above her in the evening air.

Missing Notes

DAVID HELWIG

Hugo heard a voice speaking to him, would have said that although he could make out no words. It was like the insistent noises at night in the empty house. Hugo didn't believe in ghosts of course — he sees a dim figure reflected in the old TV set as he crosses the room, and that's ghost enough for him — and yet when he heard the voice, he would not have said it was imagined.

At the time this took place, he was alone in a church. It was one of those white wooden Prince Edward Island churches, old fashioned carpentry still plumb and level, well kept up and freshly painted, and when he tried the door, it was open, and he walked in. It was the graveyard he'd come to see. He was not, in the usual way of things, interested in genealogy. It had always appeared to him a sad pastime, a hopeless primitive attempt to find a place in the cold universe, but he remembered his Aunt Claire telling him how many of their ancestors were buried in this field, and it was just along the road, and when he arrived here in the cold early spring and carried his bag into Claire's house, he found that he wished, in his solitude and confusion, to make a gesture of filial piety. He walked past the flat white stones set upright in the green grass, perfectly tended, the grass luminous with spring. He didn't care which were the ancestors, only to walk the earth over their bones. Rose was here somewhere. Was that the reason he'd come? He looked past the bare branches of a birch tree, the buds swollen but not yet open, to the frame church, the white walls caught in momentary pale sunlight shining against a background of rolling grey clouds, and he was drawn to it. He didn't expect the door to be open. The light shone down on the plain walls, the waxed wood of the floor and the pews, the pulpit from which some early Scots preacher had made the fierce assertion of John Calvin's creed. In the shed behind the house, he had found a framed motto, handwritten in ornate letters. "Flee from the wrath to come," it said, and below that, "How shall we escape if we neglect so great salvation." He stood still, and the silence sang in his ears until he heard whatever voice it was and looked around him, and there was nothing but the light and the flow of time.

As he walked back down the road to the house, he reflected on the nature of ghosts. The voices of other times, the past, the future, the voice of desire, plain and hidden, the fears which were desire in dark clothing.

2

When he found the small figure in a box in a closet, the figure of a naked woman in dark brown wax, he knew who it must be. The long neck and rather wide flat breasts, the wide hips, it was his cousin Rose. Years before, Rose had gone away to study art. In Boston. Though all that was forgotten when she came back from away, found a government job and settled down to ten years of responsible work. He held the small naked figure, perhaps two feet tall, in his hands and thought that it must be something that Rose herself had made, probably in art school. Had stood in front of a mirror and her fingers had shaped this portrait of her young body. The figure was crudely enough done; Rose had not been greatly talented. He remembered the handmade Christmas cards she would send. The last time he recalled seeing her — on a short visit with his mother, who was recovering from some disaster and wanting the reassurance of her old home — he was nineteen, and they had talked mostly about the early summers they had spent together here.

He looked at the naked figure and tried to remember if he and Rose had once undressed for each other in one of the small back rooms of the house. He thought so. It was perhaps at the end of the summer, when he was about to leave, and they both understood that he might not come back. Two small white bodies shivering and staring at each other with the same blank awareness. Adam and Eve knowing everything, nothing. He left the nude figure in the closet. Already he was too aware that this should have been Rose's house, that it had only been left to him because of her untoward death in that car accident five years before.

It was only later that she began to come to him in the night.

3

After his wife left, Hugo had quit his job as a music teacher in a good private school, left behind the house on Long Island and moved into the city, where he found an apartment in the Village, small and too expensive, but he needed the noise of the city, the traffic, the danger. The living world, city streets, cars and crowds, they made him real. He watched from his window as his neighbours passed by. The print seller going to his small shop. A man with AIDS being walked to the corner by his friend. Hugo would go out in the streets and watch the unemployed young black men playing a fast pickup game of basketball at a small court on a corner at Seventh Avenue. Himself, he could make a living of sorts editing and proof-reading musical texts. When he was in university — in Toronto that was, another stage of his wanderings — he had supported himself as a copyist. He was careful and had a good hand. Now it was done on computers. It was all but unknown for anyone to copy musical text by hand, but there was editorial work to be done, and he did it well.

Until A. announced that she was leaving, he would have said he was a happily married man. As evidence, not once in the fifteen years of teaching music to adolescent girls in a private school had he been indiscreet. A couple of times there had been pupils who were too intense, perhaps a little mad, who made gestures toward him, and each time, at the first hint, he went to the school's principal and explained the situation, made sure that she sent him a memo acknowledging the discussion and the fact that he had initiated it. He was not going to be destroyed by some hysterical girl. Early schooled in the consequences of heedlessness, he was a prudent man. He was proper and respectful, but of course he was not innocent. He had never once touched a student, had never spoken an indiscreet word, but he had looked at the girls who were coming to the peak of their physical beauty, had watched how they moved in the provokingly sexy school uniforms, the short skirts and long socks, long bare legs — Julie Christie in *Doctor Zhivago* — breathed their smell, caught the scent of a new soap or shampoo, had in fact spent all those years in the grip of a fervid erotic awareness. A hungry soul in a garden. His manner was formal, but he was sure that at some level the girls-becoming-women knew him for what he was. His classes were all the better for the soft buzz of desire in the air. A string didn't produce music until it was stretched to a very high tension. Janet Yetkind, the school's art teacher was, he suspected, much like him in this way, a lesbian who adored her disciples but kept a discreet distance. Neither of them ever had discipline problems. During his last week at the school, he had been tempted to go to Janet Yetkind and discuss the matter with her, for old time's sake, more or less, but he decided against it.

A. had brought all this up — speaking in her small, now hardened voice — when she announced she was leaving. She told him that he came home every night smelling of adolescent sex. Well, he might have said but didn't, she came home from the city smelling of ritual slaughter. That was how he thought of it, her work in the brokerage, as bloodshed. A. — well brought up in a decent family — loved danger.

The end was calm. Over the years, A. had borrowed money from him to invest along with her own savings, had even got him to borrow against his salary and pension for her, and she had made herself, if not rich, at least safe from immediate disaster, and she had paid back his loans with interest, given him the house and gone away. He was set to learn the rules of a new life. In the morning he lay in bed, cold and shaking, and he began to suffer from spells of dizziness, nausea. He avoided friends out of the fear of becoming dependent and tiresome, and he managed to silence himself each time he was on the point of telling his students what had happened to him. Every smile troubled him; the freshening girls were no longer mere leaves and flowers. His fingers had wishes, he would find himself beginning a class with tears in his eyes or sitting behind a desk to conceal a persistent erection. He knew that he couldn't go on like this for long, and so he resigned before he got into some pathetic mess.

4

How he came to spend those childhood summers on the Island: his parents had been ahead of their time in their devotion to marital disaster. Back then people stayed married, but not Ralph and Lou. They met during the war. If he had used that phrase — during the war — to his students, they would have been puzzled, but when he was growing up in Canada, even though various wars were to continue, it was understood that there was one real war, in perhaps the way that as a child he'd believed there was one real Santa Claus, in spite of the variety of department stores, each with a jolly old man. During the one real war, Ralph, who was an American sailor, got himself to Halifax where Lou was training to be a nurse, and against all sense, they had got married, Lou pregnant with his older sister, Linda. This was only the first evidence of Ralph's fecklessness. When last heard of, Ralph had been moving to New Mexico with his third wife, and now he was missing, as they said in the one real war, and presumed dead. Hugo owed to his vanished father his early musical education (by the time he was born, his father was closing out a stint as a military bandsman), a very careful nature (who not to be like), and his absurd name. His father wanted to name him after Hoagy Carmichael, his mother didn't, and somehow they compromised on Hugo, which gave Hugo, in spite of his careful nature, a dim view of compromise.

He always tells stories about his childhood in this tone. It is safest to think of it as a kind of comedy, and perhaps true.

It was in periods of maximum disorder that Hugo got shipped to the Island to stay with his mother's sister Claire, and he and Rose, much of an age, had been the closest of friends.

5

He sat down at the piano and his fingers tried to play a Beethoven bagatelle, but there were keys that didn't sound, others out of tune, and the bass had a loose vibration, as if the hammers were at the wrong distance from the strings. There were spaces in the sound and extra rattles, but he played the piece through to the end, with a certain delight in its strangeness. The spaces where the notes were silent made room for other, unwritten notes.

He was a little out of practice — he kept an electronic keyboard in his apartment, but didn't often play it — and his fingers were cold. The old furnace used a lot of oil, and he kept the thermostat turned low. Claire had let things go in the last years, probably in a kind of despair after her daughter's death, though she had taken the trouble to correct her will, leaving him the house — the farmland had been sold off years before — while her small nest egg in Canada Savings Bonds went to the church. She had called him once to tell him what she'd done. He wondered if it was a reward for the fact that he had got here from New York, a long day's exhausting trip by car, to attend Rose's funeral. When he heard the news, he climbed in the car and began to drive. Claire had recognized him instantly when he walked into the church, and she had left a circle of cousins to come to him and take his arm and lead him to the front pew to sit with her.

When Hugo heard from the lawyer in Charlottetown, a letter to tell him that he had inherited the house, he thought that perhaps Claire expected him to move to the Island and live there, and he himself had given the idea some consideration. He was alone now, with nothing to keep him in New York, but the Island had never been his home, not really, and for all his delight in its beauty and the astonishing quiet, the way he could hear the sound of the slightest breeze, the soft piping of a chickadee somewhere far off, it wasn't a place to settle. Certainly not to settle alone.

He had a phone number in his wallet, one of his former students he'd met at a concert at Lincoln Centre. Valerie Quinn: a tall elegant girl who sang alto. When he thought about her, he pictured her in her school uniform, not in the slightly military black outfit she'd worn to the concert. Recently, he'd taken to looking at the personals in the *New York Review of Books*, and the absurdity of that made him feel that it was time he did something about himself. He would sit in Central Park, watching a trim ageing woman riding her rollerblades with narcissistic abandon, and he'd think that she must be one whose brief notice he'd looked at, now just as glad he hadn't answered. Did he have the courage to start over? Dating, all the embarrassment. It was a comic muddle, this business of arranging life. Better to be in the power of the ghosts.

6

He couldn't move, and he wasn't sure whether he was awake or asleep. Something in his throat was preventing him from breathing properly, and the temperature of his body altered from cold to hot every few seconds. There was someone in the house, and yet he could see only empty rooms and doorways. The figure of the wax sculpture drifted through the rooms, in a kind of invisibility that he ought to understand but could not. There was a weight on his body that was concentrated in the impediment to his breathing, and yet he felt that if she would come and lie with him, the weight would be eased. It would melt against him and he would be safe, but it didn't come any further than the edge of his vision. If he could call out her name, she might come to him, but he was too choked to speak.

The house was shaking in the wind, and there was no hope of safety. All he could do was wait, and there was a happy sense of inevitability, he was calm, and the noise of the wind stopped, and everything was perfectly still, while the figure of the naked woman stood in the empty room. Rose was watching him. There was something she had to tell him. Then he heard a voice without speech, and she was gone. The house made a soft groaning, then a clicking in the walls, then there was the creak of a floorboard. This was the natural world calling out for the return of all that had been.

7

He stood at the edge of the garden looking down at the first dark green of the strawberry plants appearing from under the fallen leaves. A cold breeze shook the trees, a wind coming off the water, still the feeling of winter. He had never known the Island in winter. Always summer and sun as the two children sat there between the rows and picked the red berries. When Rose found a very fat juicy berry she would give it to him and watch him crush it in his mouth, the acid sweetness of the juice touching his lips and making them darker red. He couldn't understand this, how she gave him the best ones. At home with his sister Linda, he had to fight for his share of everything, had to make deals to ensure some level of fairness. Linda was fierce and determined and full of anger and cunning, and it took all his cleverness not to be defeated and become her slave, while Rose always liked to see that he had the biggest serving, the sweetest berry.

The strawberry leaves grew in sets of three, like giant serrated clover, dark green against the rusty coloured earth between the rows, and he could feel the heat of the sun through the straw hat that Aunt Claire had given him to wear. He and Rose were putting the fruit in little wooden boxes, and when a box was full, one of them would take it in the house. When there were enough boxes, Aunt Claire would make jam.

The air was full of the sweet smell of the hay that Uncle Evan was cutting in the next field. Rose was giving him another berry, but he shook his head. Her face, pink with the heat of the sun, was freckled over her nose, the eyes, blue of sky or of forget-me-nots, bright and intent, and puzzled.

"Don't you want it?" she said.

"We have to pick them."

"There's lots and lots."

She held the berry out to him again, and he took it, and her face watched with pleasure as he ate it. He lifted his head, and he could see the window of the little back room where he slept, the room next to Rose's, down the low hall under the sloping roof. When he wasn't there, the room was empty, waiting for him, the book he'd been reading spread out on the bed, or so he supposed, not being there to see. He felt someone watching him from that window. Tonight when he went to bed, he'd look out here and see the berry patch.

When they'd finished picking the berries, and maybe helping to make the jam, they were going to play their duet on the piano. He played better than Rose, but her parents said she had to practise anyway. Music was something Ralph did, and Hugo wasn't too impressed with anything Ralph did; if Hugo was clever at music, he might turn out to be like Ralph, who was no damn good. He turned and watched Rose's face under the straw hat, the way she picked the berries, carefully and with concentration, as if they could feel her fingers touching them and must not be frightened. Sometimes he would look, and find she was studying him, and then she would declare that she knew what he was thinking. He didn't dare challenge her to read his mind for fear that her claim might be true. Though he was almost sure that it wasn't. Almost.

Hugo stood alone in the yard, and the cold spring wind made him shiver as he wondered about the truthfulness of his memories. Did those things really happen? Something like that. Certainly all through the season, the two of them would be sent out to pick berries, and they would eat them for dinner and help Aunt Claire make them into jam. Later in the summer, they would drive to the blueberry barrens. It was part of the old life of seasonal necessities, a life that was gone now.

8

How he met A. and came to get married: Hugo was a music student at the University of Toronto, and A. was at Smith, but came to Toronto on a one-year exchange, and they met through a woman friend of his, a church organist who was also a don in the residence. A. was small and had a little voice, a sexy whisper that reminded him of old Marilyn Monroe movies, and her American accent took him back to places he'd lived with Ralph and Lou when they were still together. At that stage Ralph was somewhere with a second wife, and Lou was living in Oshawa and working as a nurse in one of the car plants.

Hugo never had any doubt about who was in charge. A. was. She was a virgin when they met, but it was soon clear that she had selected him to be her first lover, perhaps only because he had a basement room with its own entrance, and that allowed a certain amount of privacy. Maybe it was because his father was an American. He never knew. What he knew was that virginal A. had put herself on the pill, and then put herself in his bed. Hugo had been planning to go down to the Island after his graduation, perhaps to look for work there, someplace safe and familiar, but he and A. couldn't keep their hands off each other, and before he knew it, he was checking on whether he could work in the States. Because his father was American, it was surprisingly easy.

Two years later, they were living in a small apartment on Long Island, and he was teaching while A. was a messenger for a brokerage house, a job she got because her father knew one of the partners.

Hugo can never find the appropriate tone for this story. He's never been quite sure whether it is a comedy and if so just what kind of comedy. Once A. left, he felt that he should be able to see it all in a new light.

9

No matter how he tried, he couldn't get warm. He had two sweaters on and a scarf around his neck. He didn't own long underwear. He stood by the back window of the room where he'd slept when he was a child here, and looked out over the long grass of what had once been a lawn, past the tangle of the overgrown garden, last year's plants with a hint of green here and there. The woods beyond were misted with a light rain. Some of the spruces were dying, the branches bare, covered with fungus of a beautiful grey green. It was a haunted, ruinous landscape now, until the leaves came. The leaves were usually out before he arrived on the Island for the summer, though he was once taken out of school before the end so that Ralph and Lou could set out on some hopeless adventure, as cook and bar manager for a resort in upper New York State, something that wouldn't work out and would give them subjects for argument for the next several months. Linda would be sent to Ralph's mother and Hugo to the Island to Evan and Claire.

His Uncle Evan was a silent man, probably not unkind, it was hard to tell. Hugo knew that Claire and Rose liked having him with them for the summer, and he always hoped that Evan didn't mind. If he'd had a son, rather than a nephew from away, Evan would have started to teach him farming, but as it was, he was left to the women. He read books and played the piano, and on Sunday they all went to church. Hugo listened to the organ and wondered what it would be like to play it, but he could never bring himself to ask Mrs. MacDonald to let him try.

The raindrops were heavier now as they struck the glass of the window and hung there or slid down, and the woods were dim through the wet pane. In the ghostly grey light between the bare trees, he saw something move then disappear behind a tree. He leaned closer to the glass to try and see more clearly, then saw it again, for a moment, a woman, who stood and looked back toward the house, her eyes lifted to the window where he stood as if she could see him there. She was dressed in something dark, like an overcoat, and he couldn't make out her features, and then she walked away into the dead forest.

He was shivering as he waited to see if she would return, but there was no sign of her; there was nothing but the rain and the wet trees, so at last he turned away, went down the narrow back stairs to the kitchen and plugged in the electric kettle he'd bought and made some instant coffee. The fridge didn't seem to be working, so he was using a jar of whitener. With his hands clasped around the cup for warmth, he went into the front room and sat down at the piano. He let his hands settle on it, and he began to invent a little melody that avoided the missing notes, and as he played it through, it seemed to have words, the words of an old hymn he'd been taught in the Sunday school in that white church up the road. The odd tune shaped around the missing notes provoked equally odd harmonies, and when he had it worked out, he took a piece of paper and sketched a version of it so as not to forget. He'd never written music except arrangements for his students to play or sing. As he scribbled the last notes of a figured bass, he heard a knock at the front door. He set aside the piece of paper and went to answer it.

He didn't recognize the woman who stood there facing him. She was his age with thick blond hair and eyes of a very pure blue. There was something familiar about her face. She wore a dark overcoat, and he wondered if she could be the same woman he'd see in the woods behind the house.

"There's something I have to tell you," she said. "It wasn't the way they said at all."

"I beg your pardon?"

"The way she died, it wasn't an accident."

"You mean Rose?"

"You can't believe what people will say. They never understand."

The wind was blowing the cold rain into his face.

"Would you like to come in?" he said.

"No," she said. "One thing leads to another. It's just that you're here, and someone should know."

"Are you talking about Rose? Is that it?"

"You can't believe everything you hear."

"She died in a car accident five years ago. I was here for the funeral."

"What's an accident?" she said, her eyes looking at him and then past him into the house, as if she expected someone to appear from behind him. "Who knows what was going on in her mind, what broken promises?"

"You know about that? She told you something?"

"I've said my piece," she said, turned and walked from the door out the road, turned left and began to walk through the rain, her head down, the water soaking into the cloth of the black overcoat. It was like a coat his mother wore when he was very young, the same colour and cut. There was no sign of any car that might have brought the woman here.

"Can I give you a ride?" he shouted after her, but she didn't look back. He closed the door and went back to the piano, glanced at the notes he had written, but they seemed to make no sense. He decided that he couldn't leave the woman out there getting soaked, ran out to the rented car that was parked beside the house and drove down the road after her, but he couldn't find her.

When he got back to the house, he thought about Rose, the last disastrous seconds before the car hit a bridge abutment, the woman's hints. Broken promises. Hugo didn't make promises.

10

What Hugo sees when he wanders through the house, looking at things: in the front room was an old stuffed chair, upholstered in a dark red fabric that he remembered from visiting the Island as a child. The fabric was heavily worn, the nap rubbed off in places, but the cloth has never worn completely through. It was the chair where Evan would sit after dinner and sometimes doze off for a few minutes. Over the back of the chair was a crocheted cover in an orange and black pattern, colours that clashed painfully with the colour of the chair. Across the room was the small black and white television set, on a long coffee table and beside it a lamp with a glass shade. On the side wall was the old mahogany piano. Behind the front room, the dining room with its heavy oak table and chairs, too big for the space, the glass-fronted cupboard full of dishes against the side wall.

In the kitchen, there was a mark on the linoleum where the old cookstove had sat, and a stovepipe hole in the chimney behind, covered with a round tin cover held in place by light metal springs. The replacement was an electric stove, with various marks and stains from Claire's later days, when she wasn't in any state to keep things in order, not strong enough. The old cupboards were painted in a pale green that had faded towards grey. In places the wallpaper had pulled away from the plaster, and in others it had been glued back but with creases and wrinkles. There was a brown water stain in the shape of a bird. A church calendar hung on the wall near the back door, and on the wall a print of Banff National Park, a lake of an unnatural blue and snow-covered mountains.

On the stairs, the rubber treads were ripped, and at the top the hall was dark. The bulb in the overhead light had burned out and Hugo hadn't changed it. The top of the high veneered chest of drawers in Claire's room was crowded with family pictures. Hugo liked to study the one of Claire and his mother when they were girls, the two of them side by side in front of a farmhouse, an unknown man by the far corner of the house, staring with what might be curiosity or hostility.

The room that had been Rose's, back when they were children, was empty, except for a narrow bed and a small blue-painted chest of drawers with nothing in it. There were pictures of her in Claire's room, but here there was no trace.

Hugo had chosen to sleep in the back room where he always slept when he was sent here for the summer. There were clean sheets on the bed, as if it had been prepared for him, though there were also cardboard boxes filled with folded rags, old copies of *Reader's Digest*, odd dishes. Propped against the wall was the framed motto he had found in the shed. "Flee from the wrath to come. How shall we escape if we neglect so great salvation." The words went round in his head and made as little sense as a nursery rhyme. When he stood at the window, he saw the garden and the woods beyond. Just outside the bedroom door was the narrow stairway that led down to the kitchen.

Hugo knew that to sell the house — and that was the only thing to do — he should empty it out and leave it clean and ready for someone to move in, but he couldn't bring himself to change anything. He camped out here, in the rain and fog of a Maritime spring, as if he were waiting for something, perhaps for the leaves to come out, the wild cherry to blossom, the bed of strawberries to flower and bear fruit.

One evening, in a light rain, he walked up to the churchyard again. He'd found an old slicker of Evan's in the shed, and he wore it, but the rain blew into his face. Still he kept walking, as if he might have an appointment there, as if the anonymous ancestors were waiting for him. When he arrived, he moved among the graves that rose from the wet grass, the old white stone pitted and pocked. He stopped in front of one of the higher stones and read the names. Four children of the family had died within a period of two years, between 1892 and 1894. Little figures lying in the dark, a mother or father watching by the yellowy light of an oil lamp. A child died, a child died, a child died, a child died. What had that woman said? Broken promises. Hugo had no children. Sometimes he thought his students were his substitute, a hundred daughters, he the lustful patriarch watching their growth into beauty. They were gone now. Everything from the past was gone, and as he looked across the grass that shone in the rainy light, he was one of the dead. He saw himself standing here among the graves, as a ghost, a figure trapped between the world and memory, light shining through him, a quiet old man searching the past. Rose's grave was here, but he didn't look for it.

The rain was cold on his face and was soaking into his trousers. As he walked back to the house, he hummed the tune he'd made up, but he couldn't quite remember the words of the hymn that went with it.

11

She had come to him again. In the doorway, with the empty rooms beyond her, and with a promise of peace and calm. The body wavered between a dark figure of wax and a white figure of flesh, and he was confused about which one would come and lie with him, but he longed for her to come, and yet he was unable to move to go to her. He was paralyzed, and the figure did not come to him, yet he thought that she was speaking and that he could almost hear a strange babble of words, or perhaps not words, perhaps only the soft crooning of desire. Then he knew it was not that either, but that she was telling him secrets, offering him knowledge of death.

"Tell me again," he said, though the words were not spoken aloud.

"We are many," she said. "The wax is formed and melted and then remade."

He was at first moved by the words and then disappointed. A formula, motto from a homily.

She was lying on top of him, and her body was soft against his, sighing as she vanished, the wax soaking into his skin, as she became part of his body, and he was heavy and yet full of happiness, then he knew that she would never come back to him.

Hugo is awake, or believes he is, and remembering. The two children are on a beach. The sand of the beach is dark red and above the cliffs are a flatter more intense shade of the same colour, and the grass has a tint that is luminous, blue-green, bright. The sun is shining down, and the two children play at the edge of the cold water, and if they look up, they can look across the choppy water to the horizon, where somewhere northeast across the gulf, Newfoundland rises. Down past the beach, there is a small lighthouse, and a harbour with fishing boats. The two children are building forts or castles out of the sand, and they are dreaming of the future.

"I know what you're thinking," Rose says. "I can tell."

In the morning, he will drive to town and talk to a real estate agent, put the house on the market. There is nothing else to be done. There is nothing to be done with the past except to remember it; or to forget.

12

Hugo back home in New York: he stood by the window of his apartment and watched the man with AIDS being taken along the street by his friend. He moved very slowly now. Soon he was going to die, and his progress, step by step, was an act of fierce determination. His face was all bone, with a thin wrapping of skin. Coming the other way was a young black woman, short, with heavy breasts and hips, and it was as if she might have been deliberately set there as a contrast, an icon of the fullness of flesh.

When Hugo arrived, there were three messages on his answering machine, one from A. to call her if he wanted a good tip on the market, one from a music publisher offering him work, and one from Valerie Quinn, who said she had just heard somewhere that he was living alone — he hadn't explained anything when they met — and suggested they go out for dinner. A tall elegant girl who sang alto and would wish to make him happy. So there it was, three calls: offering him money, work and love.

The two gay men had reached the corner and were coming back. Another, older man had joined them, and Hugo thought that he knew him from somewhere.

13

His last day on the Island, he went back to the graveyard. The church, still dedicated to its imperative, now much-abandoned god, kept up his loyal rearguard, a place to listen for some transcendent voice, a place of decency and vengefulness, shone white at the end of the lane, and he stopped to look toward it through the delicate half open leaves that hung from the drooping branches of an old birch. In the morning he will leave, but this evening he has come along the road, his coat held tight around him to keep off the wind. The house was more than ever full of noises, voices of old wood crying out to him not to abandon them, but it has been put up for sale, and it will go to a stranger, and the old life will be taken from it and some new life will come.

In a week, if the weather is warm, all the leaves will be out. Already there is a dust of pale gold brushed over parts of the woodlands, but now he is in a hurry to be away. He will not wait for the beauty of the leaves. He has come here once to pay homage to the ancestors, and then he will abandon them.

Now he walks between the graves, his eyes catching a name, a date, aware of a hundred stories, untold and lost, and for a moment he has a certain sympathy for the genealogists and their brave, sturdy attempt to salvage a fact or two from the great silence, a chart that puts names in order, abstract and arithmetical, but an act of saving all the same.

A country graveyard reminded you of the old cycle of life, the rebirth of the natural world in the sap that plumped the buds, the grass that would be wild over all this if it hadn't been regularly trimmed. Yet it was trimmed, and the names were cut into each stone, the human record kept in order.

When he looked up, he saw there was another figure in the church-yard, close to the edge under the low branches of a large tree. The man was looking toward him, not so much toward as past him, as if he could see something beyond, and Hugo was convinced that the man could see Rose there, behind him, that she had returned to Hugo from another time, and that she was reading his thoughts. As he studied the man, who was partly hidden by the bare branches, Hugo heard a voice speaking to him, but the words were inapprehensible. All he can hear of the voice is the tone, the lost music.

The Party

HERB CURTIS

Shadrack Nash split Hilda Porter's wood and piled it in the shed, raked the leaves and burned them; he picked apples and banked the house, tore down the abandoned hornets' nest under the veranda floor. Then he tore up the floor itself and repaired it with newer boards he'd found in the barn. He also went to school, practiced the essentials of sexual foreplay with Bamby Dudley and played music with the Whoopsnakes. Every Friday night he went to a dance, and every Saturday night he attended a movie. The movies were either commercial-like films for various states of the USA, starring Elvis Presley, or vampire flicks. After the Elvis movies, he'd walk Bamby home to Swingtown singing "Love Me Tender," "Blue Hawaii," "Wooden Heart," or whatever; after the vampire movies, he'd walk her home glancing frequently over his shoulder, checking to make sure he wasn't being shadowed by the count.

Bob and Elva visited him and asked him to move back home. He decided against it. Brennen Siding had little to offer him, especially now in the late autumn, now that the river was cold and bleak, inhospitable. The reason he gave Bob and Elva for not moving home was school-related. He told them that his studies were improving. Being so close to the school, living with Hilda gave him the privacy and books he needed. Hilda herself, the retired teacher, was helping him with a very difficult grade nine. He did not tell them how much he admired and loved the old woman, nor did he tell them how much he felt she needed him to be there. He didn't have to. Bob and Elva were amazed to see how much the aging process had shrunk Hilda.

"Hilda's failin'," commented Bob after they left and were driving up the Gordon Road in Bob's pickup.

"Somethin' awful altogether," sighed Elva. "I never saw the like of it. Good thing she has Shad with her."

Hilda Porter had lost weight, was getting more wrinkled every day, was becoming more and more absent-minded. There was something else, too. Shad noticed that even though she could remember the past, her childhood fifty years ago, in great detail, at the same time she might forget to eat or brush her teeth; she was frequently forgetting Shad's name. He'd be raking leaves, for instance, and when he came into the house, she'd ask, "What boy is this?"

"It's me. Shad."

"Oh, yes. My darling boy. Shad."

She would sometimes prepare him a lunch, forgetting that they had just eaten an hour ago. Ask her who she taught forty years ago and she'd remember everyone in the class. Ask her who the man was that brought the mail this morning and she would have forgotten.

So they talked mostly about the past.

———

Dryfly Ramsey found himself idle as an autumn hornet, useless as an impotent crone, inactive as a Blackville cop, a sloth on pogey. There is nothing more vulnerable to melancholy than an idle sixteen-year-old. Idleness is exhibit A in the devil's trial; it kicks the winds of inspiration out of life; it is the serpent, the hoop-snake in the garden. Idleness, one of the seven deadly sins, tempts you to experiment with the other six. Bigotry is the brainstorm of an idle mind. Idleness transforms adolescents into irrational brats. God created art, music and literature to combat idleness. When Jesus said, "He that is without sin among you, cast the first stone," He looked about and was grateful that there wasn't an idle teenager in the group.

While Bert Todder, Lindon Tucker, Bob Nash and Dan Brennen teased the Atlantic salmon by placing flies here and there on the deep and dark Dungarvon waters, Dryfly spent the last days of the fishing season wandering aimlessly through the fields, skipping stones on the water, loafing about the house. Late on Friday, he got a ride to Blackville, went to Biff's canteen, sat on a stool and ordered a wiener and chips. A pretty blonde girl was both waitress and cook. She smiled at him pleasantly.

"You're new around here," she said. "What's your name?"

"Dryfly Ramsey."

"I'm Charley."

"Charley?"

"Charley."

Charley smiled. Dryfly liked her.

"Is there a dance tonight?" he asked.

"At the Public Hall. Lyman MacPhee and the Cornpoppers. Where ya from?"

"Ah . . . Renous."

"Where in Renous?"

"Ah . . . " Dryfly didn't know much about Renous, realized he shouldn't have lied. "Brennen Siding," he said, blushing.

"Brennen Siding's up Dungarvon, ain't it?"

"Yeah. The Dungarvon runs into the Renous."

"Oh."

Charley removed the wieners and fries from the grease, served Dryfly. Dryfly paid her, began to eat. Other than Charley, Dryfly was the only person in the canteen. Charley went to the jukebox, put a quarter in the slot and punched some buttons. The Righteous Brothers began to sing "You've Lost That Loving Feeling."

"Where is everybody?" asked Dryfly.

"At the rink, I imagine. The Aces are playing Doaktown."

The clock on the wall read seven. He left the canteen at seven-thirty with an hour and a half to kill before dance time. He considered going to the rink or one of the other canteens, but because he knew so few people in Blackville he decided against it. "No sense hangin' around some place where you don't know anybody," he thought.

With this in mind, he walked up the road and across the bridge to Hilda Porter's. He knocked, entered, found Shad sitting in the kitchen by the table. Hilda sat in a rocking chair by the stove. She was having a cup of tea, had just arisen from a nap.

"G'day, Dry."

"Shad."

"What boy is this?" asked Hilda.

"It's Dryfly Ramsey!" announced Shad.

"Dryfly Ramsey, Dryfly Ramsey . . . now, whose boy might you be?"

79

"Shirley's boy," said Dryfly. "From Brennen Siding."

"Brennen Siding . . . Brennen Siding . . . oh, yes! Dryfly! Sit down, Dryfly!"

Dry sat at the table across from Shad.

"What're you up to?" asked Shad.

"Nothin'. Thought I'd go to the dance. Goin'?"

"Yeah. But I gotta wash my hair, get dressed," said Shad.

Shad left the room. Dryfly waited quietly. Hilda rocked, hummed "Rock of Ages." The runners of her chair squeaked. A clock ticked.

"The Ramseys were very poor," said Hilda. Hilda had forgotten Dryfly was there. She thought she was talking to Shadrack.

"Yeah," said Dryfly, surprised that Hilda would mention such a thing so openly in front of him.

"That Buck left poor Shirley alone with twelve kids. It's a wonder they didn't starve to death."

Dryfly didn't know what to say. He had never known his father, didn't know about his father leaving.

"Buck died," said Dryfly.

"He left long before he died. Couldn't stand the hard times, I guess. They had a son, a young lad that . . . now what happened to him? His name was Bonzie."

"He went for a shit and the crows got him," said Dryfly.

"What's that?"

"Nothin'."

"Oh! Dryfly!"

"It's all right," said Dryfly.

"I'm . . . I'm sorry . . . I . . . I'm . . . "

"You got a nice place here," said Dryfly, changing the subject.

"Oh . . . yes, yes. I don't know what will ever become of it, though."

"Ain't you got a family?"

"All gone, every last one of them. It's good to have Shadrack here."

"Shad's a good lad."

"A good boy. All I have. Should go and straighten things out, look after him in my will."

"Yeah."

"Shad listens to me. He's good around the place, too. Have you ever been alone, Shadrack?"

"My name's Dryfly."

"Dryfly . . . oh, yes, Dryfly. Have you ever been alone, Dryfly?"

"Yeah, I guess so."

"It's no fun being alone . . . having nobody to talk to. I've been alone all my life."

Shad re-entered the kitchen, towelling his hair.

"You should get married," he said to Hilda.

Hilda didn't smile but somehow looked amused.

"All the men I knew were either married or drunk or both."

"A little wine never hurt anyone," said Shad.

Hilda smiled. It was this kind of conversation that had deepened her affection for Shadrack. She liked the way he never talked to her like she was an old lady. Everybody else was so careful about what they said to her.

"I'm too old," she said.

"Never too old for a little lovin'," said Shad. "What you need is to do a little partyin'."

"I haven't been to a party in twenty, thirty years."

"Well, let's have a party!"

"Oh no, Shad! We couldn't do that!"

"Why not? There's you and me and Dryfly."

"Oh Shad! I'm too old for that!"

"I'll get some wine," put in Dryfly, liking what he saw Shad doing. "And you can go get Bamby, Shad."

"Dryfly'll go get some wine, I'll get some people and some potato chips and stuff, and we'll have a party," announced Shad.

"Oh, we couldn't!"

"Why not? You need to have some fun!"

"Oh, but Shad . . . wine, people . . . we . . . "

"You get dressed in your nice black dress, and Dry and me will look after the rest."

"Well . . . well, we couldn't party very late . . . I . . . "

"We'll just stay until you're ready for bed. You just say the word when you're ready for us to go, and we'll get the crowd out of here."

Shadrack was very keen on the idea of having fun with this old woman. He was seeing a light in her eyes he hadn't seen there before.

Hilda went upstairs to change her dress and put on some makeup. For days now she had been feeling very tired. The thought of partying with young people excited her, erased her fatigue, started her adrenalin flowing.

"I'm old," she told herself, "but I'm still alive. I'll have to be careful not to make a fool of myself. They're so young and beautiful . . . "

———

The Whoopsnakes started out as a band with five members, Billy and Milton Bean, Gary Perkins, Shadrack Nash and Dryfly Ramsey. Because of the popularity of guys like Billy, Milton, Gary and Shad, within three months the Whoopsnakes had a following of half the teenage population of the Blackville area. You could always tell a Whoopsnake, or a Whoopsnake follower, by the length of his hair. Before the advent of the Whoopsnakes, the popular boys in the area wore jetboots, trucker's wallets, checkered shirts with the sleeves rolled up two wide folds of the cuff, undone three buttons from the collar. Brylcreem and cars with big engines sold very well before the advent of the Whoopsnakes.

The Beatles conceived, spawned, laid, gave birth to, inspired and influenced the Whoopsnakes. The Beatles were changing the Western world — the Whoopsnakes were changing the Blackville area. A long-haired teenager in Schenectady, New York, Olivehurst, California, or Flamborough Head, England, might be referred to as a hippie or a flower child. In Blackville, if a lad had long hair, he was labelled a Whoopsnake. To a Whoopsnake, it was cool to wear ragged bell-bottomed jeans, flowered shirts and mackinaw coats. The Brylcreemed, jetbooted boys in the big-engined cars were labelled "greasers" by the followers of the Whoopsnakes. Greasers drank Golden Nut and Hermit Sherry. Whoopsnakes and their followers drank Cold Duck.

Shadrack and Dryfly were crossing the bridge on their way to get Cold Duck, potato chips and Bamby when Billy Bean's van pulled up and stopped beside them. The side door slid open and a cloud of nutmeg smoke escaped into the frosty evening.

The van had eight people in it — two girls and six boys. All the boys had long hair, wore ragged jeans.

"G'day, boys!" yelled Billy. "Climb in!"

Shadrack and Dryfly squeezed in, the door slid shut, the van took off.

"Where you lads headed?" asked Gary Perkins.

"Goin' to get Bamby," said Shad.

"Goin' to the dance?"

"Don't know. Later, maybe."

"Why don't you come to Newcastle with us?"

"Can't. Told Bamby I'd pick 'er up."

Shad didn't think it would be very cool to tell these guys that he planned to party for a while with Hilda Porter.

"We'll pick 'er up," said Billy from the driver's seat. "She can come with us."

"What's goin' on in Newcastle?" asked Shad.

"Don't know. We'll check it out," said Billy.

"Want to go to Newcastle, Dry?" asked Shad.

"No . . . what about Hilda?"

"No, I guess we better not," said Shad to Billy.

Someone passed a bottle of Cold Duck to Shad. Shad drank, passed it to Dryfly.

"Take us to the bootleggers, will ya?" said Shad.

They went to the bootleggers. They picked up Bamby. Bamby wanted to go to Newcastle.

"What about Hilda?" Dryfly asked once again.

"She can hardly remember her own name. She's forgotten about the party already," said Shad.

They went to Newcastle.

———

Shad didn't think that Hilda had taken his party talk very seriously, and even if she had, he believed that she would forget what she was doing before she got to her room. Yet he had deceived her and was somewhat preoccupied by the thought of her possibly waiting for his and Dry's return with wine, potato chips and Bamby.

Hilda did not forget.

She went to her room to change her dress, fix her hair — she put on lipstick and rouge, a rhinestone necklace and earrings. Shad had told her to put on her black dress. "Black is not a party colour," she thought and put on a pink silk one instead. Then she went back to the kitchen.

"They might be as much as an hour," she thought. "I should prepare something. I have at least half an hour."

The clock read eight-thirty.

"Sandwiches," she thought. "Elegant little sandwiches."

She went to the cupboard and the pantry, busied herself making Kam and mustard sandwiches, cutting them small for the sake of elegance. She prepared a plate of crackers, dill pickles and baloney. She turned on the radio to CFNB, lit candles and turned out the electric lights. She sat by the table to wait, content with the cozy room.

At nine-thirty, she added some wood to the fire and sat in her rocking chair beside the stove.

"An hour and a half. They've been gone for an hour and a half. I wonder what's keeping them. Hope they didn't get into any trouble. They might not . . . "

Not wanting to concede to any possibility that the boys and Bamby might not show up, she allowed herself to drift into a reverie. She thought of spring, robins plucking worms from freshly turned furrows, fishing trout in the eddy. "I caught an eel once," she thought. "I couldn't bring myself to remove it from the hook. It frightened me. It was like a snake. I ran home. How it must have suffered there on the shore with the hook and line attached. I hated it. Then I hated myself. My greed had lured it to me; its greed urged it to take my hook. It died there on the shore. We all die on one shore or anothert . . . with hooks and lines attached . . . "

The radio announcer said, "Bringing the time around to ten minutes after the hour of ten o'clock. It's Saturday night, and John, Paul, George and Ringo are sending all their loving to you."

The Beatles sang "All My Loving."

"Ten after ten," thought Hilda. "They must have . . . what? No . . . they'll be here. They'll come, surely . . . I hope they come soon — the sandwiches will dry out. I'm getting tired. I'm too old for this anyway. At least my body is old . . . I should be in bed."

"You old, stupid, undignified fool!" she said aloud, sighed, stood and walked to the window. The breath of her passing disturbed the flame of the candle. The rhinestones glittered. She gazed out at the moonlit, snow-clad yard. What she took to be Venus shone above the barn. She swallowed. Her throat felt sore, irritated by the battle raging there — she was trying not to weep.

The lights of a car flickered on some trees across the road.

"Maybe they hitched a ride," she thought. "Maybe that's them coming."

But the car came and went, as did several more before she turned away from the window.

Hilda was certain now that nobody was coming, and the reality confused her somewhat, tossed her between anger and sorrow, dignity and humility, hate and self-pity.

"I'm too old to have to deal with such unchained sentiments," she thought. "Too old and too tired to be sitting here hoping beyond hope. At what point does one give up hope? What is hope? Is hope just another word for fear? Hope is a dream. Hope is a delusion . . . the state of mourners. When one stops hoping, one still hopes. Oh, Shad, Shad, Shad. Can one persevere without hope? Maybe Shad was just being nice to an old woman, having fun. Maybe he didn't have a party in mind at all. And then again, maybe he did and something happened. Maybe he will still show up. He always does come home, sooner or later. How's that for hope? To give up hope and wants and needs is to be God. I'm old . . . but what's the adage? The fruit ripens as the shadows lengthen?"

"I'll make some tea," she thought. "Tea will keep me awake. Not that I'm intending to wait all night, mind you. But I have nothing else to do, to wait for, to hope for. I'll give him another hour."

———

The Whoopsnakes went to Newcastle, drove around for an hour and returned to Blackville in time to catch the last half of the dance.

"I don't think I want to go to the dance," said Shad. "Let's go to my place for a while. I'll get a bottle of wine."

"Your place? What's goin' on at your place?" said Bamby. Bamby was chewing gum. Shad noticed that she continued to do so, even as she spoke.

"Nothin'," said Shad. "I just sorta told Hilda I'd . . . ah . . . be home early."

"She's not your mother."

"I know, but . . . "

"We're goin' to the dance!" Bamby had spoken her mind. She had snapped her gum for effect.

Shad sighed. He and Dryfly and Bamby were standing on the street outside the Public Hall. The rest of the gang had already entered.

"Well, you two can go to the dance," said Shad. "I'm goin' to the boot-leggers."

"But aren't you comin' to the dance?" asked Bamby.

85

"Yeah. I'll get somethin' to drink and come back. No sense you walkin' to the bootleggers."

"But you won't come back!"

"I'll be back!" Shad swung to Dryfly. "You comin'?"

"Well, ah, yeah, sure."

"You'd better come back," Bamby was saying as they walked away.

At the bootleggers they found out it was eleven o'clock. They each bought a bottle of Cold Duck and headed for Hilda's.

"Hilda gonna be up?" asked Dryfly.

"Don't matter. I can't spend another minute with Bamby, she's gonna drive me crazy. If Hilda's not up, we'll drink this wine, anyway. We'll have a say, you can stay the night. You'll never get a drive back to Brennen Siding tonight."

"Hilda won't mind?"

"She won't care."

As they approached Hilda's, they could not see the candlelight in the kitchen. The house appeared to be in darkness.

"Funny," said Shad. "She usually leaves a light on for me."

"Maybe she's mad at us for not comin' back earlier," said Dryfly.

"No . . . hope not."

They hurried up to the door, quietly opened it and stepped inside.

Across the hall they saw the candlelit doorway, the kitchen. The house seemed very warm. The radio was playing. Shad and Dry gave each other a quizzical glance and crossed the hall, entered the kitchen.

They saw the candles on the table, the sandwiches, the plate of baloney, crackers and dill pickles. They saw Hilda Porter, lipsticked and rouged, wearing her pink party dress, the rhinestones. She was asleep in the rocking chair beside the stove. A pot of tea boiled on the stove.

Shad sank to a chair as if he'd just been told some horrible news. He looked at the little white-haired lady, the tanned skin with the dots of rouge on her cheeks, the lipstick.

"She waited up for us," whispered Dryfly. "What're we gonna tell her?"

Shad was still watching Hilda, speechless. All he could do was sigh.

"Are you thinking that maybe you might be the biggest asshole that ever walked?" asked Dry, feeling Shad's chagrin.

Shad thought for a moment, then went, "Ahem!"

Hilda did not stir.

"Ahem!" went Shad again.

Hilda opened her eyes.

"You were havin' a nap," said Shad. "We got tied up, but we're here. See you made some sandwiches . . . look good. Want some wine?"

"Well . . . I . . . " Hilda did not look very happy. She could not look Shad straight in the eyes. "I thought you weren't coming."

"Yeah, well, we, ah, Billy Bean picked us up and on our way to the bootleggers, we, ah, somethin' happened to the van . . . motor or somethin' . . . "

"Well, you're here safe, that's the main thing."

Shad handed Dryfly his bottle. "Pour us all a drink, Dry," he said.

"I'm very tired, Shad. I think I need to go to bed."

"Hilda . . . I . . . I'm sorry . . . please . . . I . . . "

"I made a lunch for you . . . enough for both of you . . . Shad, I'm sorry . . . I . . . I'm so old."

If Hilda had slapped Shad's face, it would not have hurt him much; if she had kicked him in the crotch, he would have recovered quickly; if she had stabbed him in the heart, he would have felt he deserved it and died peacefully; but she laid a much worse punishment on him — she began to cry.

"Don't cry," said Shad. "Throw me out, do anything, but don't cry."

"Throw you out? Why would I throw you out? Because I'm a foolish old woman . . . I can cry if I want to . . . but what's your excuse?"

"I'm not crying . . . I've . . . got a hair or somethin' in my eye. And you're not a foolish old woman! You're not old at all! And who cares if you're old . . . I . . . I love ya. "

They embraced.

Dryfly didn't know whether to pour the wine or not. He picked up a glass, sat it down again, decided to have a drink, drank straight from the bottle. "Ahem! I, ah, I guess I'll be running along . . . I, well, you two might want to be alone. "

Shad and Hilda released each other, not knowing at this point whether to laugh or cry.

"Don't go," said Hilda. "I'm just . . . "

"Stick around," said Shad. "I've been drinkin'. I can't trust myself around this young lady when I'm drinkin'. And if she has a drink, God knows what might happen — I might even try to give her a little rub."

"Oh, Shad! Have some sense!"

"Well, I think we should drink a little toast," said Dryfly.

"Well, maybe . . . just a little."

Hilda smiled and somehow looked very pretty in her pink party dress.

Dryfly poured, being careful not to let his tears drop into the Cold Duck.

Dreaming Snow

ANNE SIMPSON

I used to read books about polar exploration. Sometimes I doodled in the margins of Fridtjof Nansen's Arctic journal, thinking of the three-masted boat keeled over slightly to starboard, fixed fast in the ice, yet moving imperceptibly with it, as it drifted from Siberia towards Greenland over the frozen polar sea, and of the men inside it, sitting in the warm, brightly lit saloon, playing backgammon, perhaps, or chess. After a while, I knew passages by heart and sometimes changed the words, re-writing it in a notebook which was a compendium of dreams, bits of fact, and odd visions. I saw it in my own way, entire in its strangeness, complete, a tale of dreaming words.

A door banged wildly against the side of the house. Aunt Maura never thought to fasten the screen door when she came in.

I would have had doubts starting off on a voyage like that, standing at the rail, watching the land recede into mist, in all its spectrum of colours, transparent mauves and blues, soft gauzy greys, moisture that lighted out of the air, stinging the skin briefly.

July 24, 1893 — The Fram *glides away from the press of people on the quay, little dabs of colour jostling together before they darken and diminish. A young woman appears in a rowboat holding a parasol, waving an embroidered handkerchief as she is obscured by mist, and for a moment only the handkerchief is visible before it, too, vanishes. On the starboard side there is a red dory, containing a golden retriever, a boy, and an old man in a makeshift wheelchair strapped to the thwarts. The old man holds up an oar and shouts something we can't make out; he disappears as swiftly as the young woman. In another boat a man in a stiff white collar stands, cheering for Nansen: "It is a great day for Norway, surely a great day. Gå fram." We float on, hovering, through silvery veils, as if there is nothing but air under us, hearing far off the staccato of the gun salute from Christiana; simultaneously, near our bows, two boats collide. A skiff overturns and two young men have to be rescued. Garbled, excited voices rise on all sides, and then fade away. We veer to the lee to avoid a startled fisherman rearing up like a walrus from the half-deck of his boat and slip into an unearthly silence, into a vague grey in which there is no horizon, only the breakwater as a marker, which we steam past. There are tears in Fridtjof's eyes as he turns to me: "So Hjalmar; we begin." It seems to me that the mist hangs with a clinging moistness, heavy as drapes.*

Aunt Maura came in to ask how I was, poor thing, such a time of it I'd had, and how was the baby today. Then she took Samuel out of his bassinet, in which he was making contented mewing sounds, and cuddled him close, with the practised hands of one who knew how to hold an infant. I wanted to hold him — I loved the touch of his warm skin, fragrant with a milky smell — but Aunt Maura told me to sleep while she fed him and put him down properly, in his own Mister Master Samuel crib, in his own wee small room. I lay back, exhausted. When Gareth came home later I could hear them talking quietly in the kitchen. Aunt Maura's sentences rose at the end, and he responded with a longer reply, which wound in and out. They were talking about me.

Gareth brought me tea, and for some reason the sight of his warm face — his hair tousled because he had yanked a sweater off — brought tears to my eyes. He was interrupted by the sound of Samuel crying and went to get him, putting him down on the bed close to me. He tickled the tiny feet. Then he took my hand and put it on Samuel's velvety head; my fingers splayed out as if in blessing.

July 28, 1893 — Within a day or so we will sight Novaya Zemlya. They will sight it first, because I am feeding the boiler's golden tiger flames. I shovel the coal until the fire blossoms up in a jungle of white-gold, orange, blue. I recall each word Fridtjof says to me, his jokes, his remarks; I laugh when he tells me that I have the eyes of a sad English sheepdog, when he calls me his good lieutenant, Hjalmar, and thumps me on the back. I watch him instructing Pettersen about cleaning the engine cylinders, marvelling at his ease. Then he climbs the ladder to the saloon, humming as he goes. He doesn't realize his stoker is a woman who is restless, ghostly, thinking of Fridtjof's hands on her skin, on her throat, along the length of her legs. I am a fire, flickering.

In the night, I turned my head to look at Gareth, lying on his side of the bed, with an arm over his face. When we made love we used to rock back and forth vigorously, holding each other. Everywhere I touched him it seemed that my fingers were made of light, leaving bright signatures on his skin. But now, lying on the white sheet, my arms loosely over my head, I could have been lying on a drift of snow.

I woke to the sound of crying.

July 29, 1893 — Late in the evenings Fridtjof sits alone in his cabin, where he has pinned up delicate pencil drawings of his wife and smooth-faced child, which he has sketched himself. He writes, yearning for Eva, always Eva. Then he scribbles over what he has written — I know what he has written — about her white arms, her shining hair, the movements of her hands, her quick fingers when she is kneading bread.

Gareth took Samuel gently from me and warmed a bottle for him in the kitchen.

I lay awake, afraid to sleep again. I thought of a green country, knit with lanes and hedges, with dusky plums clinging to branches, windfall apples in the ditches. I remembered toiling uphill on a bicycle. It was early September, the sky a mild, changeable blue, and I was on my way to Wales. By the time I arrived in Llangollen, everything was steeped in honey-coloured light. I was tired and didn't want to talk to anyone in the youth hostel, not the German teenagers, not the man reading in a soft, frayed armchair, feet propped on a stool, eating a mashed banana in a chipped bowl. In his canvas knapsack was a wooden recorder. I thought he was a native Welshman. His hair was a kind of red-gold colour like a Pre-Raphaelite hero or an Irish setter, and I had a peculiar desire to walk over and touch it. I sat watching him, eating my sandwich and soup, curious to know what he was reading. He continued to read, occasionally clinking the spoon against the bowl, and didn't look up.

When he hiked up a footpath through the hills the next morning, I followed, finally catching up with him. He told me his name, shyly, slowly — "Gaar-reth" — and said he was from North Carolina, from a little place called Pye's River. He held his hand out stiffly. As he spoke

I realized I wanted to lie down on the ground with him and make love. He was thinking the same thing. I felt it in my fingertips, which I hid in my pockets.

July 30, 1893 — We are waiting to reach the Yugor Strait, all of us tense because we have encountered ice where we didn't expect it. And there is a thick fog, so thick that it is hard to distinguish one man from another. We try to move through the ice when the fog lifts: Sverdrup spins the wheel hard starboard, then hard to port, then back again, anxious about handling the boat in the ice, until the bow runs up on it and bursts it underneath. The noise is deafening. "She's a real ice-boat," laughs Sverdrup, "rolling over it like a ball on a platter." After a day of this we are out of the ice; the fog lifts and the evening is clear. In the small hours of night, I climb the rigging and stand in the crow's nest, a hundred feet or more above the water. I am loose and free up here, suspended. There is a curl of moon, a thin peeling of light. But my hands are trembling. Last night, when I tried to talk to Fridtjof in the chart room, he turned away to check whether there was moisture in the theodolite.

Below the crow's nest, far below, the water flickers, beckons. . . . When we reach Khabarova, which is flat and grey, I am terribly unhappy. There is nothing in this landscape.

Samuel was sleeping when Gareth left in the morning. I picked up my notebook, but there was nothing to write. I looked out the window. There was still snow, which, in late April, lay in dirty patches by the shed. The garden was mottled and brown, full of the bent stalks of dead plants. Beyond the shed, the ice had disappeared from the bay, which made the steel-blue water even more forbidding. The spruce trees lifted and sagged in the wind.

When I looked down, there were triangles and loops drawn around the name "Fridtjof Nansen" on the page. I saw him clearly all of a sudden: a brown woollen hat low over his eyebrows, with reddish-brown hair curling out from behind his ears, a plaid scarf, and a faint scent on his skin that might have been buttered toast. After a moment or two, I lay down and pulled the covers up, wishing I were small again, like Samuel.

I grew up in Glace Bay, in a family of eight. My mother was Portuguese and she loved singing as much as cooking, so that whatever she cooked was full of love and devotion, full of her vibrant, floating voice. My father had once wanted to be a priest, before he settled into his life's work of selling snowmobiles. He worried about me: when I fell out of the oak tree, he ran to where I lay sprawled on the grass, asking, in a confused, strangled voice, whether anything was broken, putting his ear to my heart, without thinking to check my bones.

My brother Samuel took care of us all when we were children, straightening my hair ribbons in church, blacking Derek's shoes for school, helping with the store accounts on Sunday evening. My father relied on him, my mother tousled his hair even when he was seventeen and going out with girls, and I adored him. He and I were full of the same wildness, though in my case it had been tamped down. He was the one who found me when I took John Whybrow's rowboat and tried to row it to China, before I got stuck in the weeds by Mr. Burleigh's dock. He walked me home after that, never saying a word about it being a silly thing to do, only that I had been heading in the wrong direction for China.

Samuel was going to marry Christa MacChesney when he turned twenty-one. He knew this, Christa knew this, and I knew this, because I heard them talking about in on the front porch. I disliked Christa. I didn't like the way she looked at him. But that was before she met James Irving Morey and got all moony-eyed over him, so that I wanted to pull her hair out, strand by strand. But Samuel would sit for hours without doing anything and then get up and go hunting in his old red half-ton truck. He drove clear across the Trail to Cheticamp one day and didn't come back until evening.

October 9, 1893 — We are on the ice floe now, encased in ice, throttled by it, it glistens all around, stretching for miles in pure, excruciating whiteness, painful to look at, unless the eye falls on the shadows, which are mauve and blue. We drift through white space.

A deafening noise begins, and the whole boat shakes, lifted up with the pressure, high up. The noise subsides. And then it begins again, with a cracking, a moaning, which gradually increases, for a while it is a high plaintive sound, then low grumbling, as it steadily becomes louder: an organ played by a madman. It stops abruptly. There is an eerie sound, a long drawn-out note of pure pain, the cry of a woman.

It is quiet until the dogs begin howling; they are frightened, turning around and snapping at the air.

On Samuel's nineteenth birthday, my mother made apple-blueberry pancakes and sausages as a special treat. The warm, sweetish smell of pancake batter wafted from the griddle, mingled with the strong, slightly bitter smell of coffee. My sister Kathryn was playing a Strauss waltz on the piano in the sitting room. Samuel and my mother began to waltz around the table until my father switched on the radio and Kathryn immediately stopped playing. Through the scratchy static we heard that Yvan Cournoyer had scored a crucial goal for the Habs in the third period. My mother and Samuel stopped, her arm in a flamboyant gesture above her head. They stayed there for a moment or two: rigid and perfect. I flipped the pancakes, watching them. Then my mother began to laugh. Theresa Anne knocked her dish from her high chair to the floor and started howling.

October 11, 1893 — It is Pettersen's birthday and we are all celebrating. Bentzen plays "Napoleon's March Across the Alps" on the accordion and Juell begins to clump around the saloon in his clogs, doing a jig. He invites Fridtjof to join him and they stamp around the floor like boys until Juell falls at the galley door. They don't pay any attention to the cracking of the ice, when the pressure builds again, but I leave them to go back up to the deck. I can see with clarity because of the moonlight; each time the ice rumbles it seems that it will split the boat apart. On the port side, the ice rises in a ridge and then there is an explosion as it breaks apart. Fridtjof has come on deck during this spectacle and stands beside me on the foredeck, looking out. He smokes a pipe and I shape words of love in my mind; they are the sounds of the ice breaking and knifing into pieces.

The winter Samuel turned nineteen was unusually cold. One day in February it was so bitter that when I went out to feed the chickens, I got frostbite on the tips of my fingers where there were holes in my mittens. The snow squeaked underfoot and my eyelashes stuck together. Samuel didn't come back for supper and I was still awake waiting for him at midnight. I went out to the sitting room, where my father was staring out a dark window and my mother sat with her crocheting on her knees. In the morning, Samuel still hadn't come home. That evening the priest from Our Lady of the Sea came by the house. The Mountie at Cheticamp had telephoned him: they had found my brother. My mother began to rock back and forth as he told my parents, in that slow, kindly voice of his, that my brother was being sent to St. Martha's Hospital, and that he might not make it through the night. Father Anthony refrained from saying that they used a screwdriver to pry open the frozen door on the driver's side of the truck, parked at the look-out on French Mountain, and that there was a half-empty bottle of Captain Morgan between my brother's legs, which spilled as they moved him, so that the smell of it must have been rich and rank as skunk.

He made it through the night. That night, and all the days and nights that followed, my mother stayed with him, saying her rosary over and over. The decision was made to amputate his left hand, which my parents did not resist; later, both feet and the other hand were amputated. A few weeks later he died.

January 3, 1894 — It is pitch dark when there is no moon — there is only the faintest glow of hidden sunlight for a brief time each day. I am walking with Fridtjof on the floe, pausing occasionally as he checks the sounding equipment. Above us the northern lights are waving, folded bands of silver, changing to yellow, then green, then red. Fridtjof stands quite still looking up, but the colour diminishes. Then to the south it begins again with a few streamers of faint violet; these begin to waver across the sky in a series of soft pleats. There are hues of rose and pale yellow, rippling like silk in the darkness.

It is a dream about my life, other lives, all those who had lived before me, stretched out like a band of colours. I see my own life like a shimmering, changing thread, but it is mixed in with all the others.

"How would you describe it, Hjalmar?" Fridtjof asks me.

Gareth and I lived in an old house with a faulty wood stove at Maiden Cove. The first Christmas he ordered an electric stove out of the Sears catalogue so I could bake things to sell. When I baked, I devoted myself utterly to the process, kneading bread the way some people make love: strong, firm movements of my hands, not too hard, but just enough. The cakes were invariably light as air, and they tasted delicious but always faintly pungent and spicy, a taste people couldn't quite describe, even though they tried. That was the way it should be, to keep people guessing, my mother had taught me.

After a year and a half of saving my baking money in large pickle bottles in the pantry, I went to an auction at St. Jerome's Bay and bought a washer, a television, a crib, and a rocker. My belly was full and round by then. I marvelled at the way the skin stretched drum-tight over the baby's head. The sun slanted through the window in early April, pouring over the cat's back as it lay in the rocker, filling the petals of the rosy cyclamen on the windowsill so that it glowed. I stood by the sink in the window's warmth: I was ready, the child was ready. A few days later, I woke with pains in my back. I didn't wake Gareth. I got up and began ironing shirts, a red pleated skirt, a frilly nightgown. The pain seemed to come and go without any particular pattern. I watched a young man waver on the screen as he talked about a low-pressure system, and when he pointed to a red and orange circle that was covering part of New Brunswick, I cried out.

The labour lasted through one full day and another night. The baby was born early in the morning of the second day: small, bloody, and floured with something whitish, which made him ugly. But I thought he was radiant, beautiful. The nurses cleaned him, wrapping him in a striped flannel so that he resembled a small loaf of freshly baked bread. I held out my arms as Gareth handed me our son, Samuel.

February 11, 1894 — "I write about these lights often," says Fridtjof, looking up, "but I can never capture it." He pauses for a moment, still craning his neck to look at the lights. Then he flashes a smile and I am surprised by the white of his teeth. "These are words," he says, gesturing, "written about love — all over the sky. But there is some sadness in it."

Giving birth seemed a strange thing, as though I had gone underwater, drowned, and come up to the surface. Finally, I lapsed into sleep again, dreaming that someone was touching my face. I kept my eyes closed as the fingers travelled, slowly, over my face, as if to identify features of geography. I waited until the ghost hands stopped moving. I was afraid of this dream, afraid to look into a face which I knew was tender, with the fineness of a girl's features. The eyebrows were lightly drawn, the nose narrow, and the eyes dark blue. My brother's face. The hands stopped moving, as though something had happened, as if they had been arrested by some discovery.

I woke with deep, fierce pains in my body.

June 30, 1894 — Fridtjof is making plans to leave the Fram *sometime in the early spring of next year. I believe that he will take only one companion with*

*him. It is sure to be Scott-Hansen, I have seen them talking together for hours
as they fish for algae in the small pools by the* Fram.

It has become much too bright; the summer light exhausts me.

For a week after I hemorrhaged, the nurses gave me pills in little plastic
cups and I took them meekly, tiny capsules filled with something sour,
metallic, to be swallowed with a glass of water. When the obstetrician
came, she spoke mostly to Gareth, and once in a while she would swing
her head around to me. I was indifferent to her. It seemed as if I had been
travelling for miles. Lifting my hand was a time-consuming task, as was
turning my head to look out the window. Gareth got up to leave, kissing
me on the forehead. I closed my eyes. Nothing bothered me. There was
only the extraordinary weight of the darkness, heavy and deep as earth.

When I woke in the night, I imagined my mother sitting in the chair
by the window, hunched over her rosary. I heard the papery sound of her
whispers. I heard every prayer, over and over.

*October 10, 1894 — Today is Fridtjof's birthday: he is thirty-three. We put
a banner on his cabin door with the words, "Til lykke med dagen." In the
morning several of us go skiing, but it is colder than it has been in a long time,
about -31 degrees Celsius. After dinner Blessing pulls out a bottle of Lysholmer
liqueur, and from his pockets he takes measuring glasses, medicine glasses, test
glasses, giving each of us a dram or two.*

*Afterwards, I walk back and forth on the deck, watching for the polar bear
that has been lurking about for the past few nights. Yesterday Fridtjof asked
me to go with him when he strikes out for the North Pole. He asked me to
think about it carefully because I would be risking my life. I swing my arms
in circles to keep warm, thinking about whether I am afraid of dying.*

After two weeks Gareth took me home. He put me on the burgundy sofa
with a quilt over my knees and the cat on my lap, offering me steaming
mugs of homemade soup. And he bathed Samuel in the kitchen sink as
I watched, marvelling. But most of the time I slept in bed, deadened
and empty. When Gareth went back to work, Aunt Maura appeared. She
gave me oatmeal biscuits and tea, tucking in my blankets, telling me that
Samuel was all curled up, sweet Sammums, and far away in dreamland.

When she left, I walked to the kitchen, shuffling like an old woman,
and looked out the window at the sheets on the clothesline. The wind

whipped the first sheet, so that it wound, tortured, around the line. One edge flipped in the wind. Samuel whimpered and I waited for a moment, listening. It was silent, except for the wind. After I'd made some tea and looked out the window again, all the sheets were tangled the same way over the line. I could see the cat playing with a field mouse which was not quite dead.

I put on my rubber boots and a coat over my nightgown and went outside. I stood for a long time wondering what to do. Then I saw the sheets and remembered. It took quite a while to walk towards the clothes-line, but then I wasn't sure if I could manage to get up on the sawhorse to free the sheets. When I tried, the pain was intense. I stood up on the sawhorse and released the first sheet. Then I got down, stepping back from it as it snapped in the wind. It flew up wildly, and as it did I could see an entire Arctic landscape spread out in front of me, silvery-white, shimmering. Then the sheet flapped down, obscuring it. I lifted a corner, expectantly, but everything was the same as it had always been. The path snaked down to the beach, the sea lay dark and calm.

I freed each sheet in turn, moving the sawhorse and climbing up on it each time, trembling with the effort. When I went back to the house, I saw that the cat had left part of the field mouse's body on the step at the back door.

March 14, 1895 — I take one last look at the Fram, *which looks peculiar from this distance, slightly tilted. Its silhouette is so familiar to me: the strangely rounded hull, the three masts, the webs of rigging.*

After we have travelled for about three hours, those who are staying with the Fram *— Pettersen, Sverdrup, Scott-Hansen, and the others — shake hands with us. We say goodbye abruptly. There are tears in Pettersen's eyes, and I feel empty when they turn away, awkwardly, on their skis. When they have gone a short distance, they wave and so do we, forcing ourselves to turn in the other direction.*

Soon there is no thought of anything except keeping the dogs in line so that they don't tangle the traces. It is difficult to ski while managing the dogs and the sled at the same time. The wind is bitter driving right into our faces, which makes it hard to breathe. I drive the sled behind Fridtjof, following blindly. We plunge into white nothingness.

I was having trouble measuring distances. In the night I bumped into the bookcase on the way to the bathroom and hit my shoulder, bruising it badly. I sat down in the hallway, still holding my shoulder, wondering at the pain. Nothing could be seen for miles, except a ridge of broken ice to the south. Then Gareth appeared. He didn't seem to be bothered by the cold. I was struck by the way he walked nonchalantly over the ice in his bare feet. I put my hands out to him and he helped me up. Then he carried me back to the bedroom. With the moonlight in stripes over his head, he was Fridtjof, and then, when he moved back into the shadow, he was Gareth again.

March 24, 1895 — It is storming and the wind is whipping in freezing blasts. It has become impossible to go on in the face of it. We tried setting up the tent, but it blew down and Fridtjof only just managed to catch it before it blew away. We sit close to one another, as the dogs do, huddling for warmth. After an hour or so, the wind subsides, and we are able to put up the tent. But it is still bitterly cold. I start the stove and we heat a little broth and eat some chocolate, but then we are both overwhelmed by the need to sleep. Fridtjof's eyes are closing, even as he bites into the chocolate. We sleep from six in the evening until nine o'clock the next day.

We exist for nothing else except making our way forward, always forward. Up and over one high ice ridge and then down, and after each ridge the dogs have to be sorted out. We have to take off our gloves to untangle the lines. All my energy is spent climbing and descending the ice ridges, trying not to break the sled or my skis.

April 5th — The ice conditions are making our journey extremely difficult. Already the first week of April has nearly passed. We are working our way further to the west, hoping that the hellish ice ridges will disappear, but the ice becomes more broken as we go, as if some giant had crumpled it in his fist. I long to lie down and sleep. This journey is almost more than I can bear.

We will not be able to go forward much further. The ice continues to get worse.

April 7th — 86 degrees, 14 minutes N. Fridtjof has decided that it is impossible to continue towards the Pole. We are turning back.

On top of the last ridge I see a rocking chair and a crib. The chair rocks slightly. We descend the broken ice, going southwest. I look back, but there is only a pressure ridge of ice.

April 29ᵗʰ — We have to kill another dog. Bruin is so weak that he can't even hobble. It is not easy to kill these beautiful animals quickly, but we have to. The knife is no longer sharp, but I have learned precisely where to thrust it.

May 10ᵗʰ — We must kill the last dog today.

May 26ᵗʰ — Perhaps one day we will reach Spitzbergen. I hope I will not die here, with nothing around me. There is, I know, a reason why I must return, but I have forgotten what it is. My mind is playing tricks. I imagine that I am walking naked across the ice, that the cold does not affect me. I walk towards Fridtjof and he is also naked. He is not surprised by my body, which is shaped and curved like a woman's body. We lie together, side by side on the ice, without touching. He turns his head and I see Gareth's face.

We make love on the ice, which is surprisingly soft and warm underneath us. My fingers, as they touch his body, flicker with little flames.

May 30ᵗʰ — We should have reached Spitzbergen by now, unless we are further to the east then Fridtjof imagined. But we have sighted eider duck far off in the sky, so there must be land, though it evades us. Fridtjof is going off to the west to see if he can locate it. But I am suffering from the onset of snow blindness. I will stay here and sleep.

I wake to the sound of a Strauss waltz, and when I unfasten the tent flaps, I see a girl — with braids like my sister's — sitting at a piano. My father is sitting on the burgundy sofa, turning the knobs of the radio on the walnut table beside him. Further away, where the ice is flat, my brother Samuel is dancing with my mother. She is wearing her long blue bathrobe, which swirls around her like a ball gown. Her dark hair falls out of its bun and down to her waist, swinging as she dances. Both of them are laughing.

I hear something behind me and turn, thinking of bears, but it is a golden plover, beating its wings overhead.

June 5ᵗʰ — In the vague distance, in a haze of white, I think I can see Fridtjof returning, a dark figure making a wide detour around a pool of water. I ski towards him slowly, like someone in a trance. Perhaps he has found land.

I reach the last hummock of ice, unfasten my skis with difficulty, and climb up, losing my balance now and then because of the mist over my eyes. When I haul myself to the top of the ridge, no one is there.

June 9th — I have spent two days looking for Fridtjof, to no avail. He must be dead. For some reason I feel no sadness.

June 14th — It is almost warm in the middle of the day and the ice is frequently a soft mush, making it difficult to ski. The dark shape on the horizon has become a solid mass. It is land — probably Franz Joseph Land — but it will still take time to get to it. It may not be land; I may be dreaming it.

June 19th — I have reached land. I leave the sled and skis behind, taking only what I need as I walk towards the southeast. It must be night, even though the sun is just going down. There is still a great deal of light so I keep walking, scraping my hands as I clamber over ice and rocks. The horizon is crimson for a while, until it softens to beaten gold. Some ivory gulls wheel above me.

There is much less ice the further I walk in this direction. I see stones on the beach, each one distinct. There are many birds overhead: some gulls, an eagle. The wind is from the south. It is strangely familiar.

June 22nd — In the distance, I see a small shed near the edge of the cliff. As I get closer, I see an old farmhouse. But I am dreaming the path winding up to it. I am dreaming the clothesline, the sheets snapping in the wind. Flowers curl out of the earth in brilliant colours.

I wait for it to disappear.

But it is still there. I see a woman working in the garden. Her dark hair is coiled up out of her eyes. She sits back on her heels for a moment and picks up a rattle for the baby lying on a plaid blanket. Her gaze is alert and calm.

As I move towards her I become lighter, so that I am nothing more than a breath of wind she feels for a moment, as it lifts her hair.

Batter My Heart

LYNN COADY

You see it there, every time on the way back to the old man's. Put up by Baptists or the like, about twenty miles or so from the tollbooths. What always happens is that you go away and you forget that it's there until the next time. Just when the fog and eternal drizzle have seeped deep enough inside your head and sufficiently dampened your thinking, it leaps out from the grey and yellow landscape — the same landscape that has been unravelling in front of your eyes for the last three hours. Lurid, oversized letters painted with green and red and black:

PREPARE
TO MEET
THY GOD

Then the bus zips past almost before you can be startled. And it makes you smile for a moment, just like it always has, and then you forget about it, until, presumably, the next time you've gone away and then come back again.

By the time it gets dark, you are driving through Monastery, so called because there is a monastery. You know when you're passing it because there is a large cross lit up by spotlights positioned on either side of the turn-off. Earlier in the day, the driver slowed down and the people oohed and pointed because a small (it looked small, in the distance) brown bear was scampering towards the woods. Just before disappearing, it turned around to glare. These are all the signs.

The monastery you remember from twice in your life. Once, a pious little kid with your family. You saw the crosses marking the graves of

103

dead monks, you saw the building but didn't go inside that day. It hadn't looked like a monastery. Industrial, like a hospital or a prison. It had been built some time in the fifties. You drank water from a blessed stream.

Now they run some kind of detox program there, the drunks living with the monks. The second time, you were a less-than-pious teenager there to visit both your boyfriend and your history teacher. The two of them were actually related somehow — same last name. He had told you it was a disease that runs in his family. The history teacher, far worse than him, older, having had more time to perfect his craft. The monastery like a second home. Word was, this time it was because he had showed up at an end-of-the-year staff party at the principal's house and walked directly through a sliding-glass door. He had a Ph.D. and spoke fluent Russian. You walked into the common room with your boyfriend and the history teacher was sitting at a table playing gin rummy (ha, ha, ha) with the other drunks. You and he chatted a moment, he condescending, as usual. But not nearly so much as when he was drunk. You can't remember why, but the last thing he said was that you would never make it in the big world. You could only agree, pliant. You still agree. What did that mean, though, *make it*? Did he think you would shrivel up like an unwatered plant? But at the time, you didn't care, you didn't care to defend yourself, you didn't care about any of it. It was liberating, that. It was almost fun. All of a sudden you didn't have to be nice to the boyfriend who used to seem so sad and fragile, who used to get drunk and then go and take a dirty steak knife from out of the dishpan and look at it.

———

Now about Daddy, different people have said different things. He is the kindest man you could ever know. Well — he's got his own way. He's got his own opinions and, goddamit, he's not afraid to express them. With his fists if it comes down to that. Quite the temper. Quite the mouth, if you get him going. A good man. The only honest man in town. A visionary. A saint. Would do anything for you, but if you disappoint him, I guess he'll let you know it. Stark raving mad. One mean son of a bitch.

You get home, and Daddy's throwing a man off the step.

"Mr. Leary, I implore you." The man is filthy, flabby, pale.

"Get offa my step, you goddam drunk."

"Mr. Leary, I've changed. I've turned over a new Jesus leaf."

"And what d'ya know, there's a bottle of Hermit underneath it!" (a sometime wit, Dad.) "You're more full of shit than my own arse. I'm through wasting time with you, Martin. Offa my step."

"Another chance, Mr. Leary, that's all I ask." The bum straightens himself with boozy dignity.

The old fella has caught sight of you. "Hello, Katey! Martin, I'm telling you for the last time to fuck off. I won't have my little girl gazing on the likes of you."

Martin turns, he seems to bow, but may have just lost his balance. "Hello, dear. I'm sorry not to have a hat to tip at you."

Daddy steps forward with a no-nonsense air. His fists are clenched, his jaw is clenched. It should be laughable in a man this side of sixty, but here is the truth: he is terrifying.

"I'm not gonna tell you again," his voice breaks a little, as though any minute he's going to lose control. Again, it seems so put on that it should be ridiculous. You would think that, anyway. Martin is no fool. He retreats into the driveway.

"Mr. Leary," the bum says, actually resting his hand on his heart. "You were my last hope. I went around tellin' everybody who would listen, Jane at the hospital and them, I ain't worried, no matter how down I get, I know I can count on Mr. Leary to come through for me."

"Don't you try to make me feel guilty, you sick bastard!" Daddy shouts. "I broke my ass for you, Martin, I put my ass on the line!" But Martin is stumbling down the driveway. He has his pride.

"Jesus bum." Dad looks like he wants to hit something. He always looks like that. "Come in and have a bite of tea, now, Katherine."

———

Daddy had done all he could for Martin. This is what you hear over tea and bannock and cheddar. Put his ass on the line. Tried to get him straightened up. On his Jesus feet again. Martin lived in an old pulp-cutter's shack out in the woods with no water or electricity. His wife dead of a ruined liver. Both boys in jail for the drunk driving. His girl off living with someone. Dad spits, sickened.

Dad normally wouldn't have done a blessed thing for the drunken idiot, but there had been something rather enchanting about him when they had met over the summer. "Lyrical," Daddy says around a mouthful of bannock, surprising you with the word. Daddy had been on the river helping out a friend with his gaspereaux catch. This was etiquette — everyone who had a fish trap helped everyone else load their vats. Daddy didn't begrudge his friend this, particularly because his own catch, brought in last week, had been larger.

Dad had been sitting on the edge of the trap once the last vat was filled, wiping sweat from his pink, hairless forehead, when Martin Carlyle appeared from out of nowhere and greeted him. The two men had never actually come face to face before, but, as both had attained a kind of notoriety within the community, they recognized one another, and each knew the other's name. Now Daddy puts on a show, acting out the two parts:

"Good day, Mr. Leary, sir!"

"Hullo, Martin."

"By the Lord Jesus, it's a beautiful day!"

"Yes."

"Did you catch a lot of fish today?"

"One or two, Martin, one or two," Dad says, squinting up at the man, who had a terrible matted beard and pee stains on the front of his pants.

Now Martin stands in silence, weaving just a little bit, and appears to be thinking very deeply about something.

"Mr. Leary," he says at last, "I put it to you. Would this not be the perfect day to be bobbing along the river in one of those vats with a big blonde in one hand and a bottle of Captain Morgan in the other and a pink ribbon tied around your pinocchio?"

Daddy concludes the performance, sputtering bannock crumbs from his laughter. "Lyrical," he says. "That's what you would call lyrical, isn't it, Katey?"

———

There you were in the monastery, once upon a time, a walking sin.

Defiling the floor tile upon which you tread. A sin taking life in your gut. No one can see it, which is good. Being a girl is bad enough, in a monastery. The drunks turn and stare.

Martin Carlyle among them at the time. A pink ribbon tied around his pinocchio. Sitting on the bridge that crosses the blessed stream as you and the boyfriend traipse by along the muddy path. Spring. Grimy, miserable season. You irreverently spit your gum out into an oncoming mud puddle, and he shoots you a dirty look. Impiety. He's religious now, after two weeks among them. Martin is on the bridge with a fishing pole between his legs. He calls:

"Hey-ho, Stephen, boy!"

"Martin!" Raises his hand.

"Whee-hoo! You got a little friend!"

"How are you, Martin?"

"Ready to break into the vestry, that's how. Get meself a little taste of wine!"

"Don't do that, Martin, don't do that now."

"No — "

Together, you walk up the hill to look at the stations of the cross. He is insistent that you pause at every station. The women clamour at the feet of the suffering Christ. He keeps telling you how different he is. He keeps saying things like: "I pray now. I honestly pray," and, "Everything seems right. Like all my problems are meaningless."

And you say, "Of course it does," and he says, "What?" and you say, "You get to be in a monastery."

He tells you, "The monastery doesn't have anything to do with it. You just have to learn to pray. I mean really pray. What that means is accepting God."

Well, you are certainly too much of a hardened and worldly wise seventeen-year-old to go for that. "No way," you say.

"Why?" He gives you a gentle look, and you see that he thinks he is a monk. Wise, wizened. Sleeping in a narrow bed, in a little cell, humble. But when you spit your gum out onto the path, and were impolite to Brother Mike, he wanted to hit you. You could see that. Any fool could see that.

"Nothing to accept," you say.

"You can't believe that." Misguided woman. Is there no one left to condemn you? No one, Lord. Then I will condemn you.

"Belief," you say, "doesn't come into it."

He attempts to look at peace with himself yet disappointed with you all at once. Then: "Do you want to go see the shrine to the Virgin?"

Why not? Very nice, very pretty. Easily the prettiest thing here in manland, white stones and plastic flowers all about. He tries to hold your hand, to create some kind of moment, sinner and saviour. He looks over: "Do you want to kneel?"

"No, I don't want to kneel!"

———

He smiles when you leave, all benevolence, alongside of his favourite monk, Brother Mike. He had wanted you to talk to Brother Mike for some reason, but you said no. He was disappointed, but he said he understood. He thinks that you're making the wrong decision, going away, but he understands that too. He understands everything. He and the monk stand side by side waving goodbye.

When you first arrived, it was Brother Mike who intercepted you. You had gone into the chapel instead of the main entrance, and stood overwhelmed by the height of the ceiling, the lit candles, the looming statures of saints looking down from every corner, the darkness. For want of something to do while you waited for someone to come and find you, you went over and lit a candle for your dead Gramma.

Brother Mike had been kneeling up front, but you didn't even see him, it was so dark. He was standing right beside you before you noticed him. He spoke in a natural speaking voice, not a whisper, which in a church seemed abnormal. "Are you Katherine?"

He led you to the common room, and that was when, watching your feet hit the grey industrial floor tile, it occurred to you what a desecration your presence constituted. Every heartbeat, every snoutful of sanctified oxygen you took went blasphemously down into your bellyful of sin to give it strength. Brother Mike looks around to see if you are still following and gives you a kindly smile.

"Well, the boy had a lot of anger when he came here. A good deal of anger with himself and the world. I think you'll see a big difference."

Now, a few years gone by, the phone will ring late at night. Not often, but every now and again. Bitch. Heartless, stupid . . . Just like old times!

The day after you arrive is Sunday, and it is clear that he expects you to accompany your mother to church. No argument. My, hasn't Katey changed. Because then it used to seem like there was some kind of moral imperative to jump up and down on the backs of their sacred cows. Isn't it, you used to argue into Daddy's pulsating face, more of a sin to be sitting there thinking the whole proceeding is a pile of shit than to just stay at home? And now you don't care if it is or not, sins and moral imperatives alike being figments of the past.

But when the choir isn't present, ruining the peace, church can be nice, the sun coming in through the fragmented window. You can sit alone among everybody, enjoying your mild hangover. Everybody murmuring responses to the priest in unison. You do it too and are not even aware. That's nice. The powdery smell of clean old men and old ladies all around. The feel of their dry hands when it comes time to extend the blessing to one another. You love the sight of old men in glasses, kneeling, fingering their beads.

But one of the last times you went to mass, also sixteen, Mommy insisted for some reason on going to the early one and there you are with the worst hangover in the world. Ever, in the world. Mother, God love her, with no idea. You say in the car: Hm, Mom, I'm not feeling so good this morning. She says, Yes, Margaret-Ann's kids are all coming down with the flu.

Inside, everything makes you nauseous. You remember that your Gramma had this bottle of perfume that she only wore on Sundays, for mass. She said that she had been using the same bottle for thirty years, and only on Sundays and for weddings and for funerals. You remember that because it smells like the old women sitting on all sides of you must do that too — don thirty-year-old scent for mass. Everything smells putrid. You think that the old man in the pew ahead must have pissed himself a little, as old men will. The priest waves around incense. You stand up, you sit down, you stand up, you sit down, you mutter the response to the priest. You turn to tell your mother that you need to go outside for air — dang flu bug. Halfway down the aisle, bile fills your cheeks.

Outside, you run around to the back of the church where no one will see you because it faces the water. It's February, the puddle steams. Your breath steams. You eat some snow and gaze out at the frozen strait, mist hanging above it. Hm, you think.

Today, it's not like that. You feel pleasant, dozy, as soon as you take a seat beside your mother in the pew. You pick up the Catholic Book of Worship and read the words to the songs. You've always done that, ever since you were small.

Sadly, the choir will be singing today. The well-to-do matrons with sprayed, silver hair and chunky gold jewellery. Most of them are members of the Ladies Auxiliary. You don't know what that is. Mrs. Tamara Cameron approaches the microphone and tells everybody that the opening hymn will be "Seek Ye First." This is the one where they all try to harmonize one long, high-pitched "ALLLLL-LEEEEE-LOOOOO-YAAAAA" with a whole verse. They think it sounds ethereal. The organist is a stiff, skinny fifteen-year-old outcast who appears to be scared out of her mind. You lean over to ask Mommy where the real organist is, Mrs. Fougere, who has been there for as long as you can remember, and your mother whispers that she is dead, as of only two weeks ago.

The first chord that the fifteen-year-old hits is off-key, causing Mrs. Cameron to glower. The girl is going to cry, maybe. No — the song begins.

The congregation has always liked the choir because it means they don't have to sing. They are content to stand there, holding their books open in front of them. But Mommy always sings, choir or no, and she holds her book at an angle so that you can see the words and sing too.

A wonderful thing happens now. You notice Martin Carlyle, shuffling unobtrusively into the back row of the choir box. He is wearing the same clothes as you saw him in yesterday. He blows his nose quietly, with deference, into a repulsive piece of cloth and then tucks it back into his sleeve, where he got it. He picks up a hymn-book, flips it open to the correct page after peeking at someone else's, and decides to join in on the high-pitched "Alleluia" rather than the regular verse. Except that his voice isn't high-pitched, like the ladies'.

Seek ye first the Kingdom of God
And his righteousness
And all these things will be offered unto you
Allelu, alleluia.

Mommy says into your ear, "There's Martin," unsurprised, which must mean he shows up for this every Sunday. That is why Mrs. Cameron has failed to glower, and only looks a little put out. What can she say? They are all God's children.

———

After you've been around for a while, Martin seems to turn up everywhere. He's the town drunk, is why, and the town is small. Every Sunday, you see him at church, singing in the choir, his voice even more off-note than the ladies'. Half the time he doesn't even know the words and sort of yah-yahs his way through. One day you do an experiment and go to the nine o'clock mass instead of the later one. There Martin is, singing away.

He never recognizes you, even after the time on the step. One time you see him at the bar bumming for drinks and you are so pissed that you say to the assholes you are with: "Look! It's my soulmate," and you go over and fling your arm around him and call for two scotches and sodas. You remember him blinking at you with reservation and saying, "Thank you, dear. Thank you, Miss."

Another day you go to the bar — even though you have been saying to yourself all along: I probably shouldn't go to the bar — and of course on that day you see him there and he comes and sits down at the table you're at. So then you go and sit down at a different one but then he comes and sits down there too. All he does is look at you and smoke. It is the first time you've been face to face in two years. At a third table, he sits down right beside you and tells you, in a number of ways, that you are a terrible person and why. The assholes you are with examine their drinks. If one of them would at least move, you could get up from the table.

———

For a long time, nothing much happens.

Then, word comes around that Martin has shot himself in the head. Doctor Bernie, a second cousin, calls from the hospital and informs Daddy that the patient has been asking for him.

"Holy shit!" says Dad.

"Yes," the doctor replies. He has an implacable, sing-song voice which has always annoyed you and your father equally.

"He's been asking for you ever since they brought him in here, Alec."

"Well, holy shit, Bernie, is he going to live or what?"

"Oh yes, he's sitting up having a cup of tea."

Dad has to get you to drive him to the hospital because he is "so Jesus pissed off I can't see straight."

"Holy shit," he keeps muttering, and, "Stupid bugger."

In the hospital, you hang around the reception desk listening to his voice resound in the corridor. It is a small hospital. Nurses rush past to silence him, not understanding that their pasty, wrinkled faces and harsh, hushed voices and fingers pressed against their lipless mouths are just going to make him angrier. You remember this from all your life. Shrinking down in the front seat of the car while Daddy yells at a careless driver. Shrinking down in the wooden desk while Daddy yells at your math teacher. Shrinking down into the chesterfield while Daddy yells at the television. Everything making him angrier and angrier and nobody getting it right.

But when Daddy emerges, trailing flustered and ignored nurses, he is laughing.

"Leave it to Martin," he says. "Shoots himself through the head and even that doesn't do him a bit of good."

"So are you going to help him again, Daddy?"

"Well, Jesus Christ, Katey, what are you gonna do, you know?"

———

He doesn't really know what to do any more, he's done so much already. He used to drive Martin to AA meetings (much as he had hated them himself in the old days) but was soon informed by such-and-such that Martin took advantage of the trips into town to visit the liquor store and drop in at Buddy's Tavern. And everything ended up like that. Daddy had badgered social services into boosting Martin's allowance so that he could buy some soap and deodorant and Aqua Velva and clothes to get himself cleaned up for the job Dad had managed to get him sweeping up at the mill. Then, when Dad heard about the new public housing units that were going up, social services found themselves duly annoyed into putting one aside for Martin, even though they were being clamoured for by single mothers and the like.

So Daddy drove out to Martin's shack in the woods, which had no water or electricity, and laid all of this at his feet.

"By God, Martin," he said, "you'll get the new place all snugged up nice and pretty soon you'll be having your daughter over for Sunday dinner."

"No, Mr. Leary, my daughter wouldn't come over so she could spit on me."

"Well, goddammit, you can have me over to dinner!"

"Proud to, Mr. Leary."

Daddy handed him the keys and, looking around at the differing piles of junk that served as Martin's furniture, told him to just give social services a call once he got everything packed away and ready to go. They'd come and get him moved in. "By the Jesus, I'll come and help too," he added.

"God bless you, Mr. Leary."

"Aw, well, what the fuck."

Dad left, feeling good, stepping over Martin's sick, emaciated dog, King.

But months went by and social services called up: "Mr. Leary, there is a list of people as long as my arm who are waiting to get into that unit, and it just sitting there . . . " Dad barks something that shuts the sarcastic bastard right up, and then hangs up so he can phone his buddy at the mill. How has Martin been getting along? Martin Carlyle? He didn't show up, Alec, and I wasn't expecting him to.

Outside the shack with no water or electricity, Daddy found Martin asleep on the ground while King sniffed daintily at the surrounding vomit. Martin's drinking friend, Alistair, was leaning against the side of the house, taking in the sunshine. A beautiful spring day. He was not passed out, but cradled a near-empty bottle of White Shark against his crotch, serene and Buddha-like. He squinted up at Daddy and said that himself and Martin had been having "a regular ceilidh" all month long with the extra welfare that Martin was now getting. Daddy kicked the dog into the woods and threw the bottle of White Shark in after it. This having been the incident that preceded the throwing of Martin Carlyle from Alec Leary's step, where you came in.

———

Daddy has a sore knee. It makes him hobble when he walks, and it makes him angry. You have to go out and help him bring the wood in because none of your brothers are about. If you were one of them, it would be a bonding moment between you and he. It might be anyway. He likes you when you work. Here is one thing you know: Men love work. You might not know anything about what women love, but men love work.

You can always tell when it's Martin phoning, because Daddy's tone will become reserved. You hear him say things like: Well, I'll do what I can, Martin, but I'm not making any promises, you hear me? I can't just give give give. Then Dad will hang up and turn to you.

"If that Martin Carlyle ever comes around when I'm not here, don't you let him in."

"No."

"Do you know what he looks like?"

"Yes, I've seen him a million — "

"A big, fat hairy ugly bastard and he's got a hole in his head" — Daddy points to a spot above one of his eyebrows — "where the bullet went in."

Daddy is busy these days with Little League. The head of the recreation department called him up and asked him to coach. "Nobody else wanted to do it, I suppose," he grunted into the phone. "Selfish whores."

And your mother, observing that you never seem to go out any more and have absolutely nothing to occupy your time, ever so delicately suggests that it would be nice and he would like it if you attended the games. So you do, even though you have no understanding of baseball and don't know when to cheer or when to boo and are the only woman there who isn't somebody's mother and almost get hit on the head with a foul ball twice. You watch him hobbling back and forth in front of the dugout, hollering at both teams and causing the little guy at bat's knees to knock together. At the end of every game, win or lose, he takes them to the Dairy Queen and buys them all sundaes. You get to come along too. You have coffee. The little boys look at you and ask you questions about yourself. Are you married? What grade are you in? They can't quite figure out where you fit. You answer every question as honestly as you can, but it doesn't help them any.

Soon, you're attending the practices. Maybe you are the unofficial mascot. Dad gets frustrated with them one day and steps up to the plate to show them how it's done. He can't throw any more because his arm cramps up when he raises it above his shoulder, and he can't run because of his knee, but he gets the best pitcher on the team to throw him one so they can see how to hit. The clenched fists and clenched jaw all over again — overweight, balding man clutching a child's tool in his large, pink hands. When he swings the bat, it makes a sound that frightens you and you look up from picking at your nails and see that all the little round faces are turned upward in awe.

Grieving Nan

DONNA MORRISSEY

Despite everyone's worries about me and Josie, it was a good year that passed. Shine never came back. Doctor Hodgins came faithfully twice, sometimes three times, a week, and had supper with us. Old Joe and his brother kept bringing out truckloads of birch, and there was always someone dropping off a fresh fish, a bottle of beets or a chunk of moose meat. Aunt Drucie dodged over every morning, sometimes after I had already left for school, and she went home again right after supper each evening. Her sleeping sickness kept her occupied most of the time that she was with us. Feeling all tuckered out from her walk over, she liked to take a nap in the rocker to get her breath back, giving me time on the weekends to get the dishes washed, beds made and floors mopped. By the time she woke up, she'd forgotten that she'd seen an unmade bed and was telling everybody in Haire's Hollow how clean me and Josie was, and how we were the nicest girls in the world to work for because we never whined, mouthed back or asked for anything.

I took to watching how she cooked, and before the year was up, I could make a pot of pease soup, scrape and fry up a salmon, or throw together a pot of moose stew as quick as Nan; anything to get Aunt Drucie out of the house early. Not that I minded her so much, but I could best hear Nan when I had the place to myself, and when I could best find comfort. Sitting in her rocking chair, with the fire crackling in the stove and the wind hurtling the snow against the window, I could forget that she had passed on and feel her humming all around me, and see and hear everything she ever did and said, like looking at a picture, only I saw it in sounds: the creaking of the floor beneath the weight of her step, her ongoing arguing, the twittering in her throat as she sucked on the hard

115

green candies, and the rumbling in her belly while she filled up with gas. And it's like there's a smell that comes with the picture — a mixed-up smell of powder and skin and oily hair. And sometimes, when I just happened to be sitting there doing my homework or listening to the fire crackling, something — like the whistling of the kettle or a whiff of dried salt from the starfish nailed to the inside of my room door — would trigger the picture and bring a feeling over me, like something soft, and nice, and big — so big that it felt like I was going to see something, like when you have a dream sometimes and you wake up and you can't remember it, but the feeling is so strong that it's almost as if the feeling is the dream itself. And then, when I get that feeling, I get another one that hurts all over — like a big ache. And no matter how well everything was going with Aunt Drucie and school, that's what I felt like every single solitary minute since the day Nan passed on — like a big ache that hurt all over.

One night I woke up to the sounds of the rocker creaking. It was one of them nights where it felt as if Nan had lain with me and I felt warm no matter how cold the canvassed floor. Hopping out of bed, I crept down the hall and looked into the kitchen, half expecting to see her sitting there. It was Josie. A thin shaft of moonlight shone through the window, outlining her bulky form in the rocker next to the cold stove. She was still mad at me for Nan's passing, and I thought to go back to bed. But she looked cold, and Nan wouldn't have wanted her feeling cold. I took a step towards her and yelped as she suddenly reached out and grabbed me and pulled me into her arms. Still yelping, I scrabbled to get away, but she pinned me to her chest and started rocking. Hearing her sob, I went still. I noticed that the smell of fermenting dogberries wasn't so strong. And I noticed that she had laid her chin on the crown of my head, like Nan used to do when I was little. Despite feeling a pain in my side from where her fingers were digging into me, and despite my being too big to fit even a small bit comfortably on her lap, that aching feeling came in my throat and I stayed still for a long time with her rocking me like that — rocking and weeping, rocking and weeping. It was almost dawn when her arms slackened and I nearly slipped to the floor. Creeping back to bed, I listened as she soon got up from the rocker and went down the hall to her room.

The next morning she stomped past me in the hall and started cranking splits into the stove and lighting the fire like she always did before Nan's passing. And I made her tea and toast like I always did since Nan's passing.

Yet despite her getting over her anger towards me, she hardly did any of the things she used to do while Nan was alive, like bounding up and down the gully, racing noisily across the house with muddied feet, barking out that crazy laugh at just about anything or shoving her face up to mine and sticking out her tongue. Mostly, she just sat in the rocking chair, or trudged off down the gully somewhere for hours on end. I couldn't think what she did with her time. Doctor Hodgins said she was seeking solitude to grieve Nan's leaving and it was best to leave her be. So I left her be. One small blessing that came with her not doing any of the things that she used to do was that she never went off with the men when they came blowing their horns up on the road any more. And the smell of rotting dogberries slowly disappeared from her body.

One evening in late September, just a year since Nan's passing, I was coming down over the bank from the road, just home from the store, when I caught sight of Josie treading across the meadow towards the secret path leading to Nan's partridgeberry patch. I always remember the way she looked walking off across the meadow that day with the grass up to her waist, and the sun, a bloody red, going down behind the hill, touching on her hair and making it look like a flame that burned smaller and smaller the further she went. I told her that when she came home for supper. We were eating baked beans and Aunt Drucie was dozing in the rocking chair.

"Who looks like a flame? You looks like a flame!" She slapped her hand on the table and stared at me. I stared back. She had freckles that had faded and were now blended into her skin so's you couldn't see the spots any more, you just saw that she used to have freckles. Her teeth were jumbled in front and her eyes were a greenish brown with queer yellow flecks spotting them. Sometimes she had a way of staring at you till it felt like the flecks were small beams of yellow light shining straight through your head, lighting up your very thought. Then, most times she'd just walk away, leaving you wondering if she knew what you had been thinking, or if it just felt that way.

"What do you look like?" she demanded, slapping the table harder.

"Like Nan," I said, eyeing her carefully as I placed a forkful of beans into my mouth. She went silent at the mentioning of Nan's name, and sullenly picked at her bread. I thought to ask her then who my father was. But I remembered Nan once saying to Aunt Drucie that that would be like asking which bean in the can made her fart.

117

My father! From the first day I entered the schoolyard I was told by Margaret Eveleigh, and everybody else around me, that I didn't have a father. Then, when Josh Jenkins figured out everybody got to have a father, him and Margaret pinned me in the corner, sizing up my features and trying to figure out whose father I looked like.

"You don't look like nobody," Margaret had said accusingly, and I ran off home to Nan, crying that I had a father and that I didn't look like nobody.

"Aye, it's not just the youngsters sizin' up your features," Nan had said. "For sure they're all frightened to death that you're goin' to start lookin' like one of theirs someday."

I suddenly lost my appetite for the plate of beans before me and left Josie siting at the table forking around hers. Shoving another junk of birch in the stove, I smiled at Aunt Drucie as she sputtered awake and, pulling on my coat and boots, wandered outside looking for Pirate. I liked to think I entered the gully the same way as he — just appeared one day, with an offering in his mouth. Only I wouldn't wish it was a half-dead robin. Aside from his not wanting anyone to touch him, it was the one thing I didn't like about Pirate — his killing instinct.

After I had pried the robin free from his jaws, I had put it in a box and kept it in my room, feeding it a little water and a couple of small worms, cut up like sausages. It never ate the worms, but it beaked back the water. When it got stronger, I'd chase Pirate out of the house and put the bird on my finger, lifting it gently up and down, till the air stirred its wings, and soon they were flapping a little more each time. After a week, it was flying off my finger to the table or the top of the chair. One day Pirate was waiting just outside the window, and when the robin flew off my finger to the windowsill, he lunged and caught it in his mouth. This time the little bird wasn't so lucky. I ran outside screaming, but Pirate was gone. The only thing left was a few feathers resting on the windowsill. I put the feathers in the special box where I kept my pieces of broken coloured glass.

Not finding Pirate spooking through the timothy wheat edging the meadow, and not particularly interested in walking far in the dull, grey evening, I wandered back inside the house. Josie had gone off somewhere, and Aunt Drucie was gone home for the day, leaving me to wash the supper dishes. She was sleeping more and more this winter, and cooking and cleaning less. Because we lived outside of Haire's Hollow, no one actually knew how much time Aunt Drucie was spending at our house or hers — which worked out fine with me. I'd taken over most of the chores by now and was only too happy to be sending her home more and more. Doctor Hodgins's wife had worsened considerably this winter and his visits were kept down to one, sometimes two, a week. And when he did come, he couldn't stay for long. And what with my mother taking off down the gully all the time, I was mostly alone. And that's when I liked it best — when I was alone, feeling Nan's humming all around me as I sat quietly by the crackling stove doing my homework and reading.

The one problem that kept upsetting things was when Josie forgot to split the firewood. She didn't usually. Cleaving wood was her one chore since she was a gaffer, and one she was always intent on doing. And during that first year after Nan's passing, she most always kept the woodbox filled and splits ready for the morning's fire. But it appeared as if she became more and more despondent over time, and chopping wood became another one of those things that she didn't care about any more. And try as I might, I just couldn't get that damn axe to slice through a junk of wood, getting it caught instead on a knot, or jammed at such an angle that no amount of prying could get it freed. On those evenings during the second winter without Nan, after Aunt Drucie had gone home and there wasn't enough wood to keep the fire going, and the wind was whistling in through every crack in the house, it was Pirate that kept me warm. Stretched across the foot of my bed, his was a quiet presence that brought comfort to a cold night. Crawling beneath my bedclothes and shoving my feet down beneath the spot where he was lying, it felt like Nan had already been here, leaving behind a tea plate, heated and wrapped in a towel for me to put my feet on — like she always done in the winter time. On nights like this I stared at the orange speckled starfish shining dully through the dark, and wished that Pirate was a cat that could be touched.

It was after such a night that Doctor Hodgins came to visit. Buffing his hands from the cold, he stood in the middle of the kitchen, his breath spurting out in puffs of white.

"Good Lord, why's the fire out?" he asked, glancing at the empty woodbox behind the stove.

"I was up studyin' half the night and burned all the wood," I say.

"How you going to get to school on time with no fire lit and kettle not boiled?"

"It's Saturday."

"Heh, so it is." He scratched his head, looking a little confused. "Perhaps I should have come over and split you a cord."

"You knows she likes to do it," I said, nodding towards Josie's room door. He stood quietly for a minute, rocking back and forth on his heels, and I noticed that his hair was tangled, and his shirt was unbuttoned at the top, and wrinkled. "Is something wrong?" I asked.

He started buffing again, pacing the room.

"Nothing you can help with, I'm afraid. It's Elsie." His eyes darkened and his voice lowered as he turned to me. "She's took a turn for the worse. I'm taking her home to St. John's. There's a good hospital there. Plus her sister." He shrugged. "We'll just have to hope for the best."

"Will you come back?" I asked, suddenly terrified.

"Of course I'll be back," he said, trying hard to sound convincing. "Just as soon as she's well again."

"Will that take long?"

"Maybe." His voice deepened further. "Maybe not." A look of unbearable sadness passed over his face and he moved quickly around the room, buffing his hands all the harder. "You make sure Josie keeps the woodbox filled, and that Drucie don't go to sleep while she's stirring the gravy." He jammed his hands in his pocket and looked at me with a forced grin. "I'll be back as soon as I can."

I forced a smile.

"We'll be fine," I said, not feeling fine at all. "You just take care of Elsie."

He smiled at me then, a sad little smile that did little to lighten the look of gloom around him. Trying hard to think of something to say, something that might make him feel better, as he had with me so many times, I ushered him out the door, making small of his worries about the unlit stove.

"You go on now, and don't go worryin' about us. It's nothing for Josie to split a load of wood. And Aunt Drucie will be here any minute, rousin' her out of bed."

"Mind you don't catch cold," he said, nudging me back inside from the winter's wind. Giving me a pinched look, he pulled the door shut behind him, sending an icy draught around my bare feet and legs. I shivered, huddling my arms around myself for warmth as I watched him through the iced window, trudging up over the snow-beaten path. More so than anyone, his was a presence that was deeply felt in the gully, in this house and in me — like the fire that had always burned steadily in the stove when Nan was alive. It was only after she has passed on did I feel the canvas cold beneath my feet. Even when I was the first one up in the mornings and the coals in the stove had gone out during the night, I had never felt the canvas cold beneath my feet. And now, watching Doctor Hodgins walk away from the gully to some distant city that I had only read about in books, I felt another coldness, one that touched me deep inside, drawing a small shiver of fear down my spine and leaving me feeling as cold as Nan's brow as she had lain in her coffin.

The Coinciding of Sosnowiec, Upper Silesia, Poland, 1942, and Banff, Alberta, Canada, 1990

J.J. STEINFELD

After a Saturday-morning argument with another artist about the relative merits of certain painting styles — a stupid, too-emotional shouting match — and a futile effort to paint at his studio, Aaron took the bus to Calgary. He did not want to get drunk in Banff, anywhere near his studio or other artists. Between the first and second bars, he stopped into a second-hand bookstore to look for art books but instead saw a paperback copy of *The Yellow Star* in a bin of specially reduced, slightly damaged books. As he was purchasing the book, Aaron told the salesclerk that his parents' and grandparents' pictures might be in the bargain-priced book. The salesclerk, wearing a large button stating READ!, smiled defensively and handed the change to the talkative customer. But his grandparents, all four of them, were dead, Aaron informed the salesclerk as he took the change, and offered to tell the story of his famous grandfather, the one, according to Aaron's father, whose paintings had been destroyed by the Nazis in 1942 but whose paintbrushes had been saved. Aaron even drew a map where his grandfather's paintbrushes were buried and gave it to the salesclerk, along with a quick geography lesson on Sosnowiec, Upper Silesia, Poland. The original map, drawn by his father twenty-five years ago, Aaron explained, was in a safety-deposit box in a Winnipeg bank.

Between the second and third bars, Aaron stopped in front of a travel agency and looked at the posters in the window, with their enticing claims of warmer climes, carefree destinations, travel adventures of a lifetime, unforgettable visits to distant lands.

A short time after Aaron, carrying his recently purchased book, had entered the travel agency, a travel counsellor stood up from her desk and came to the front counter. Aaron was at the display racks to the left of the counter, looking through the rows and rows of brochures, picking out ones that interested him. Maybe they would give him ideas for paintings later on, suggest places to go — if not actually, then in imagination — to paint trees. He found it important to paint trees.

"Can I help you with anything?" the travel counsellor asked.

"You have any information on Poland?" Aaron said, without looking at the woman. He was already mildly drunk and had every intention of becoming fully so before the evening was over.

"We used to have some pamphlets but I think we're out of them."

"You happen to know the airfare to Poland?"

"No trouble finding out," the travel counsellor said and returned to her desk and the computer on it. She tapped expertly at the console keys. "When would you be going?" she asked from her desk.

"I'm not certain. Eventually."

"Poland is supposed to be an interesting country. Everything that has been happening in Europe makes people more aware of Poland," she said, continuing to work with her console.

"So does Auschwitz," Aaron said, selecting even more travel brochures.

The travel counsellor did not seem to know what Aaron had meant but nevertheless smiled at his remark and said, "We don't get large numbers of people from around here wanting to go to Poland, not like to England or Florida or any places like those."

Aaron turned and looked at the travel counsellor for the first time. She told him the airfare to Warsaw during the different travel periods.

"You going for a vacation to Poland?" the travel counsellor asked, returning to the front counter.

"I have to do some excavation work there. Some old paintbrushes I want to dig up," Aaron explained, looking directly at the travel counsellor. "If I come back to Banff next year, I want to paint with those brushes."

The travel counsellor turned to the wall clock and saw it was nearly time to close. "You want me to book a seat for you, sir?"

"I need some time to think about when I can go. I'll have to get my shots first."

"You don't require any shots for Poland," the travel counsellor said with a seriousness that almost caused Aaron to laugh.

"I do," he said and left the travel agency, *The Yellow Star* gripped tightly in one hand, the other full of travel brochures to the far corners of the world.

———

Aaron was at his easel early Sunday morning. He stepped back from his painting and counted the trees already on the canvas — the fifteenth of his series of sixteen paintings. He better add some more, he thought. He wanted to have the impression that trees were the entire world, an unending forest. No one painted trees more skilfully than he did, the artist believed. These were trees in summer, painted from photographs he had taken in British Columbia, where he had been living the last three years. He had already finished the paintings of trees during the other three seasons and in different parts of the country. Four paintings for each season: there would be sixteen in all when he was done, three completed during his stay at the Banff Centre for the Arts, if everything went smoothly.

He had a slight hangover, much less than he was expecting after spending Saturday afternoon and night bar-hopping, but he did not allow the discomfort to keep him from his work. Up early as he was every day, no exceptions: this he had learned from his father, who had survived because of his work. Now his father was retired, missing his work. Aaron wanted to finish this painting as soon as possible and get on with his next one — the last painting in the series — before leaving Banff. He had been productive, if not happy, here.

Rather than continuing to paint, Aaron spent an hour reading and looking at the photographs in *The Yellow Star*. He was amazed that he had not forgotten the book or travel brochures at one of the bars yesterday. He was even more amazed that he had made it back to his studio in Banff in one piece last night. At one bar he had attempted to show some of the pictures of Jews persecuted under the Nazis to the other patrons and was asked to leave. "You can be thankful I don't drown you in schnapps for your callousness," he had said as he was escorted out of the bar by the owner. At another bar, where the indifference of the table dancers mocked his pain, he was physically pushed out by a bouncer who declared that this wasn't a library show-and-tell. He was threatened with

125

arrest at a third bar, a quiet lounge, when he refused to stop reading loudly from the book, but had managed to leave before the police arrived. They weren't his favourite bars anyway. What had started him drinking this time? The need to make his weekly telephone call home the next day? The pressure of getting a solo show ready? The argument that morning with one of the other artists? The article about vandalism in a Jewish cemetery? Maybe he should avoid reading newspapers and stop listening to news reports. Maybe he should paint trees night and day.

Aaron stopped reading but kept looking at the photographs in *The Yellow Star*. He had seen many of them before, in one place or another, in his nightmares, in his waking fears. Where are the photo-takers now? He imagined the photo-takers, their eyes looking into cameras, focussing, observing life ending, sense dissolving, snapping the pictures and turning away to another direction, another photograph. . . . He imagined his family and himself being photographed.

Aaron wanted to telephone his parents early, to get his weekly call over. It was already nine in Winnipeg, he thought, but decided to wait another half-hour. His parents were always up early, even on Sundays. They slept no more in retirement than when they ran their small dry-goods store. His mother never slept more than two or three hours a night, unless she took her medication. Aaron could remember waking up in the middle of the night when he was a child and his mother standing over his bed, watching, just watching. It was his earliest recollection. He quickly became used to her nighttime presence.

Near the end of the book was a map of the major camps, labelled "Reich 1942." Eleven years before he was born. When his mother was eighteen and his father twenty-one. Aaron had seen similar maps before, numerous times. This map had small black squares and small black triangles to indicate the locations of camps in Europe. Squares for the extermination camps, triangles for the concentration camps. Tiny circles for the towns. Sosnowiec, the Polish town where his father's family was from and where his grandfather's paintbrushes were buried, was not listed. But it was on the map that Aaron's father drew for him twenty-five years ago and the son kept in a safety-deposit box in a Winnipeg bank. Aaron put a dot on the map of the major camps, Reich 1942, where his grandfather's paintbrushes were buried. 1942, he thought, was the year the Nazis returned for a second horrifying incursion into Sosnowiec, on May 12, when his father hid as his family and fifteen hundred other

Jews were taken to the black square called Auschwitz. When all he saved from his own father's studio were his paintbrushes. Ironically, Aaron's father, who hid and escaped that day, wound up at Auschwitz all the same. He survived to meet years later in Canada the woman who would become his wife, and who he had not even known was going through the same hell as he.

Aaron counted sixteen triangles and six squares on the map. He started to say the names of the camps as he painted, and managed to finish another tree, but could not work too long that morning.

At first he said the names as if he were reading from a telephone book. Then from the script of a play. And later from a part of the heart that was hidden from thought and logic: *Papenburg . . . Neuengamme . . . Bergen-Belsen . . . Ravensbrück . . . Stutthof . . . Sachsenhausen . . . Dora-Nordhausen . . . Buchenwald . . . Gross-Rosen . . . Theresienstadt . . . Flossenbürg . . . Natzweiler . . . Landsberg . . . Dachau . . . Mauthausen . . . Plaszow . . . Chelmno . . . Treblinka . . . Sobibor . . . Majdanek . . . Belzec . . . Auschwitz . . .*

Soon Aaron did not need to look at the map. He said the names of the camps faster, went deeper into the past. He thought of doing a painting with twenty-two monuments, each with the name of a camp. He wanted to set the painting in a remote corner of the world, a land whose inhabitants felt protected and unthreatened. Then he decided that twenty-two flowers would be better. Each flower different, an exotic plant. He would find a good reference book on world flora and select the flowers for the painting. Suddenly the painting seemed wrong and overly simple, and he abandoned the idea.

Aaron attempted to return to the present — forced himself back. When he behaved this way, acting as if he were in Europe during the Second World War, as if the past were more important than the present, he became frightened, more now than ever before. He felt no stronger now at thirty-seven dealing with the past than when he was twenty-seven or seventeen . . . or when his mother stood over him at seven. He wanted to believe that this mood would pass, as others like it had. The doctor in Winnipeg told him to confront his fears, to fight against his demons through art. Art isn't magic, Aaron had argued. Make your art magic, the doctor encouraged. The last time Aaron went to him, the doctor told his patient, "You are guilty about not being able to sufficiently ease the burdens your parents feel. Not an unusual feeling for the children of

Holocaust survivors. You would like somehow to make up for what your mother and father suffered in the concentration camps . . . " I'm not *that* kind of painter, he had told the doctor, and never returned to his office.

Aaron became trapped at his easel, no longer speaking, thinking of the camp names, caught in the past. He struggled to remind himself that he was in an artist's studio in Banff, Alberta, and it was the fall of 1990. "Banff," he said in his loudest voice. "Banff, Alberta, Canada." He imagined a map of Banff, a beautifully drawn map, but other maps superimposed themselves in his mind on the Banff map, maps with black squares and black triangles, maps with blood-red rivers and death-marked towns. . . . Into his thoughts came a concentration camp named Banff in the darkest part of Poland, and he, finding it difficult to breathe, saw himself there, as thin as his mother and father had been. He looked at his left forearm but there was no tattoo. "Banff . . . "

At nine-thirty he went to a nearby pay telephone and started to dial his parents' number but hung up and returned to his studio. He was unable to call until ten-thirty, eleven-thirty in Winnipeg. His father answered the telephone, sounding in good spirits, saying that he and his wife would be going to a movie in the afternoon and then to dinner at a nice restaurant. Aaron had *The Yellow Star* in his hand, confused by why he had brought it with him to the pay telephone. He mentioned his grandfather's buried paintbrushes early in the conversation. His father again promised that he would return to Poland one day to unearth the treasure and bring the paintbrushes to Canada. Aaron wanted to get the paintbrushes on his own, for his father and for himself.

Thinking of the map in the book, Aaron asked his father if he had ever heard of Gerhard Schoenberner, the author of *The Yellow Star*, and Aaron's father said no.

"You want me to read this book?" Aaron's father asked.

"Best not, Papa," Aaron told him. The son was careful with the books he recommended to his father. He remembered reading parts of a novel years ago to his parents, scenes set in Auschwitz, and the strain it had caused on his parents, especially his mother. Trying not to let his thoughts become too despairing, Aaron told his father that he was almost done with his second-last painting for his next show and was eager to tell his mother about the progress.

"She is not too bad this morning," Aaron's father told his son. "She knows it is Sunday and you would call. Wait, I'll bring her to the phone . . . "

Aaron told his mother about his latest painting. "I'm doing more trees than ever. I must have chlorophyll in my veins, Mama," he said, making a half-hearted attempt at a joke. He tried to sound confident and uplifting, and told her that he had one more painting to do after this one and then he would be ready for his next show. "You'll get the first invitation, Mama. I'll deliver it personally. . . . I couldn't come back to Winnipeg to paint. I had to come to Banff to work," he explained to his mother, even though she had not asked him, not this time. When he left Winnipeg to live in Toronto . . . Toronto for New York . . . New York for Vancouver . . . there were the painful explanations, the Sunday telephone calls collect.

Aaron's mother did not react to what her son was saying — he had expected her to be excited and ask questions — but she did start to talk about events from Aaron's past: his Bar Mitzvah, graduation from Hebrew School, graduation from university, his wedding. . . . She talked about them as if they were all going on at the same time and were occurring while she spoke.

Aaron patiently listened to his mother talk about the past — did not remind her that he had quit school at nineteen after doing poorly during his first year at university and was divorced three years ago — and then she said, her voice betraying no emotion or depression, "Listen to the rabbi, Shmuel. The rabbi is a wise person. You can't do everything the way you want, Shmuel . . . "

Aaron held back from correcting his mother, allowed her to call him Shmuel. She talked about having made love with Shmuel, about how, lying in bed, they whispered to each other in Yiddish. She had been engaged to Shmuel after the war. He had committed suicide before their departure for Canada, but desperate to leave the Old World behind, she went alone. In the middle of a sentence Aaron's mother became silent a few seconds later his father took the receiver from her.

"Write us a good long letter soon. Your mother loves your letters," Aaron's father said. "With drawings, don't forget to make drawings."

"I'll write . . . " Aaron hung up the telephone and immediately opened *The Yellow Star* to the map of the major camps, Reich 1942. Why couldn't he paint anything of what had happened to his parents during the war? he asked himself. What if the paintbrushes really did exist, had remained undamaged for forty-eight years in the cold Polish ground? What if he took the map his father had drawn and went to Poland?

Aaron rushed back to his studio and put *The Yellow Star* on the same shelf as he kept his books on art. Refusing to allow his mood to darken further, he looked at his painting of trees in summer. Green is such a colour of affirmation, he thought. He picked up the travel brochures from where he had thrown them last night and put them neatly away. He promised himself that after his next show he would take a trip to Poland. And even if he couldn't find his grandfather's paintbrushes, Aaron thought as he finished the last tree in his current painting, he could do some paintings of the trees in Poland.

Mr. Manuel Jenkins

BUDGE WILSON

I remember well the day he came. It was autumn, which starts early in Nova Scotia and is always for me a time of joy and bitterness. The onset of winter is hard to accept after a summer that is so short and a fall that is so brilliantly beautiful. And in some parts of the province, winter can seem as forever as dying. As early as the second week in August, my mother would say, "I feel fall in the air," and my heart would lurch a little.

It was late September, and some of the low-lying bushes were already scarlet against the black of the evergreen forest. Dried flowers waved stiffly against the blue of the bay, but the gulls were acting as though nothing had changed, as though sailing above on the wind currents were enough for them, now and for always.

It had been a bad day for me, and the splendour of the afternoon rebuked me. Beauty can be an aching thing when you are unhappy, and I have always welcomed fog and rain — or better still, a storm — when I am sad. Otherwise, I can feel a pull back to balance; and misery, for me, has always been half in love with itself.

The reasons for my depression were not dramatic. No one had died; the house had not burned down; I hadn't failed a test in school or lost a boyfriend. But I was fifteen, a time of limbo for me and a period of trigger-happy nerves. Neither child nor woman, I wanted to be both and sometimes neither. For one thing, I longed to adore my mother again; but she irritated me almost beyond endurance, with her obsession with food and cleanliness and good behaviour — and with her refusal to listen to what I was or was not saying. I wanted her to see right into my head and heart and to congratulate me on their contents. Instead, she ignored or misconstrued or *misdirected* even the things I said aloud. For

131

instance, that morning I had said to her, "Mom, it's such a divine day. I'm going to take the boat out to Crab Island and just sit on a rock and be me all day long."

To which she replied, "You can be you right here in the kitchen this very minute and help me defrost the fridge." Which I did. After that she said, "What's the use of going out to Crab Island all by yourself? You could at least take Sarah with you. She's been galumphing around the house and driving me crazy. If you go alone, she won't even have the boat to play in." And where did that leave me? Either I stayed home and nursed the hot ball of resentment that inhabited my stomach almost constantly of late; or I went to the island with Sarah, age twelve, whose main characteristic was never shutting up for one second, and who always wanted to be *doing* something — like *exploring*, or *skipping stones*, or writing Xs and Os on the granite cliff with rocks — *scrape, scrape, scrape* — when I'd be wanting to soak up the stillness. I opted for home and the hot ball of resentment.

My mom was the big boss in our home. Do this, do that, and we all did it. Jump! and we jumped. Even my dad jumped. He had a slow and kindly heart, unending patience, and a warm smile. That had been enough for me for years and years. But suddenly this year it wasn't. I wanted him to look my mother in the eye and say, "I live here, too. I caught that fish you're frying in the pan. If I want to go hunting this afternoon, I'll go. And you can just stop ordering me around like I was in kindergarten." But that morning he'd spoken to her as she was thunking down the rolling pin on the cookie dough at the kitchen table. "Gert," he said slowly, tentatively, as though he already anticipated her answer, "I thought maybe I'd go over to Barrington this afternoon and see old Sam Hiltz. Haven't had a visit with him for near two years. I'm kind of tuckered out. Feel like I could sort of use a day off."

"We could all use a day off," she said tartly, no softness in her anywhere. "If women ever took a day off, their families would starve to death in twenty-four hours. And by the time they got back, they'd have to spend longer than their day off cleaning up the bathroom and the kitchen." She delivered to him a piercing look. "Why, I can go shopping in Shelburne for two hours and come back to find the kitchen sink looking like the washbasin at the drive-in." She stopped attacking the dough and started forming shapes with the cookie-cutter. No diamonds or hearts on that pan, ever. Or chickens or gingerbread men. All her cookies were round. "And do you think these cookies drop out of the sky?" she went on. "Chocolate chips all firmly in place? Or that an angel flies down and deposits your clean laundry on the bed each Monday evening? No siree. I need that car this afternoon to pick up a parcel at Sears. Old Sam can wait till the next time you feel a holiday coming over you. And if you've got that little to do, how about bringing in some water. Or wood. Or lettuce from the garden. Or *something*."

I wanted to take the pans of round cookies, all the same size, all placed exactly one-half inch from each other, and throw them through the window. I imagined the crash as they hit the window, visualized the little slivers of glass protruding from the dough. And I wanted to yell at my sweet and silent father, *Do* something! *Answer* her! Say, It's my car. I paid for it. Go to Sears *tomorrow*. Old Sam is ninety-two years old and sick, and he might die this afternoon.

Or he could have said, To hell with all that food! Curses on your stupid cookies! We're all overweight in this family, all six of us. And we don't need to be that *clean*. Even without any plumbing, some people live to be a hundred and ten years old. Sit down. Fold your hands. Take the time to talk to us a spell. Or better still, to listen.

But no. Off he went, down to the government wharf to discuss the day's catch with his friends.

And outside the kitchen, the soft gold September sun shed radiance upon the face of the sea. The sky was cloudless and almost as blue as the bay. Such beauty was beckoning, and not one of us could see it.

And then he came. Straight up to the front door, where no one ever came. Knocking three times, he waited, hat in hand, and I opened the door.

The loveliness of the day had left me, but there was no way to escape the beauty of the stranger who stood before me. He was tanned and shining, face strong and gentle, body tall, hard, powerful.

"Got a room?" he said, rolling a toothpick around in his mouth.

"Pardon?" I asked. My mother's zeal for food and cleanliness stretched itself to include language. She never let anyone forget that she had once been a schoolteacher.

"Got a room? I bin lookin' all over. I'm workin' on th' new road and need a boardin' place."

I hardly heard what he said, I was that busy looking. Even the toothpick wove a spell for me, probably because of the way his lips moved around it.

"Well?" He grinned. "Cat got yer tongue?"

"Just a minute," I said, and went to deliver his message to my mother.

"Certainly not!" she snapped, wiping the flour off her hands with a damp cloth. "As if I didn't have enough to do as it is."

I wanted to get down on my knees and plead. Please, Mother. I'll do anything if you'll just keep him. I'll come home from school and cook his meals. I'll do his laundry. Only please, Mom. Can't we let him stay, for a little while anyway, just so I can *look* at him?

She came to the door, still wiping her hands. The toothpick was missing, and the beautiful stranger stood before her, quiet, still. I watched her, hope waning. But a flicker remained. I knew that we needed money. I also knew that my brother's room was empty. I stayed close to her, as though hoping that some of my eagerness would seep into her.

Even in her apron, with the white kerchief tied around her hair, my mother was a pretty woman. At forty, she still had a young face and firm skin. She was tanned from hours of blueberry picking and from weeding the garden, and the only flaw in her face was a line between her brows — a mark of worry or of irritation, which came and went. She reached the door, the line intact. And then her face changed. I cannot say how it changed. The line was still there, and she was not smiling. But for a few moments, there was something about her that was unfamiliar to me.

Then she said, with more courtesy than I would have expected, "I'm sorry, but I have four children at home and too much work to do already. You could try Mrs. Schultz across the way."

"I tried Mrs. Schultz," he said. "I tried everyone. I bin everywhere. I even bin to Mr. Snow and asked him if I could sleep in th' barn. Please, ma'am" — he smiled — "I wouldn't be no bother. I could cook my own meals. Just a room would be fine."

"Well . . ." she said slowly, as though to herself, "there's Jeffrey's room empty, now that he's away in Upper Canada . . ." Then she was silent for a moment or two, staring across the bay, with that line deep between her eyebrows.

"Yes," she said suddenly, but sighing. "I guess we could manage. But you'll eat with us." No way she'd be letting any stranger go messing around in her kitchen. "Will you be needing the room for long, Mr. . . . ?" she inquired.

"No, ma'am," he answered. "Two months maybe. Could be three.

Nothin' you can do, once the frost hits hard. Manuel. Manuel Jenkins. I'm much obliged."

He picked up his suitcase and walked in, filling the kitchen with his beauty, blessing the walls, casting light and gladness upon stove, table, electric clock. Like one of the wheeling gulls, I flew out into the back field and up, up to the top of the hill, running all the way. There I threw myself down among the high grasses and the late goldenrod, face turned to the sky. Nothing mattered. Nothing. My mother could crab and fuss and complain all she wanted. My dad could roll over like the Jacksons' yellow dog and wait to be kicked, for all I cared. The beautiful stranger had come and would live in my brother's room for two months. I would hear him moving about next door to me, doing his mysterious ablutions. Through the vent I could maybe hear him breathing. He would be there at suppertime, casting a benediction upon us by his presence, with his smile, his dark skin, his enormous hands with their oddly graceful fingers. I turned over and pressed my face into the grass, blinded by so bright a vision.

———

Our first meal with Manuel Jenkins was an event to remember. My mother sat at one end of the table, straight as a stick, company manners written all over her face. My father sat at the other end, comfortable, relaxed, slumped in his chair, waiting for the mashed turnips to reach him. When they did, he lit into his food as though, if he didn't attack it immediately, it would vanish from the plate. My mother often reprimanded him about this. "I've spend a long hour and a half preparing this meal," she'd say. "There's no law that says it has to disappear in nothing flat." Or "This is a dining room, Harvey Nickerson, not a barn." To which he paid not the slightest heed whatsoever. It seemed to be the one area where she couldn't move him. Tonight I looked at him and thought, C'mon, Dad. Just for the next couple of months, let's eat slowly, like fancy people. Mr. Jenkins is here. What will he think if we eat like savages?

What indeed? I looked across the table at Mr. Jenkins, and watched him stuff his napkin in the neck of his T-shirt, revealing a veritable carpet of black hairs upon his chest. Then he ate. Holding the fork in his fist like a trowel, he shovelled Mom's enormous meal into himself in perhaps five minutes. And noisily, with quite a lot of smacking and chomping. And, when drinking his hot tea, slurping. I didn't mind. He could have eaten his entire meal with his bare hands, and it would have been all the same to me. But I dared not look at my mother. She would never allow anyone to live in our house with table manners like that. Then out came the toothpick, and I watched entranced as it wandered around his mouth without the aid of his fingers. It was as though it had a life of its own. Then he wiped his mouth with the back of his hand, pulled one of Polly's pigtails, smiled his dazzling smile, scraped his chair back, and said, "Much obliged, ma'am. That was some good." And was gone.

I looked at my mother. What would she say, feel, do? Mr. Jenkins had just spent the mealtime doing everything we had always been forbidden to do. Would she make him leave? Would she hate him? But she was just sitting there, arms and hands slack, staring at the tablecloth, registering nothing. After all, she had said he could stay. If she kept her word, she was stuck with him. The kids, who had spent half an hour with him before dinner, were all aglow, loving his cheerfulness, his handsome face, his bigness, his booming laugh.

Then he was back.

"S'cuse me, ma'am," he said, "I'm forgettin' m' manners. This here's a lot o' people and a lot o' food. Like you said this morning, you're a hard-workin' lady. You must be some tired." Then he picked up his dishes from the table, washed them in the kitchen sink, and placed them with amazing delicacy in the dish drainer to dry. "Why, thank you, Mr. Jenkins," said Mom, her face expressionless, although for a moment the line disappeared from between her eyebrows. But I remembered his dirty fingernails, and I wondered how she felt about having them in her clean dishwater. Later I saw her change the water before she washed the other dishes.

"Seems like a nice enough man," said my father, as he stuffed his pipe full of tobacco. Then he pushed away the dishes on the table to make room for a game of cribbage with Julien.

———

We were given three and one-half months with Mr. Jenkins. The frost kept off, and the early winter was as mild as April. We had him with us until January sixth. Three months, fifteen days and six hours.

Except for my father, we all called him Mr. Jenkins. He was, my mother surmised, about thirty-eight years old, and therefore we were to treat him with the respect befitting an older man — although we all called Aggie Crowell's grandmother Susie, and old Sam was always Sam to us kids. I tried to keep my face inscrutable, but maybe Mom saw the glint in my eye and wanted to place distance between me and him. In any case, I used to call him Manuel privately, when I was alone in my room. "Manuel, Manuel," I would whisper, rolling the name around my tongue, loving the sound, the taste of it.

But it didn't really matter what she made us call him. Calling a man mister couldn't change the way the rest of us felt about him. Even my dad. I think even he was half in love with that towering stranger, in a way that had nothing to do with sex. He grew to love him the way you love a rocky cliff, or a heron in flight, or a sunfish turning its giant body on the surface of the sea. Or a clown dancing on the street in the midday sun.

Most of us, of course, didn't see him too often. All the kids except Polly were in school, and that just left weekends and suppertime and a small slice of evening, before he'd go up to his room and read his *Popular Mechanics* magazines and listen to his radio. And my dad was always off fishing by six a.m., gone all day. Mr. Jenkins got his lunch at our place, but no one was there except my mother and Polly and the dog, unless it was on weekends.

Weekends were heaven for me. He didn't have much to do with me directly. But I watched as he made our home a sunshiny place, filling our little house with his huge and animal grace, his laughter, his easy way with life and living. He's like an enormous cat, I thought, a panther, maybe. Working when necessary, but knowing how to relax, how to play, how to soak up the sun, letting his cubs crawl all over him as he radiates serenity. Our kids all followed him around like the Pied Piper, and he never seemed to mind. Polly was four, and he'd sit with her on his lap and talk to her as though she were twenty-five years of age. "How was your day, Polly girl?" he'd ask, and then he'd really listen when she told him about her dolls and the dog and the drawings she had made. I wondered about her sitting on his dirty overalls in her clean dresses, but my mother made no comment. Politeness to guests was almost as high on her list as cleanliness.

Julien had Mr. Jenkins up on a pedestal so high that it's a wonder he didn't fall right off. The two of them would go out before supper and play catch, and once Mr. Jenkins took him to show him the front-end loader he worked on. He let Julien sit way up on top in the driver's seat, and waited around for a whole half hour while Julien pretended he was driving it. When Julien came home, his eyes were like pie plates.

Even Sarah. Gabby old Sarah who never shut up. He'd sit on the old swing with her, chewing a blade of grass, while she'd talk on and on and on. And he'd smile and nod, saying things like "That so?" or "Well, well," or "I bet you enjoyed *that*!" Never once did he fall asleep in the middle of all that talk, which is what all the rest of us always wanted to do. And Mr. Jenkins was a man who could fall asleep on the head of a pin in the middle of a thunderstorm, if he wanted to.

Happy though I was, I never got over the small niggling fear that Mom would finally make him leave because of all the bad things he did. He left his shoes around where you could trip over them, although I tried to protect him — and us — by putting them by the doorway every time I found them in the wrong place. He chewed gum with his mouth open and passed some around for all of us to do the same. My mother would chew hers with her small mouth tightly shut, slowly, as though it tasted either very good or very bad — I could never be sure which. And his belongings — his magazines, his clothes, his tools — littered the house, or decorated it, depending on your point of view — from top to bottom and side to side. My mom, I thought, must have needed that board money really badly.

One evening, early on, during maybe the third week of his stay, my father came home extra tired from lobstering. It had been a day of driving rain, and he was chilled to the bone and grey with fatigue. Everyone was supposed to take off shoes and boots at the door, and he always did; but on that day he sort of moved like a person in a trance, right into the middle of the kitchen floor. My mother flew at him and pushed him backwards to the doorway, her voice hard, as if it were hammering on something metal.

"Inconsiderate! Always inconsiderate! Not one thought for the length of time it takes to scrub a floor! You get out into the back porch and take those wet clothes off before the kitchen looks like a slum. And hurry.

Dinner's ready. You're late! I'm not going to wait two more seconds." My dad just stood there for a moment, as though he had been struck physically, and then he turned toward the porch.

Then Mr. Jenkins spoke.

"Jest a sweet minute, ma'am," he said, his mouth soft and coaxing. "We all knows you works hard. We're all right grateful to you for your good food and all that scrubbin' and polishin'. But anyone can see with half an eye that that man o' yours is three-quarters dead with bein' tired." He said all this in a lazy quiet way, but his eyes, always so kind and warm, were steely cold and serious as death.

"Now, Sarah girl," he went on, "you jest get up and wash them few dirty spots off your mom's floor. Won't take but a minute. And Julien — I think your dad could use some help. Maybe you could put his wet boots out behind the stove to dry them out a bit. And you, m'girl," he said, turning to me, "how about a bottle o' beer for your dad, before he falls right over dead." He said all this from the couch by the back window. He never moved a muscle. Just sort of organized the whole lot of us into a rescue brigade. I thought that would be the end of Mr. Jenkins. I'd never my whole life long heard anyone tell my mother to shut up, and that's really what he was doing. But she just turned quickly back to the stove and started shoving pots around, this way and that. When we all finally sat down to supper, there wasn't any tension left at all — not in me, anyway. Mr. Jenkins sat up, talking with his mouth full, and told us about life up in the James Bay territory, when he was working on the new highway up there. His huge brown body, sandwiched between Julien and Polly, was like one of the statues I'd seen in our ancient history book. I was sick with longing for him, but also oddly content just to sit peacefully at a distance and feast my eyes upon his grace of body and person. For me, the slurp of his tea was like background music. I always avoided my mother's eyes at the dinner table. As time went by, I knew she would not evict him, but I felt I could not bear it if she scolded him, like us, for his table manners.

When Christmastime came, Mr. Jenkins said he was leaving for the four-day holiday. The kids all kicked up a terrible fuss, and my dad begged him to stay. "Surely they can do without you at home just this one year," he said.

"Well," said Mr. Jenkins, grinning sheepishly, "truth to tell, home is where I hangs my hat at any given time. If you wants me to stay, that I will do, thanking you most kindly." Then he excused himself and took the bus to Yarmouth and was gone for ten hours.

On Christmas Day, we found out what he had done with those ten hours. He had gone shopping. And shopping and shopping. He bought extra lights for the tree and a wreath for the door. He supplied a bottle of real champagne and another of sparkling wine that I was allowed to taste, and there was pink lemonade for the kids. He had even bought tall glasses with stems — seven of them — for all of us. He gave Polly a doll that said six different things when you pulled a string in her back. For Julien he had an exact model of his front-end loader, and I thought Julien might possibly faint for joy. Sarah got three Nancy Drew books, and for me he bought a silver bracelet with "Sterling" written inside it. He gave my dad a big red wool sweater to keep him warm in the lobster boat, no matter how cold it got. To my mother, he presented a gold chain with a small amethyst pendant. We all had gifts for him, too, either bought or made or cooked, and the day was one of the single most perfect days I have ever known.

If Christmas was a perfect day, the day that came two weeks later was a terrible one. We all knew he had to leave soon, that the deep frost would not stay away forever. But when he actually stood there in the kitchen, holding his suitcase, it seemed that all that was warm and beautiful in our lives was about to abandon us. I could not imagine the supper table without him, the couch empty, the silence that would strike me from Jeffrey's room. He shook hands with my dad and my mother. My dad pumped his hand and said, "Come again, Manuel, and good luck." My mother stood erect as ever and said, "It was a pleasure to have you here, Mr. Jenkins," and almost sounded as though she meant it. Polly and Sarah cried, and he hugged them both. Then he tossed Julien up in the air and shook his hand. Julien didn't say a single word, because it took his whole strength just to keep from crying. Then Mr. Jenkins came and shook my hand and kissed me lightly on the top of my head. "Have a good life, m'girl," he said, and smiled such a smile at me, oh such a smile. Then he walked to the door.

A lot is said about the value of strong, silent men. Me, I think that men who are silent about things that matter just don't have the strength to say what they really feel. Manuel Jenkins turned around at the doorway and said, "Thank you. I'll be missing you a whole lot. I loves you all." Then he was gone. I put on my warm jacket and boots and went back to the old sawmill and sat inside on a bench. Over by the breakwater, the gulls were screaming, screaming, and I could hear the winter wind rattling the broken windows. I had taken several of my dad's big handkerchiefs with me, because I knew I was going to be doing a lot of crying.

The whole family just sort of limped through the next few weeks, but gradually we emerged from our grief and got on with our lives. My mother would say things like "My word, he was only a man. Perk up, Julien. It isn't the end of the world." Or to Polly and Sarah, "For goodness sake, stop sighing. At least we're not falling all over his shoes, and there's a lot less work for me to do." And to my dad, "Don't look so sad, Harvey. He's not the only one on earth who can play crib. C'mon. I'll have a game with you." One day she said to me, not unkindly, right out of the blue, "He was too old for you. You'll find your own man sometime, and he'll be right for you. Let Mr. Jenkins go." I wasn't even mad. I didn't know why.

One day in early February, I was sent home from school with a high fever. The vice-principal drove me to the front gate. I entered the house by the back door and took off my boots in the porch. Then, slowly, because I was not feeling well, I dragged myself upstairs. At the top of the stairs I stopped short, unable to go forward or back. There, to the right of me, beyond her doorway, was my mother, sitting in front of her dressing table. Her forehead was right down on the tabletop and was lying on her left hand. The other hand was stretched out across the top, and was in a tight fist. I was very frightened. I had never before seen my mother in any state of weakness whatsoever. She seemed never to be sick, and I had never heard her give voice to any physical pain. She was always strong, sure, in perfect control. A heart attack, I thought, and dared not speak lest I alarm her. Then, as I waited, a long terrible sigh shook her, and she opened her closed fist. Then she closed it and sighed again. In her hand was the gold chain and the amethyst pendant.

I crept down the stairs in my stocking feet and put on my outdoor clothes in the back porch. Then I retraced my steps to the front gate, fever and all, and slammed it shut. Returning to the back porch, I stomped the snow off my feet on the stoop, and entered the house, banging the door behind me. I was long and slow taking my clothes off, and by the time I was hanging up my scarf, my mother appeared in the kitchen.

"What's the trouble?" she said, her voice warm and concerned. "Why are you home so early?" I realized for the first time that she had become gentler, and that she had been like that for a long time. Even to my father. Possibly especially to my father. As I mounted the stairs to bed, I pondered these things; but none of them made much sense to me.

You maybe thought I was telling you this tale about Mr. Manuel Jenkins because there was something secret and terrible in his past that we eventually found out about. But no. Or possibly you were looking for something dramatic at the end, like the Mounties coming to get him, or a tragic death under the front-end loader. But none of these things happened. He just came. And then he just went. None of us, not one of us, ever saw him again. He never wrote to us, which seemed odd to me at the time, because he was a great one for saying thank you. So I think now that perhaps he didn't know how to write. Maybe those big hands of his never held a pencil. Come to think of it, he never would join the kids when they did their crossword puzzles. "Too hard for me," he'd say, chuckling, and we always thought he was joking. No. He just left. Disappeared down the road in his front-end loader and was swallowed up by the hill behind Mrs. Fitzgerald's house.

I'm forty-one years old now, and from time to time I still ache to see Manuel Jenkins. I've been happily married for sixteen years, and I have four beautiful children. But I feel as though something is unfinished. Does that seem curious to you? It's like seeing a really great movie and having to leave the theatre ten minutes before the end. Or like wanting a pony all your whole life long, and not ever having one. Or like yearning to see, just once more, the rocky coast where you grew up. And I'm exactly the age my mother was when he left. Sometimes I think that if I could see him just once more, I might understand everything, all of it. And that then I could put the memory of him away where it belongs. Although I live on a farm in the middle of Saskatchewan, I have a notion that one of these days I'll just turn around, and there he'll be at the back door, filling the kitchen with his size and with his grace.

It could happen, you know. I feel it could.

from The Afterlife of George Cartwright

JOHN STEFFLER

In the morning light, the Thames was opaque grey. It seemed thicker and slower than he remembered it. A completely different species of river from the Charles in Labrador. But the bustle of shipping, the traffic on shore was exciting. It was what he'd hoped for, everything operating full tilt. He turned to Caubvick and Ickcongoque beside him at the rail of the barge, Ickcongoque holding little Ickeuna tightly by the hand. It was their faces he wanted to watch. "How do you like it?" he asked in Inuktitut, and glanced again at what they were looking at, the north bank near the Tower, and saw what they saw without their having to tell him — angular rocks, cliffs with countless caves, a jumble of scree.

"So many boats," Caubvick was saying, "I've never seen so many before."

"Look," Cartwright pointed, "those are all *houses*. Not cliffs and rocks. All houses that people built up stone by stone." The women's eyes widened, but it seemed to be more in response to his tone of voice than to what they were seeing.

They weren't looking at things the way he wanted them to. Instead of admiring the steepled sky-line, they would stare down at bits of rubbish floating by in the water, or study the clouds, or look at the caged eagle, the dog, the trunks and bundles they had with them on the barge.

Attuiock and Tooklavinia had been worse. On the previous day, Cartwright had left the women on board ship at Gravesend and had gone ahead with the men in a post-chaise to find lodgings in London. The streets had been crowded and hectic, but the men had slept most of the way, or pretended to. Even when he shook them to point out sights such as the Tower of London or St. Paul's Cathedral, they only opened their eyes a crack, nodded, smiled, and closed them again.

143

He wanted Ickcongoque's and Caubvick's first encounter with London to be more satisfactory. This was why he had chosen to bring them into the city by boat. The approach would be more spectacular. It would be slow and relaxed, there would be time to marvel at things. Mrs. Selby, at least, was enjoying the ride, seated along at the prow of the barge.

Now they passed under London Bridge, fighting the current, without his Inuit friends noticing what was overhead.

"What do you think that is?" Cartwright asked, pointing back.

"Rock," Caubvick said.

"Ice," said Ickcongoque. "Water has carved it out. It will fall down in the summer."

Cartwright tried to convince them that men had made it, carved the individual stones and stacked them up, but the women laughed and covered their faces. They thought he was teasing them.

When they went under Blackfriars Bridge, he insisted they focus their eyes as he did. He showed them the joints in the stone-work piers, the marks of the masons' chisels on the massive blocks. He lifted his arm and face toward the arch overhead, the hundreds of fitted stones. His companions followed his gaze, and he turned and looked at them. What their faces revealed was a kind of revulsion, a kind of fear.

They landed beside Westminster Bridge. Cartwright stepped ashore carrying the eagle in its cage and leading his Eskimo dog, which was three-quarters wolf. The crowd at the fish market alongside had seen them coming, and by the time Cartwright got to the top of the stairs that ran up from the river he was surrounded. He turned and beckoned to Mrs. Shelby to hurry. She was coming behind, escorting the Inuit women. Ickeuna, holding her mother's hand, was finding it difficult to lift her feet high enough to get up the steps.

"C'm'ere an' look! A wolf! A man's got a wolf! And Africans, look! Are you from Russia, sir? Those aren't Africans, they're Chinee! GIVE YOU A QUID FOR THE BIRD! Are they cannibals, those? Red shank slamkins, they are. Are they men or women? ARE YOU FRENCH? Are you actors? 'Ere, does yer dog like fish?"

Cartwright waved his arm, bidding the crowd make way — without effect — but the people fell back conveniently from in front of his dog when he roused it by shaking its leash and crying, "Up, boy, up!"

It took time to get coaches in through the mob along Bridge Street and to make arrangements for the servants to follow with the trunks. And when they had finally managed to wrestle themselves into a vehicle, along with the dog and eagle, and had pulled the doors shut and were on their way, they discovered the eagle was missing a number of feathers, and Ickeuna's small whale-bone doll had been stolen out of her hand.

All afternoon and evening Cartwright's friends and acquaintances came to the second-floor rooms he had rented in Leicester Street to look at the Inuit. The five of them sat in their sealskin clothing on the settee and upholstered chairs shyly smiling while dozens of strangers stared at them and endless questions were asked. In the midst of the goings-on Mrs. Selby and a couple of servants tried to proceed with unpacking the trunks. Mrs. Selby's temper was short. She would take out a jacket or dress, shake it sharply in the faces of the milling visitors, push her way wordlessly through to one of the adjoining bedrooms, and stride briskly into the parlour again straight to the trunks.

"Are they cannibals?"

"No. They are gentle if treated gently, and respectful of human life."

"Have they discovered fire?"

"Yes."

"Do they understand English?"

"A little."

"Get them to say something in their language."

"They're rather shy right now. Um . . . Attuiock, tell them where you are from."

"Netcetumiut."

"What did he say?"

"Netcetumiut."

"Oh."

"Have they invented the wheel?"

"No."

"Are their sexual parts the same as ours?"

"Yes."

"Do they worship idols?"

"No."

"Do they play a version of cricket?"

"Don't be daft," another says. "They probably haven't invented the ball."

"Or the wicket."

"Do they eat raw meat?"
"Sometimes."
"All bloody?"
"Mm."
"What do they use for napkins?"

On their third day at the lodgings the landlord made his way through the ever-present crush of visitors, looking distressed. He drew Cartwright aside. He was sorry. It couldn't go on, he said. Complaints were coming from every quarter. The street outside was obstructed night and day by chairs and carriages; the continual concourse was disturbing the other tenants. Even the neighbours across the street and next door were protesting, threatening legal action. His lodgings were not for the use of freak shows and charlatans. They would have to go.

Cartwright rented a furnished house in Oxford Market, and Mrs. Selby packed their trunks again, violently, surrounded by many observers. The number of people wanting to see the Inuit continued to grow. The street in front of their new residence became blocked as before. There were fights between carriage drivers. Attuiock and Ickcongoque began refusing to come out of their room. Mrs. Selby and Cartwright rarely spoke except to shout over the heads of their guests about ordering food.

In the bedroom, Attuiock looked out the window. Cartwright stood beside him, sharing the view — a tangle of horses and carriages. "It is hard to travel in London," Attuiock said. "Why do your people go everywhere with those animals dragging those things? They are always caught on one another. If people got rid of them, they would be free to walk."

At Mrs. Selby's insistence, Cartwright posted a notice restricting visits to Tuesdays and Fridays, and everyone relaxed. For two days they did nothing but eat and rest. They set a washtub up in the parlour and all took turns bathing. The Inuit combed one another's hair for most of one afternoon. Cartwright brought in a tailor and had them measured for English attire so they could go out in public undisturbed. He also bought bolts of woollen and flannel cloth, beads and embroidery thread, and brought some furs from the warehouse where his own supplies were stored. Ickcongoque and Caubvick studied the cloth, considering colours and weights, then set about cutting and stitching new clothes for the family, garments they trimmed with beads and furs in exquisite style.

Their old sealskin clothes, which they'd worn all through the crossing, they cut up and burned in the fireplace when there was a good draft.

1772. December. Wednesday 30.

Among those who have come to observe the Eskimos during the past week and a half was a young artist who asked permission to draw their portraits. He was first here a week ago Tuesday, when he worked assiduously with his chalks and pencils while all around the usual questions were asked and comments were made. On Friday he returned, presented his subjects with miniature portraits of themselves, and delighted Ickeuna with the additional gift of a small copper bell. He then sketched the group in watercolour the whole of that afternoon. He was here again yesterday.

An engraver's apprentice was how he described himself, and confessed that his master believed him to be drawing effigies in Westminster Abbey rather than here making portraits of Eskimos. His interest, he said, is in innocent people uncorrupted by civilization. When I attempted to inform him that crime is not unknown among the Eskimo, he asked if they had churches and armies, and when I said no, he nodded as though his point had been confirmed. He also asked if I intended to make slaves of them, and when I answered that I did not, he said he hoped I would abide by that intention. He then shook my hand, as well as those of the Eskimos, and took his leave.

———

The King and Queen attended the opera on the same night Cartwright was there with his Labrador entourage. When the royal couple entered the box, the house rose and broke into applause. The Inuit's eyes shone at the sight of this spectacle. Whatever they thought of London's traffic and buildings, its social glitter clearly appealed to them. In the same way, although it exhausted them, the attention they drew in high society, the gifts and invitations that flowed their way, pleased them immensely. It suited the way they preferred to think of themselves: not as curiosities or captives, but as dignitaries, representatives of their people.

Caubvick especially took to the new way of life. She wanted dresses like those of the ladies she saw at the theatre. She got Mrs. Selby to take her to a hairdresser and came back with her glossy hair swept up in an impressive chignon. She was remarkably beautiful, Cartwright saw.

They made a striking group at Covent Garden where they went to see a performance of *Cymbeline*. Caubvick's hair was gathered in braids and ringlets behind her ears, and her white sequined gown was cut low to show off her smooth shapely shoulders. The rest of her family were wearing their newly made parkas and boots. When they entered their box, the audience greeted them with enormous applause. Attuiock and Tooklavinia sat proudly erect during the tribute, then remarked to their wives that they had been welcomed with as much respect as the King.

Ickeuna watched the play's action open-mouthed, never taking her eyes from the stage. When the sword-fight between Posthumus and Iachimo began, she let out a scream that brought the performance to a stop for over a minute. Then she buried her face in Mrs. Selby's breast and went to sleep.

They were invited to dine at the home of John Hunter, a famous surgeon and anatomist. Joseph Banks and his friend, Doctor Solander, were there asking eager questions across the table. "What vegetables play a part in their diet in Labrador?"

"To what extent and by what means do they heat their houses in winter?"

"Do they have legends of early encounters with Europeans?"

"Do any of them alter their bodies surgically through tattooing, circumcision, that sort of thing?"

"Where do the souls of their dead resort to at death?"

Attuiock left the table to visit the privy, then almost immediately rushed back into the room, his face rigid with fear. Ignoring the company, he rounded the table to where Cartwright was rising to meet him, gripped Cartwright's arms and spoke close to his ear. "They plan to eat us here! I have seen the bones! Inuit bones. I know whose they are."

He tugged Cartwright into the hall, into Hunter's study. There were human skeletons in glass cases on two of the walls.

The attendant was there at his elbow. "You may approach his Majesty." then being led through the reception hall's multitude, the high murmur pierced by laughter echoing from the frescoed dome, around groups in close conversation, the blur of marble floor, backs of satin jackets, movement of lace, into a circle of courtiers — the King raising his hand in generous greeting.

Cartwright bowed deeply.

"So these are the Eskimo-Indians everyone's talking about. . . . Do they speak English? No? Tell them, then, that I give them my personal welcome to England . . . that I am pleased to accept them and their countrymen as subjects . . . and that as such they shall enjoy the full protection and . . . elevating benefits . . . of English law.

"What curious people. Bright and good-looking, wouldn't you say?" He drew a murmur of assent from his courtiers. "Tell me," he looked at Cartwright, "are they physically constructed like a European, in all particulars?"

Cartwright bowed. "They are, Your Majesty, except they seem to have a greater tolerance of cold, and a more sanguine complexion."

"Are they a numerous people?"

"No, Your Majesty. Their exact number is unknown, but I would estimate no more than three or four thousand."

"Good. How are they governed?"

"Only by heads of families and village leaders."

"Do they use money and value precious metals and gems?"

"No, Your Majesty. They value steel because it is useful to them."

"Have they a form of writing?"

"No."

"May I hear their language spoken?"

Cartwright turned to Attuiock, Caubvick, Ickeuna. "The King wishes to hear you speak," he said in Inuktitut.

"We could sing," Attuiock said.

"What's that?" The King tilted his face inquiringly. Attuiock looked at the floor while the rest of the family giggled amongst themselves.

"Well then ask one of them to count." The King sounded slightly impatient.

Caubvick counted to twenty-one in her language.

"Why did she stop?" he asked.

"Their numbers only go to twenty-one," Cartwright explained.

The King pondered this information a while. "What was their number for twenty?"

"*Awatit*," Cartwright said.

The King repeated the word.

"What was their number for two?"

"*Malrok.*"

The King repeated it to himself, then gestured significantly to the Inuit, collecting their full attention. "*Awatit-malrok,*" he announced. He showed them his outstretched fingers once, twice, and held up the first two fingers of his right hand while casting a pleased grin to the courtiers on either side. He dropped his hand, signalling that the interview was about to end. "There. I have advanced the cause of knowledge in their civilization. I trust I'll be remembered as the Eskimo Euclid."

The courtiers laughed with vehement appreciation.

"You're doing good work, I'm told." The King let his last words drop as he turned away. Someone or something else drew his attention. "Whatever assistance you need shall be given. Arrange Lord Dartmouth Board of Trade."

"Excuse me, Your Majesty, I have a . . . "

The King turned to Cartwright again.

"I have a gift for the Queen." He reached behind him and lifted the wicker cage containing the eagle. "Also, I hoped, I wondered . . . you do collect guns, I understand."

A dog had begun barking in shrill bursts somewhere nearby.

In the midst of the racket the Queen, who had been chatting with another group to the rear of the King, was sought out.

The King slipped away as a servant accepted the cage from Cartwright and held it for her inspection. "My, what a remarkably . . . cross-looking bird." The Queen glanced about, trying to guess from whom the gift had come. The dog continued to bark. "Thank you, Mr. . . . "

"Cartwright," someone said.

She nodded, smiling. "I shall have him placed on a mantel somewhere. . . . Or mounted on a wall."

———

With the window open cold air poured into the study, but the moon was full and the night was perfect for using the telescope. Banks aimed the instrument and adjusted its focus, then invited his guests to have a look. Cartwright was there with his Inuit friends and his brother John. Solander peered through the telescope and began talking with Banks about the Mare Imbrium. John took a look. Cartwright beckoned to Attuiock. "A close look at the moon," he said.

Attuiock put his eye to the viewing piece, then straightened and nodded. "The moon's *house*," he said, correcting what Cartwright had told him. "I have been there. I have gone inside and met the moon."

Everyone gave them gifts. Clothing and combs for the women, mostly tools for the men. Banks gave Attuiock a set of saw, chisels, and hammers that fitted into removable trays inside a chest. Cartwright's brother John gave Attuiock a heavy knife and an Irish Ordinance Department medal. He'd won the medal years before in a bet, and although he didn't value it much — it was only silver — he thought Attuiock would be glad to have it.

Attuiock and Cartwright looked at the medal together. On the back was a shield with field guns, a harp, a crown above palm and laurels. On the front, the royal arms, and the motto "DIEU ET MON DROIT." "It means 'God and my right'," Cartwright explained. "It's the King's power. The power he gives the British."

In the small house in London they were all more confined than they were used to.

Mrs. Selby went to stay for a few days with her brother. When she was gone, Cartwright announced he was taking Caubvick to the theatre so she could show off her dress. None of her family seemed to mind being left behind.

The two of them dined at an inn, polishing off a platter of beefsteaks and roast potatoes. This was the food Cartwright dreamed of during the winter in Labrador, what he most often boasted of eating in vast quantity. It was clearly a passion he shared with Caubvick. She matched him steak for steak, squinting and giggling as her jaws worked, catching the juice from her chin with the back of her hand.

"Do you miss Labrador?" he asked.

"No." She showed her graceful mastery of knife and fork. "It's better here."

In the room upstairs she didn't resist his caresses, but insisted on taking her dress off to keep it from being mussed. He wanted her to keep it on so he could run his hands over her shoulders and breasts under its white sheen, so he could lift it over her hips and take her on his lap. Instead she hung it over a chair and pulled him down on the bed on top of her.

"Come on, hurry," she told him. "I want to go the theatre like you said."

———

Attuiock's hunched back bounced and swung in the saddle in time with his horse's long stride. Cartwright, his own horse galloping flat out, watched him from well behind. Attuiock with Tooklavinia slightly ahead of him disappeared into a shallow glen following the hounds whose ragged braying echoed up from behind the trees. Cartwright, too, plunged into the glen, lurching precariously over his mount's neck, raked by branches of hawthorn and wild pear.

The Inuit's riding style was far from graceful or orthodox, but it did the job. They managed to get their horses to go wherever the fox and the hounds went, and just as fast, down no matter what kind of embankments, through every thicket and hedge. They didn't know it wasn't normally done.

At the top of the next rise he could see them again, clumps of turf flying behind their horses' hoofs. Sometimes a foot of sky showed under Attuiock's rump. He seemed to be flying parallel with his horse, only holding on to the reins. Cartwright had argued with him about the length of his stirrups, but Attuiock had wanted them long, saying he needed to grip the horse with his legs. Tooklavinia's style was different again. He rode like an overweight jockey, bent over his horse's neck, his stirrups short, the reins bunched up with a handful of mane.

Cartwright ducked a branch, reined sharply around a stand of trees, laughing to himself. Remarkable talent, he thought. This was only their third time on a horse. And their commands were all in Inuktitut.

What splendid light cavalry they'd make! He watched them gaining on the hounds across the meadow, the fox clearly in view and losing ground. He pictured a squadron of Inuit men in their boots and parkas, their long hair streaming, armed with sabres and carabines, himself at their head, thundering down on the French or the Austrians. Even the pandours, the hassars would have been put to flight. *Ayeeee-ya-ya-ya-ya*! Swinging their sabres overhead. Unmatchable savagery!

The fox was already dead when Cartwright came up and dismounted beside the stone wall at the edge of the field. Tooklavinia was holding the slight red body up by its tail. His eyes and Attuiock's eyes were beaming, their faces flushed and bright. Since they'd all left London and come up to Marnham, the change in the Inuit was remarkable. The size of the fish in the brooks and the fact that they couldn't hunt deer were disappointing to them, but just being able to roam through the fields and woods every day had lifted their spirits. They'd fallen in love with horses and hounds.

Attuiock was scratching one of the hounds behind the ears, the dog grinning and panting, gazing up at him adoringly.

"They are skinny dogs," Attuiock said, his breath making long clouds in the damp February air, "but they can see with their noses better than any dogs I've known. As well as a hawk can see with its eyes."

Other men who were part of the hunting party arrived. John Lilly and his son, from the neighbouring village of Skegby, dismounted heavily and were followed soon after by Edward Wright and John Popple.

"Didn't come down through Handley's forest, did you?" Lilly asked.

"Yes." Cartwright lifted his horse's left front hoof to see if a stone was lodged there. She had been limping slightly. "Easy country," he said, "compared to Labrador."

"Bloody madness," Lilly snorted. "Break your neck. . . . Were your Indian chaps in at the death along with you then?"

Cartwright let go of the horse's hoof and straightened to watch Lilly's face. "Actually, Tooklavinia and Attuiock were the only ones in at the death. I couldn't keep up with them."

Offended, Lilly turned to meet more of the party as they arrived. Servants ran up, collecting dogs for their masters, putting their leashes on.

Lilly had moved a few paces off with his friends. "Yes, very poor outing," Cartwright could hear them saying, "bit of a run for the dogs is all . . . no, couldn't call it a hunt. . . . " Their hounds gathered, the men mounted their horses and began heading home. Lilly paused and turned in his saddle. "Oh, George, refreshments at my house. Do join us, won't you?"

Cartwright declined.

Tooklavinia carried the fox draped over the front of his saddle as they rode back to Marnham Hall. The dogs, tired but satisfied, were content to lope alongside, close to the horses. Attuiock looked at the dull yellow stain in the clouds where the sun was hidden. Fields and groves sloped away to their left toward the Trent. "It is all *made* here," Attuiock said with a slow sweep of his arm. "The land is all made by hand."

It was what Cartwright had tried to tell him about St. Paul's.

Tooklavinia was leaning over his horse's neck, stroking her shoulder as he rode. "My beauty, my beauty," he was saying in Inuktitut. He caught Cartwright's eye. "I would like to bring her with me to Labrador," he said. "And four of those good-nosed dogs."

"It would be possible," Cartwright said. "But you would have to live differently for the sake of the horse. You would have to build a house to live in, and feed her grass and grain. . . . I could show you how to grow grass and cut it. And you could buy grain by trading furs."

One Saturday

HELEN PORTER

The sun awakened Kathleen very early on Saturday morning. The bed-room windows were far too big, making the house chilly in winter, but it was nice now, in May, to feel the warmth streaming in. For a few moments she felt good, luxuriating in the knowledge that she needn't get up yet. Then she remembered her dream.

Once again she had dreamed of having a small baby. It was a boy this time, a round little brown-eyed boy who looked a lot like David had looked when he was a baby. She recalled the feeling of pure joy the dream had released in her, that sensation she had basked in after the birth of each of her children, especially David, the youngest. It was like lying in a warm pool, with sunlight pouring down the way it was pouring through the windows this morning. Each time she'd experienced it she had wished the feeling would last longer.

In spite of the sun the bed felt a little cold, perhaps because Jim was not there to warm his side of it. He had not wanted to go away without her, or said he hadn't. She would have enjoyed the two days on her own in Toronto while he went to his meetings, and the nights in the hotel. But she hadn't been able to go with him because of Gran.

Gran. She had almost forgotten about her. She hoped Gran wouldn't get up too early this morning, at least until she'd finished her own breakfast. Sometimes, as soon as she sat down at the table, she'd hear Gran's cane pounding. Gran rarely rang the little chrome bell they had put on her night table. She liked to keep up the pretence that she could look after herself.

Kathleen burrowed down into the blankets again, trying to get back into the dream. Sometimes when she dreamed of having a baby she was glad to wake up, for the dream often ended with something dreadful happening to the child. This time it had been all pleasant. Nothing else mattered except herself and the little brown-eyed boy. But she knew that as soon as she was fully awake she'd have to contend with memory.

When she opened her eyes again she found herself staring at the calendar on the wall opposite the bed. In just six days she would have a birthday. She wished it would just pass like any other day, without any-one noticing it. Who wanted to celebrate a fiftieth birthday? For weeks now it had been at the back of her mind, especially when she woke up in the mornings. In fifteen years I'll be sixty-five. A "senior citizen." In twenty years I'll be seventy.

Kathleen wasn't a vain woman, had never worried a great deal about her appearance. It wasn't what she looked like that was bothering her. Slogans that she had never seen or read kept framing themselves in her mind. "There's a funeral in your future" was one of them. Every night when she lay close beside Jim, her hand in his, his body heat warming her, she would think of the nights that must come when she would lie without him, or he without her. So many people she knew had died in their fifties, including her own mother.

Was that Gran, trying to make her way out to the kitchen? Surely not already. Perhaps she was only using the commode beside her bed. Jim had made it the summer before when they had realized that Gran couldn't keep hobbling to the bathroom four or five times a night at the insistence of her old, wasted kidneys. Gran had protested at first, as she protested every symbol of her increasing dependence on others, but in the end she'd probably been glad to give in.

Kathleen sat up. The bed no longer held any comfort for her. She pushed her feet into slippers, pulled on her old red chenille dressing gown and went to the bathroom. Gran's door was wide open; since she'd had the stroke she was afraid to have it closed at night. She was lying on her back in the middle of the bed, her mouth open, snoring slightly. She fell asleep easily, like a small child, but rarely slept through the night.

As soon as Kathleen had settled herself at the kitchen table she heard Gran's cane knocking. Damn. Why couldn't she ring the bell instead of pretending that the cane-thumping was accidental? She decided to ignore it for a while.

The cane was pounding now. Kathleen got up from the table, threw her tea into the sink and started toward Gran's room.

The old woman was sitting on the edge of the bed, struggling with her dressing gown. The familiar lump of irritation rose in Kathleen's throat as she went to help. It was the same every day. Only screaming or shouting or crying would dissolve that lump, but she rarely screamed or shouted or cried. Unless she was out walking, struggling against the wind in a fierce, noisy winter storm, or in the basement with the radio turned up very loud.

Now that Kathleen was in the room, Gran seemed in no hurry to move. This pattern was the same every day, too. More and more lately Gran reminded Kathleen of a very young child who'd do anything for attention.

Kathleen slid the pail out from under the commode, emptied it into the toilet, ran hot soapy water and disinfectant into it and replaced it in its groove. By this time Gran seemed ready to move. Kathleen bent to take the old woman's arm, and together she and Gran made their slow progress to the kitchen.

"Did you hear from Jim yet?" Gran asked.

"No, he's not going to phone. I told you that. He'll be back tomorrow night."

"I suppose he got there all right. Where are the boys?"

"Bob had to work today, and David is gone off somewhere in the car."

"When is Alice coming home?"

"Not till next Friday, Gran. I told you that every day this week."

Why do I have to let it show so much? Kathleen asked herself as she eased Gran into her chair at the head of the kitchen table. The old woman smelled strongly of stale urine, as she did most mornings.

"Where's David gone in the car? I'll be worrying about him all day now."

And I suppose I won't be. Kathleen felt her face tighten. Gran must think her flippant and hard, the way she always made a point of not showing concern when the children were away. The more Gran fretted, the more callous Kathleen forced herself to feel.

She poured Gran's orange juice and tea, gave her some bran flakes and counted our her blood pressure pills. Then she poured more tea for herself, made fresh toast and sat down opposite the old woman.

Is she my punishment for what I did six years ago? Gran, of course, knew nothing about that. She thought Kathleen had gone into the hospital for a tubal ligation. She would have been appalled at the idea of abortion.

Kathleen remembered the dreadful story about her own abortion Dory Previn had told in one of her books, when the priest with the kindly-sounding Irish name had screamed at Dory that what she'd done at seventeen was the same as taking an infant and bashing its head against a concrete sidewalk. She'd been given a penance and cast out of the confession box.

Kathleen had never in her life tried to get pregnant. It had always amused her to hear about people who had trouble conceiving. When, at forty-four, she'd found herself pregnant for the fifth time, she couldn't believe it. She had always been very careful, she and Jim had been elaborately careful, but the pregnancy had happened anyway.

They had been camping when it happened, she and Jim. David had been with them but had left the camper to play baseball with some of the boys he'd met in the park. Kathleen had almost laughed aloud as she recalled how she had enjoyed that session more than she'd enjoyed sex for months. It sounded so Total Woman, husband and wife alone in the wilderness, she making herself into a vamp for him. It also reminded her of what some of her mother's friends used to say about paying for your pleasure.

She looked now at the old woman eating her cereal, drinking her tea, her eyes wearing that glazed-over expression they had worn so often since the strokes. Gran had experienced more hardship in the twenty years after her young husband was killed than most people did in a lifetime. But she had never known the guilt of deliberately cutting off the life of another human creature.

Gran seemed to have finished her breakfast now. She was sitting back in her chair, her head nodding forward, her tongue protruding through almost-closed lips. Kathleen knew that soon she'd begin to drool. She looked quickly away.

The baby in the dream had looked so much like David. Where was David today? She hadn't been able to resist letting him have the car, with the weather so beautiful. She didn't really know where he had gone, as she so often didn't know, those days, about what David and Bob were doing. On weekends especially she found it hard to get to sleep, and had over and over again imagined the knock on the door, the policeman and the minister waiting when she opened it, just as they had been waiting for Mary Lawton the time her son and his friend had been killed when their car went over the bridge after they left the Ocean View Lounge.

When Kathleen finally heard the basement door squeak open, and David's heavy footsteps as he pounded up over the stairs to the bathroom, or Bob's quieter, slower ones, she would whisper silently "Thank you, Jesus," too full of relief to even laugh at herself for saying it.

Gran was ready to go back to the bedroom now.

"What's it like out?" she asked as they walked through the hall. She asked that every morning.

"Nice and sunny," said Kathleen, her throat hurting again. "A bit cool, though."

"We won't get out today, I don't s'pose. Not with the car gone." Gran sighed heavily. "It's going to be a long day for me."

And what kind of day do you think it's going to be for me, you smelly old thing? Kathleen was always glad nobody could hear what was in her mind. Do you think I exactly enjoy staying here looking after you, too much to do, not enough to do, worrying about David and trying not to let you know it, grieving over things you know nothing about? Do you think it's going to be the highlight of my life or something? She turned away so that Gran wouldn't see the anger in her face.

She thought of a television program she'd seen a few nights earlier, the one about that near-saint Mother Teresa, who was spending her life looking after the sick and the dying. It must be done with love, she had insisted, this frail, sexless creature in her long, loose robe. Didn't Mother Teresa ever get angry, frustrated, annoyed in spite of herself with the poor pathetic creatures who were dying all around her? It's probably easier to help people to die than to help them to live, Kathleen had thought as she watched the program. And then had felt immediately ashamed of herself.

Lately she'd been reading a lot of magazine articles that advised her, and other women like her, not to be too hard on themselves. She remembered one piece titled "The One Person You Can't Forgive." Well, the Right to Lifers didn't make things any easier, that was certain. Almost every time she opened a newspaper these days she'd see a letter headed "Baby Murders Must Stop!" or "Gas Chambers Next" or "Abortion Today, Euthanasia Tomorrow!" That last one almost made her laugh, when she could stop being angry or keep from crying. Here she was, tied day after day to the needs of an old woman who could no longer look after herself. And she'd been doing this for five years.

She thought again about Dory Previn and wondered if she herself had agreed to look after Gran as a kind of penance for her own "sin." She had never been a Roman Catholic, but the stern Protestantism that was her background could be even harder to live with at times, the way it left everything up to your conscience.

Gran's bell rang, sounding louder than usual. Kathleen swore to herself and tried hard to arrange her features in a pleasant expression before she went into the bedroom. At least she'd abandoned the cane-knocking strategy.

"Where's Bob today?" Gran was sitting up again now. She never stayed lying down for long.

"I told you, Gran, he's working. All day."

"Poor boy, he's going to wear himself out, working and going to university too. It's too much."

"He needs the money." Kathleen wondered what would have to happen to her before the old woman saw *her* as tired, weary, exhausted? To Gran, Kathleen was a provider for Jim, David, Alice, Bob, herself, the cat, and Margot by a kind of remote control. What could she do if I collapsed on the floor in front of her eyes?

"Did you hear from Margot this week?"

"I had a letter yesterday, Gran. Don't you remember? I showed it to you."

"If you did I couldn't read it. My eyes are shockin' here lately."

Kathleen picked up a crumpled tissue from the floor and threw it into the wastebasket. She found balled-up tissues like that every morning, sometimes several. Did Gran cry in the night?

She helped the old woman to get dressed. Afterwards Gran, exhausted from even that much effort, lay back on her pillows.

Back in the living room, Kathleen sat down in the armchair and closed her eyes. She thought of the hours she'd spent sitting in that same chair during those horrible weeks after she'd had the abortion and tubal ligation. Every day she'd put in the morning talking to her sister Audrey and her friends Jean and Daphne on the telephone. Not Angela, though. Angela was a practising Catholic. Those conversations had helped her to get through the hours until Dave came home to lunch.

Gran's bell rang again. She was sitting on the bed, her eyes staring straight ahead at something that wasn't there. Her eyes, and the set of her shoulders, reminded Kathleen of a sheep that she and Jim had come upon once when they were walking over the hills in Brigus. Or maybe it had been a lamb. Gran was obviously waiting to be led out to the living room. Why couldn't she stay in one place?

On the radio in the living room, the announcer was reading a short item about the ever-increasing price of gold.

"Can you buy five-dollar gold pieces now?" Gran asked. "I had a five-dollar gold piece once," she went on, not waiting for a reply. "Poor Eldred gave it to me. I treasured it for years, but then one time when I was having it hard I had to spend it on groceries." The old woman's eyes filled with tears; they didn't look like a sheep's eyes, or a lamb's, any longer. She reached into her cardigan pocket for her glasses. Her brother Eldred had died in the First World War.

Kathleen didn't know if she wanted to cry herself, or scream. She was used to most of Gran's stories, but this was a new one. She turned and went into the kitchen to make lunch.

The rest of the day passed slowly. After lunch she settled Gran down in the big armchair, her puffy feet on the carpet-covered footstool Jim had made for her. Kathleen herself lay down on the chesterfield. She was always tired these days; Dr. O'Malley thought she might have a thyroid deficiency. She let her eyelids drop as she listened to the regular Saturday afternoon music program on the radio.

The sun was still streaming in through the picture window. Basking in the sun this way, basking almost as a cat basks, she could forget for a moment that it wasn't really very warm out, that it was just a trick of sunlight through the glass. She felt herself relaxing as she almost dozed, listening to the Nashville performers sing of poverty and desertion and lost love. From her almost-sleep, she glanced across at Gran. The old woman's eyes were closed, her mouth slightly open. She seemed at peace, for the moment.

Loretta Lynn's true country voice came over the airwaves, tuneful and clear:

> *They say to have her hair done Liz flies all the way to France,*
> *And Jackie's seen in a discotheque, doing a brand new dance,*
> *And the White House social season should be busy and gay,*
> *But here in Topeka, the rain is a-fallin',*
> *The faucet is a-drippin' and the kids are a-bawlin',*
> *One of 'em's a-toddlin' and one is a-crawlin'*
> *And one's on the way.*

A cloud passed over the sun; Kathleen brushed hot tears from her eyes. Nowadays she often got weepy, especially when she passed the school where her children had gone, wishing back the days when they'd all been dependent on her. When she'd actually been living through those days she couldn't wait for them to end.

Strange, wasn't it, to have such mixed feelings about one's children? After they were born it was difficult to remember a time when they hadn't been around. To realize that they might never have been born, that chance plays so crucial part in the making of a human being, was almost impossible. Yet, when her pregnancy had been confirmed six years before, when she'd realized it was possible for her to have a therapeutic abortion, she had known immediately that she would not have this baby.

Now Dolly Parton was singing "Coat of Many Colours." That woeful, strangely poignant story about a child's shattered pride in a new home-made coat brought her attention back to Gran. Jim often joked now that he and her brother Albert had once shared a coat. The old woman was hunched forward in the chair now, her eyes open, staring at the window.

"Do you want anything, Gran?" she forced herself to say.

"No, nothing I can have. I wouldn't mind a new pair of legs." Sometimes Gran chuckled when she said things like that, but not today. "What wouldn't I give to be able to go out. People with nothing wrong with them don't appreciate what a blessing it is to be able to go and come when they want to." For once Kathleen had sense enough to say nothing.

Sometimes she felt herself rushing headlong into old age, following the path that Gran had worn for her. How long would it be before someone had to lead her from room to room, help her to get dressed, empty her slops? Of course Alice or Margot or Bob or David wouldn't ever have to do for her what she had to do for Gran. She'd rather die, or go into the most impersonal institution in the country. She would make her own decisions, not force others to make them for her. Or so she believed now.

The music was soft and seductive; Kathleen felt herself being lulled into sleep. The room, with the sun still pouring in, looked strange and foreign almost the way an operating room and the people in it look as the patient is being sucked under by the anaesthetic.

When she woke up, the sun was gone. It wouldn't be dark for hours yet; daylight saving time had started a week before. But there was something about the suddenly heavy sky, the dark clouds, the absence of sun, that reminded Kathleen of an evening in winter. Perhaps it was going to rain, or even snow. She hoped it wouldn't snow before David got back with the car. She had told Jim it was too early to take off the snow tires. They often had snow in May.

The menace that had been hovering over her all day came closer as she started to get supper. Perhaps it was the sudden blackness of the sky or her preoccupation with David and the car. Would he and his friend Mike stop for a few beers? Were they even now rolling joints for themselves? The cigarette papers that she had noticed in David's room a few days before were not there today.

Kathleen fixed her eyes on Gran, sitting across from her at the kitchen table, eating with appetite the cod chowder Kathleen had put in front of her. Food was one of the few things left for the old woman to enjoy.

Bob phoned to say he'd be staying the night at a friend's apartment. He often stayed downtown on weekends. Kathleen had almost given up speculating about where he was or what he was doing, reminding herself that most young men of twenty-one did not even live at home. Gran often asked Bob why he didn't get a nice girlfriend for himself; even though the question always angered Kathleen, she couldn't help wondering the same thing herself.

She was really beginning to worry about David now. Just as she had expected, it had started to snow; the flakes were getting thicker. He'd had his driver's licence for less than a year.

What's it all about? she asked herself, staring through the window at the snow. We're born, we grow up, we have children, we worry about them, they grow up, we worry about our parents, they die, we grow old, our children worry about us, we die. How senseless it all is.

"Isn't David home yet?" Gran called from her chair in the darkening living room. She hadn't wanted the light on, claiming it hurt her eyes.

Kathleen considered telling her a lie but instead decided to be flip. "So that's your worry for today, is it, Gran?" she said lightly. She thought of the little wooden plaque she'd bought for Gran on her last hurried trip out of town. "Don't just sit there, worry," it said in large, fancy letters, cut deep into the wood.

"It must be wonderful not to worry," Gran said, tightening her mouth.

Yes, thought Kathleen, it must be.

As she and the old woman sat watching television, Kathleen tried hard to concentrate on the *Barney Miller* rerun that even Gran was laughing over, but she couldn't keep her mind off the slippery, winding road that David must be driving over. If something happens, it happens. Worrying won't prevent it. All the clichés she used on Gran and other people crowded into her head, but, like most of the clichés used in times of stress and sorrow, they did her absolutely no good.

When she had finally made up her mind to call Mrs. Burton, mother of David's friend Mike, she heard the familiar squeak of the basement door. David ran up the stairs and bounded into the living room.

"What have you got it so dark for?" he asked, switching on the light.

"Where *were* you, David?" his grandmother asked. "I was so worried about you."

"Yes, you know what Gran is like." Kathleen was surprised at the ease of her laughter.

"What's for supper, Mom?" David went into the kitchen. "Hi, cat, what're you at?" He picked up the cat, who had followed him upstairs, ruffling the thick black fur.

"There's some chowder on the stove," Kathleen said. "But perhaps you'd rather have bacon and eggs. I didn't know what time you were coming." She kept her voice light. "You didn't tell us where you were."

"Oh, here and there. And I'd love some bacon and eggs, if it's okay with you. Sunny side up now, remember." He grinned at her, his brown eyes shining, and Kathleen thought of the baby in her dream.

"You've got great times," she said to David, putting the iron frying pan on the burner and remembering her mother saying the same thing to her.

Mike came over, and he and David spent the evening in the basement recreation room. The sound of rock music and laughter thundered up through the hot air vents. Jim phoned, although he'd said he wasn't going to. Even more surprising, Margot, who rarely called home, phoned also, sounding a little bit lonely. Then, just before Gran went to her room for the night, her only daughter, Jim's sister Iris, called from Montreal, where she'd been living for five years.

"Good-night, now," Gran said finally into the phone, her voice sounding stronger than it had all day. "We're doing well with the phone calls tonight," she said to Kathleen. Just for a moment there was a kind of camaraderie that existed so rarely between the two women.

"Good-night, now," Gran repeated later as Kathleen tucked her into bed. She seemed about to say something more but changed her mind.

"Good-night, Gran." Kathleen felt inclined to kiss the old woman. Instead she smoothed her hair and adjusted the two pillows under her head. "I hope you sleep well."

"So do I," said Gran, turning on her side.

In the living room the drapes were drawn, shutting out the dark and the snow. From the basement Pink Floyd sang out a musical sermon to the materialistic world. The boys were laughing a lot; Kathleen had heard that smoking pot made people laugh at nothing. She wouldn't worry about that tonight.

She got some orange juice and chocolate biscuits from the kitchen and settled down to watch television. Another night that there'd be no clergyman and policeman at the door to bring her bad news. As for the bad news locked up inside her, that was contained, for the time being. "Thank you, Jesus," she whispered, giggling to herself. And, for once taking no thought for tomorrow, she leaned back against the cushions, an unlikely lily of the field.

Heavy Ice

WAYNE CURTIS

Heavy ice," Tom says. "She could go tonight as well as not if the water keeps on raisin'." He turns his back on the river and talks to us over his shoulder while he urinates into the rotting snow. "I hope there ain't much damage done."

Yellow water covers the ice; the shores are open, black. The river looks to me like a giant snake, twisting between the hills, waiting to erupt in anger and shed its cover at any minute.

"Boy oh boy," Danny says, "I hope it goes today. Once the ice is gone, it's really spring then."

Raindrops cling to the stunted cedar on the riverbank. The tall juniper sway, dropping showers on the dirty snow. Insects crawl beneath the trees — sap flies. There is a scent of woodsmoke that mixes with the sour dampness.

"Boys, I tell ya, one spring she jammed in here on the flat. What a mess."

"Way up here?"

"Oh hell, yes, right where we're standin'. Took out every bridge on the jesus river. What a son-of-a-whore of a jam that was."

"How long ago was that?" I ask.

"Now let me think. It was twenty years ago, before the war. Around '35, I guess it was. I had logs piled here on the bank and the ice took 'em. Lost everything that year. A whole winter's cuttin' down the goddam river."

Tom turns and faces the river once more, lights his pipe with a wooden match scraped on the seam of his wool pants, cups the flame in his palms and draws it into the bowl. Grey hair on the back of his hands covers the freckled veins. He puts his thumb over the pipe bowl and puffs, talking now without taking his eyes off the river.

"Boy! I can't wait till it starts," Danny says in his high young voice. "I hope it goes before dark so we can see it." He makes snowballs with his bare pink hands and hurls them out onto the ice.

A wooden bench sits upright on the ice near the shore: bench, ashes and a coil of rusted wire. I think of a January night and the game of hockey, two-on-a-side, boots for goal markers. It seems like years ago already. Back then, the ice was a playground and the communities facing each other across it were one. Now, it's a different ice, angry and suffering, worn thin by the currents. The horse and sled tracks on the ice have moved so that the road up the hill and the one on the river are separate. The manured sled tracks on the ice are like a railway switched toward open water. There is no way across except for the cable bridge down below the next farm.

Unlike the rain that comes in winter and brings a cold dampness, this has warmth and a light hollowness that makes thin sounds echo beyond where we can see. We reassure ourselves that this is not a winter's thaw. We check for spring signs. The shingles on the south side of the shed are blackened with rain. We listen for crows hollering, higher pitched than the raven. We check the willows and find tiny rabbit paws of hope, white along the black stems. And there are tunnels from the manure-stained brooks that zigzag beneath the pathway. Visible beneath the ponds on the flat is spongy grass: dirty blond hair waving under glass. The yellow stubble that emerges on the flat is a contrast to the baring furrows on the plowed land, and while the snow remains deep in the woods, the swamp shows visible kinks of alder like the claws of ravens. We watch the signs strengthen with each warm day.

Tom coughs and clears his throat with a long deep snort, spitting into the snow. "Yessir, boys, a long cold son-of-a-whore," he murmurs.

Down on the highway, a car grinds past, its fender rattling. It splashes muddy water over decaying snowbanks. I can see Cindy Long, who is walking, stepping off to the side to let the car pass. She lives across the river and has crossed the wire bridge. She turns in our driveway up ahead and goes into the house.

A dark cloud blows low over the treetops and the rain drifts slanting across the shabby fields and river. The large drops are cool against our faces as they hammer like kernels of grain upon the steel roof of the barn. We're getting soaked through, but we don't hurry. Getting wet in the April shower is a small price to pay for spring, a pleasant discomfort.

Tom begins to sing. Catching the words in his shaky voice, he murmurs bits and pieces of his favourite song. Some of the words are shrill, others are lost altogether in the slump of a footstep or a cough from his tobacco smoke. It's like someone singing in his sleep. "Ka-ka-ka-Katie, beautiful . . . You're the only one that I aaddooorrhhh . . . "

Danny and I poke along behind, quiet. The song brings our three souls together, I think. As we reach the dooryard, Cindy slips out of the house, and when Danny sees her he lifts his thin chest and joins Tom in the song. "I'll be waitin' at the ka-ka-ka-kitchen doooorrhh." They go into the house, singing.

Cindy's blonde ponytail spills over the short winter jacket that doesn't cover her tight blue jeans. She smiles when she speaks, her forehead furrowing. "So how's it lookin', anyway, the ice?" she asks.

"Oh, it's all open at the shores," I say. "Tom thinks it could go today if the rain keeps up."

"Let's go down, Stevie. I wanna see it," she says. But she has just come across the bridge. I say nothing and nod okay.

We walk over the ploughed field toward the river. Culverts bubble and chuckle beneath the pathway as flooding swamp brooks boil yellow in deep brown ponds that flood our footsteps. We're balancing each other around ponds, and she clings to my jacket to keep her balance. Nearer the river, Cindy slows, losing interest in the ice.

"D'you have any tobacco?" she asks. "I'd give anything for a smoke."

"I have two tailor-mades," I say, "hidden there in the millshed."

We walk in that direction. I'm taking short steps, packing them firmly so she can follow in my tracks. Edges of furrows are now showing through the hail, and we make greasy footprints, slumping through in places, tracking mud onto the snow.

The day is all soft and fresh with dampness. It is the kind of dampness that you can smell and taste everywhere. My jeans are clinging wet, my wool coat is steaming from the rain, and I'm uncomfortably sweaty beneath it.

The old millshed haunts the upriver corner of the ploughed field. Black and rain-soaked, it has a forlorn magic around it that pulls me in if I am anywhere near. I lift the latch and the sagging door falls open. A gust of wind against the shed lashes us gently forward. Inside it is dark, the only light from the empty windows and the wide horizontal cracks. There is a strong musty smell of cat urine, old clothes and wet sawdust floor. Two cats scamper out past us, moaning and snarling as they run. We sit on an old car seat and light the cigarettes.

Cindy has her eyes closed, enjoying the smoke, not talking. I ease myself back beside her, stretching my legs upward to reach an old metal trunk. I inhale the smoke, holding it deep in my chest before blowing it toward the wavering rows of rusted nails that splinter the board roof. My secret from the family; I am sharing it with Cindy. It gives me a feeling of independence. I relax, enjoying each dizzy puff to the fullest, watching the grey smoke curl upward in streams. Cindy unfolds beside me, her eyes still closed. She has a pretty dimpled face, one which I haven't really looked at much before. She used to have freckles. I can smell something sweet and fresh in her hair. She's become very attractive, I think.

"Steve, gimme a kiss," she says without opening her eyes.

The smoke catches in my throat. "Huh?" Her eyelashes flicker. One pale hand moves toward me across the old vinyl seat.

"I wanna kiss. Kiss me?"

I kiss her cheek, then drag roughly on my dying cigarette and grind it out on the damp sawdust floor.

"No, a real kiss," she says. This time she turns her head, and I kiss her on the lips. "Gimme a hug," she says.

I put my arm around her, I kiss her again, and we're holding each other tightly, her leg draping over me as if she suddenly can't get close enough. Beneath the open jacket, her snug red sweater has lifted from her jeans; I ease my hand under it and touch her smooth back. She presses down now with hot kisses, and my cold fingers work stiffly on the alien hooks of her bra.

"I never done this before," Cindy whispers. "Stevie, you gotta stop it." But she wriggles closer with more of those kisses, her bra opens beneath the sweater. All I can hear is our breathing. My hands move down her back, down to the small waist of her jeans. "This feels so good, Stevie, you make me feel so good."

"Cindy, you're beautiful," I stammer.

"Oh, Stevie, Stevie, stop it. You're so bad."

Are either of us listening to our own words? "I've been thinking about you," I say. "I'm glad you're here."

"D'you always do this with your girlfriends?"

"Just the special ones."

"You're sweet, Stevie, very special." Cindy's hands tighten across my shoulders. "I really like you a lot."

"You do?"

"Oh yes, I like you so much."

Suddenly from behind the shed there is a hollow crack like the sound of a rifle, then a rumble that makes the millshed tremble the way a siding house is jarred by a passing train.

"Ha whooo, hu, hu," someone far across the river whoops. A voice on this side echoes, louder, "Ha whooo, hu, hu!" The world is deafening; churning, crashing, cracking. I pull away from Cindy and look out the window. Tom and Danny are half-running, half-slumping across the field to the river.

The ice is running.

"Oh, my God, I gotta go! I gotta get across! The bridge might go!" Cindy scrambles to her feet and pulls at her clothes. We hurry out the back way, and Cindy hurtles over the field to the highway.

The ice has broken into wide zigzags across the river. As I watch, the water is piling thick chunks into house-high heaps. Above, in the bend, it has broken up in smaller ice slabs upending and bucking, dirty water spilling ahead of the jam. Heavy triangles crowd the banks, scraping the bark from trees and lodging high in the bushes. The constant rumble is like a summer night's storm, like Niagara Falls.

"Stand back!" Tom shouts a warning. "Stand well back. She's a wild ol' bitch today, boys."

A tall spruce snaps beneath a sliding cake of ice and falls full length into the jam, leaving a splintered stump in front of us. Tom's eyes sparkle with excitement. He clenches his fists and shouts as though the angry river is challenging a new kind of spirit in his old body. "Lord God Almighty, what a jam! God be praised!"

Danny and I stand safely back on the hillside above the bank, drawn close together by the crash and thunder of the river. Danny points to things adrift in the current, a few boards scattered on the ice. "Look! Look, there, it's an old shack goin'," he says. "Lookit out there!"

"Boys, there goes Harrison's Road," Tom says, the tension leaving him now. "Poor ol' Maggie grounded now agin fer the summer. Good God." He sighs and turns toward the house, the excitement ended.

As the ice breaks up, it moves along more freely, more quickly. And behind the jam there's black water.

"Look up there," Danny points. "It's all open."

We leave the river. In our minds the ice has gone, though the floes will be running for days. Tom has already made his way up the hill, and I think I can hear him playing "Katie" on his homemade flute. Danny and I follow, glancing back at the open river as we walk.

Cindy waves to us from the other side; with her brother, Nick, she's climbing the hill to their house.

In the evening, the rain stops and the clouds scatter and drift away, letting the sun cast a sudden warmth against the far shore and its hillside. The breeze carries a false scent of summer as it catches the new water, making patches that sparkle like jewels. In the dooryard I can hear the tiny jingle of the wind chimes, like glass birds hanging behind a web of Virginia creeper. And beneath the hill, in the alder swamp, the season's first robin begins to warble and chirp above the sounds of the freshet.

Dance the Rocks Ashore

LESLEY CHOYCE

I think I love him more now that he's losing his mind than I did when I first married him. Pretty funny how things work out that way. He says he doesn't want to go to a doctor, and I don't blame him for that. Never know what they'll do to you. We never went to doctors much the whole time we have been married. Just the way we were, the two of us.

Hard to think ahead about what might come next. Tough enough to focus on the here and now. But I'll tell you, I can see every little detail of our past life together like it's right here before my eyes. The first time I laid eyes on Jim. Getting married before the judge, just the two of us before him in that big empty room. Of course we'd already been living together. Then there's all those pictures of him and me swimming around in my head.

Or sometimes I see pictures of just him. I can see Jim and the dog rolling around together in the yard. We always had a dog because we couldn't have kids. Usually the dog would come with us when we took those long morning walks to the wharf, with the sun just barely fending off the shivers with its thin, grey-silver light. I don't need to get out the photo album to see all that.

Of course I'm not a hundred per cent sure that it's him who's crazy. Could be me. Caught myself staring straight into the TV set the other day and it wasn't even on. I was entertaining myself, I guess, with my own reruns of the past. Better that way, maybe. No commercials, no inter-ruptions. But I don't think that makes me crazy. Jim's the one who wakes up some mornings, and, if I don't wake up myself, he'll be all done up in his rubber boots and sea pants, picking up his gear and heading out the door to his boat.

Only there is no boat. Well, at least, she can't go anywhere. She sits up on land now. The boat's too old and too dry to ever go back into the water. Jim said it wasn't worth keeping her in repair. Like us. Jim and me. Old, tired a lot, one or both of us crazy.

Jim started to lose a grip on things when the fish gave out. Oh, we'd seen it coming for a long time. Jim came home one day, and he sat down on that piece of lawn furniture he'd built out of alder saplings, and he just looked at his hands.

"What is it?" I asked him. I knew something was wrong.

"It's over," was all he said, but I knew what he was talking about. I'd been catching bits and pieces of it on the CBC radio.

"What do you want for your dinner?" I asked him, putting my arm around his shoulders.

"Nothing," he said.

I had to walk away then 'cause I didn't want to have to look at him. I didn't want him to have to see me watching him cry. You know what I mean, what I'm trying to say. About men and all. I went inside and closed the door and let out this big sigh of relief. I could never come out and admit to him that I was secretly happy that it was over. He'd be safe now.

Yes, he did cry. I know that. A man isn't supposed to cry, but I think he can handle it as long as he thinks no one is watching. Jim always cried when the dogs died. Trouble with dogs is that you outlive them. We outlived three, Jim and me. All died of old age, but they died just the same. We have three good dogs buried on the edge of the forest here. Don't know exactly why we never replaced Beauty. She was the last one to go.

I guess Jim never had any real thoughts about what he'd do once he stopped fishing. But it wasn't like he planned to die at sea. Jim had sense. He came home one day with a survival suit that the government helped to pay for. "A man could stay alive in this thing for days at sea if he had to," he said. "Got pockets for food and everything." He put the ridiculous-looking thing on, and then he put his arms around me and hugged me tight. "I'm never gonna drown like them other silly bastards. I couldn't bear the thought of leaving you alone. If my boat ever goes down, you better bet on me out there bobbing around like a cork, waiting for that Jesus helicopter ride. Just make sure I got plenty of sandwiches, in case. I'd hate to be out there without food. That's the only thing that scares me. The thought of missing lunch."

Jim was always a survivor. Nothing got him down. He had that suit ready to just jump into the sea with my sandwiches in his waterproof pockets. He even had radio emergency gear to signal the coast guard by way of a satellite in space. Jim was not a man prepared to go down with his ship. He'd never be that mean to me.

That suit is still hanging upstairs on a hook. Jim never had to use it. It was always with him on the boat, though, ready to save him and keep me from being lonely. It was the suit that got us both going on that conversation, you know the one. "If I go first I want you to . . . " Every married couple goes through that.

"If I go first, I want you to find some sensible, pretty woman and marry her," I said.

"Not possible," Jim said. "The two never go together."

"What's that supposed to mean?" I snapped back, pretending to be insulted.

"What I meant to say was that a man can find a woman with those two qualities only once in life, and I found her."

"You're a liar," I teased. I wanted more of the flattery. Jim never was good at flattery, never said a whole lot about how I looked or if he liked my hair or dress. I learned to live without the language of flattery.

"If I go first," he continued, "you have to do something you always wanted to do but never did because of me."

Funny thing, but right then I actually thought about a whole list of things we never did, things that maybe I would do if he was gone. Drive to Halifax and go to a symphony concert, eat breakfast some day in a fancy restaurant. The whole time we were married, we never once ate breakfast anywhere other than at home, and half the time we were eating it in our kitchen with all the lights on because the sun wasn't even up yet.

Jim saw the look in my eyes, dreaming up a list of things. "If I go first, I want you to do whatever you want. Just be sure to bury me out there with the dogs. I'd like that. They were good dogs."

All he had to do was mention the dogs and I started to cry, feeling awful guilty for even thinking about Jim dead.

"If I go first," I said, "I want you to take good care of yourself." That was all I could get out. Then he gave me a hug and went out to mow the yard with the lawnmower.

I need to explain about the place we live in. It's a house Jim built — well, I helped him build it, too — about thirty years ago. It sits on five acres of land that goes right up to the inlet, with a big lawn stretching down to the sand and the water. Jim has about ten pieces of lawn furniture out there made from those alders and young birch trees. Stick furniture it's called, although the name doesn't do it justice. People admire the chairs because they look like they are still wild and alive. Jim would mow the grass with a gasoline mower, and it would stay green right up into December. We'd go out there on one of those rare, warm days in late fall, and he'd say, "It feels just like summer." The grass was a rich green, the water in the inlet was a piercing blue. Those were good moments. Those were better than any old breakfast in a restaurant.

———

So hard to think of all the good things as being behind us. If we had kids like other people, maybe we'd have that way of talking about the future, seeing it in our children and grandchildren. But we don't have that, and I'm not gonna go worrying myself about what might have been. Like I say, I've got Jim to focus my worrying on.

It was a couple of weeks after the news that the cod were all gone. They might not be back for ten years, a hundred years or ever, that's he way the government man said it. Jim sat down in the yard on his chair with a pile of newspapers he'd pulled out of the wood shed. And he started to read them. Those papers were probably three years old or older. But he just sat down and started to read one after the other — the news, the classifieds with boats for sale, the sports. I didn't say a word about it. What was there to say, anyway?

Later that day when I was in the kitchen making a soup from an old ham bone and some stuff from the garden, Jim was walking around the house from room to room, like he was looking for something. He opened drawers and peered into cabinets, and when he was on his second circuit, I asked him what he was searching for. Jim seemed startled, and he looked at me with this odd blank stare on his handsome face. He tried to shape some words in the air with his hands, he stuttered, and finally he just said, "I don't know."

I saw the fear on his face, and it scared the living daylights out of me, but I didn't let on. I laughed and chastised him for being so absent-minded. "You'd lose your head if it wasn't held on by your neck," I said for the five-hundredth time in our marriage.

———

One night I woke up and touched him on the shoulder. He didn't notice, I'm sure. His breathing was so slow and steady, just like that of a child. I needed to talk, and I guess it didn't matter much if he was awake or not. I'd been feeling guilty for some time about the whole fishing business. Like it was my fault or something that the cod had all gone away. Jim, I said to my sleeping husband, when you said it was all through with the fishing and the boat and hauling off in the morning in the dark to risk you life at sea, I had to hold back from smiling. I had to hold back from going bloody wild with happiness now that I'd never have to worry about you at sea again. Pretty selfish, I know, 'cause I wasn't thinking about how you were feeling but thinking about me. I had you all to myself and wouldn't have to share you with the Atlantic Ocean ever again. Well, I got that off my chest. Knew I had to say it to him some day because it had been burning a hole inside me. But now I didn't feel so bad. Jim was safe, and I would have him with me twenty-four hours a day.

But I guess I was fooling myself somewhat on that. It was like I was going to be punished after all for my selfish, foolish thoughts. The next morning Jim woke up first. When I opened my eyes he was sitting bolt upright in bed, and he was looking around the room in a strange way. I knew already what the look was about. He didn't know where he was. I took a deep breath and sat up. Jim edged away slightly and turned his piercing blue eyes in my direction. I thought they were going to drill right through me. "Who are you?" he asked, his voice almost shaking.

I knew that this would happen sooner or later, and I had been practising in front of a mirror for my own way of dealing with it. I'd read a little bit in the *Reader's Digest* about the disease that was affecting my poor husband's brain. I didn't understand it real well, but I knew there would be these lapses. His memory would go away, and it would come back, a little bit at first, a little more later. Something like the tide going in and out, but it would get more drastic over time. The tide would someday slip out and never come back at all.

"What am I doing here?" Jim demanded as I tried to get a grip on myself.

Here goes, I said to myself, putting into action my little plan. Now, the experts had said, stay calm and reassuring, slowly and carefully remind the person of who he is and where he is. But I wouldn't do that and rob my husband of whatever dignity still threaded its way through his brain.

Instead, I slapped him playfully on the leg, then tickled him under the ribs. "Don't be silly," I teased. "What games are you trying to pull on me?" Then I traced my fingers once through his thinning hair and ruffled it up like when we both had been twenty years old and he had had this big, shaggy mop of thick, curly brown hair.

Truth is I'm a lousy actress, always was. Couldn't recite a couple of lines from a play in school in front of a class, couldn't pretend to be anybody other than who I was in my whole life. This was a real test, I'm telling you.

I'm not sure Jim figured out much of anything in those few seconds except for the fact that he was safe and this was where he was supposed to be. If I'd have asked him, he wouldn't have known his own name, I think, and it would have scared me to the root of my being, but I wouldn't let that scene happen. If Jim was going crazy, then I'd have to go halfway crazy with him if we were going to work it out. One foot in crazy, one on solid ground, that was my plan.

"Let's not get up right yet," I said, and I tickled him some more and wrestled him down under the covers until I got him stirred up enough so that we made love. That was something we didn't need any talk for at all, and whoever the hell we both were right then didn't seem to matter much. Everything worked out just fine. It pulled us both back into some warm, secret world full of tenderness and light.

Afterwards, Jim reached over and flicked the shade on the window so it flipped up in a snap. The late November sunlight came flooding into the room like a big, friendly, happy dog. "What's for breakfast, woman?" Jim asked in his pretend-to-be-tough voice. I had always liked the way he did that, mostly because it was pretend stuff. Jim was tough, all right, but tough deep down in some strong way that few men on this shore would ever know.

"Anything you want," I answered, pretending to be the dutiful wife who only took orders.

At breakfast, Jim talked to me like there was nothing wrong at all, and I knew that I was going to be able to handle whatever the memory eater could throw at me. I even believed that, if I fed Jim enough of the right food and took good care of the old guy, everything would work out fine. That's why I fried up some of the cod tongues we'd kept hoarded away in the freezer for special occasions. Jim loved fried cod tongues for breakfast the way some rich people must love their caviar. But caviar could never compare with cod tongues done up just right. When breakfast was over, I checked the stock of what was left in the freezer. It was a hard case of reality coming back to haunt me. We had maybe a dozen more feeds of the blessed stuff in there. It dawned on me then that, with the cod all killed off, I might not ever be able to replenish the supply. I'd have to dole it out carefully and make it last as long as I could. Cook it up only on extra-special occasions like this.

Jim saw me standing there with the upright freezer door open and cold smoke pouring out over me like a spring fog. I quickly closed the door before he might begin to consider what I was worrying about.

"I'd like to go down to the boat," Jim said to me, and I didn't know if he was still thinking she was in the water afloat or if he could remember that those days were all over. But then he added, "Good day for a walk. Maybe you want to come with me."

"I'd like that," I told him, and began to take the plates off the table until Jim stopped me.

"I'll take care of this. Go get yourself ready."

––––––

Out on the road that morning, we walked the same path Jim would have taken every working day, winter or summer, whenever the weather allowed the boats to go to sea. Despite the cold, the sun felt hot on my face, and I felt young again like you wouldn't believe. Everything made me smile. Jim holding onto my arm, the McCarthy's big stupid dogs yapping at us as we went by, the sunlight sparkling off the ice crystals that grew like diamonds in every blooming pothole on the road. It was a day to be fully alive. It was a cold but clear day, not a touch of wind. I was all bundled up, but Jim had on nothing more than his old ratty wool pullover. We walked down the gravel road that leads from the highway to the fishing wharf. Beyond that point, the road dwindles off to nothing. It doesn't exactly come to an end, it just fades to nothing that looks like a road, just a patch of stubbly stones and a stretch of flotsam and sand. Further beyond is a stretch of rocks sticking up out of the water like broken teeth. That's all that connects what's left of Crofter's Point to the mainland. Still farther out is what's left of the headland where Jim had grown up, on a farm at the very tip of the land named for his family. Unfortunately, the sea has swallowed up most of the old farm. It's hard to believe that in forty short years the Atlantic could have been so hungry as to chew up a barn and a field and so much land. Every time I thought about that place through our entire marriage, I had this sneaking suspicion that the sea had stolen Jim Crofter's family farm and that it was anxious to snatch him away as well. Even though I loved the ocean for its beauty, I never trusted it once in my whole life. We were sworn enemies, she and I. Both of us had wanted Jim, but I had won.

Our home was halfway out from the highway to the wharf. For Jim, it had been a kind of retreat back from the high hill of the headland where he grew up, a safer haven along the less troublesome, less greedy tides of the inlet, with its crystal clear water, its ribbons of eelgrass and its millions upon millions of underwater snails. We had a nice little house set back from the road and that big green lawn that he was always so proud of spilling down to the edge of Five Fathom Harbour. At the sandy shoreline, we had a grand view of every sunset of the year and all the privacy and beauty anybody could cram into a single life-time.

———

When we arrived at the boat, Jim's own *Just My Luck*, it was like a big dark cloud suddenly came swooping across the sky even though the sun was still out bright. Jim sucked in his breath and reached up to put his hand on the bare, weather-stained wood of the gunwale. That touch and the look on his face was something I care not to translate. I was sure he was about to slip into one of his episodes and lose himself, either that or explode like some kind of volcano. Ever since the fishing had gone bad it was like everybody around here was ready to go off like a firecracker. Who the hell was to blame, anyway? Government, politicians, Spanish trawlers, the Russians? Was it us or the sea itself? Nobody could pin it down, and that frustration made some of the men go right crazy. Billy Jobb taking a hammer to the RCMP car one day for no obvious reason. Kyle McCurdy beating on his poor wife until she had to leave him and move to Truro. Stammy Woodhouse, who had always lived alone, just boarded up his house one day and took off in his four-by-four. Nobody ever heard from him.

Jim had his own way of dealing with it. He didn't hardly talk to me or anyone for about ten days. And then he started to lose his memory.

I pried Jim's hand off the side of the boat. We both looked like a pair of prize idiots, I know, standing there in the blasting sunlight staring at the side of an old boat whose paint was peeling badly. All that blue and yellow giving way to grey boards beneath. It seems that every damn thing along these shores of Nova Scotia first turns grey before it eventually gives up the ghost.

Jim turned away from the boat finally and followed the track of where the boat had been hauled up from the inlet, skidded up on parallel logs leading ashore from the water line and the tidal zone, rich green with algae and slime.

"Tide's real low," Jim announced.

"Hardly ever gets that far down," I offered. When you live all those years as a fisherman's wife, you learn that any discussion of tide is a serious matter.

"It does. A couple times a year. Easy to make a mistake coming in past the point. When she gets this low, you don't want to trust the markers."

That's when I noticed Jim had turned his attention seaward. He leaned against *Just My Luck*, and I watched as he drifted off back home, to his first home, that is, on Crofter's Point. A lot of people consider it an island now, since the rocks that connect it to the mainland are underwater most of the time.

It had been a long while since Jim had gone home to what little was left of his old place. The last time he had gone there alone on his boat and rowed the skiff ashore. He never told me more than five words about his visit that time. I looked off to where Jim was staring, and I could see what he had discovered. "You could walk there today, if you don't mind high-stepping all those slippery rocks."

"And if you get there and back before the tide slips."

Once the words were out, there was no turning back. I hated trying to walk on slippery, stony shorelines more than anything else, and there was probably some ice on some of those stones today as well, but like I say, there was no turning back.

"I haven't been home in a long time. Maybe there's still something left."

It was a difficult trudge for me, a real battle of body and mind just to keep from crashing down and breaking a leg or an elbow, but Jim held me steady and had no trouble at all, except for the fact that I was slowing him down. It took forty-five minutes from the end of the road, and it wouldn't have been possible except for the extreme low tide.

Crofter's Point, once a hundred acres of beautiful green pastures just poised above the sea, was now whittled down to a third of that size. Barely anchored to shore by that backbone of boulders and stones we had just travelled, it was as if the place was prepared to let slip from the mainland altogether and drift off to some other continent. Where the hills once curved smoothly and gently down to the sea, now there were ugly, scalloped red dirt cliffs and, above, a dagger-shaped plateau of land that was being hacked away by every storm and wave the world could conspire.

Jim and I climbed up the lowest slope, him holding fast onto my hand as we set more stones free to rattle against their cousins beneath. Jim's parents were long dead, no brothers or sisters left. He still paid taxes on this place and had never argued to have them reduced because of the fact that it was shrinking. We both knew that it would disappear forever without a trace not too many years after we were gone.

The gulls were the true owners of this property now. They nested here on the grass in the early summer, their young ones grew, and those who survived took their first flight at the cliff's edge. They swirled and shrieked about our ears as we walked through the tall, brown grass and dead thistles. I smelled the crush of bayberry plants beneath our feet. "This was quite a place for a boy to grow up," Jim said as his eyes followed the swoop and flow of the gulls around us. Some looked like they were brazen enough to dip down and stab at us with their beaks, but it was as if an invisible barrier prevented them from getting dangerously close. It was obvious they didn't like us being here. They didn't trust us, and I could understand why. I'd seen fishermen shoot gulls for fun, a sickening game. Jim had gotten into a fight more than once with someone over that. He hated seeing anything killed without good cause.

"It was heaven or hell," Jim continued as we walked on to where the family homestead had been. "Heaven on a summer day with blue seas stretching to the horizon. Swimming in the pools with the fish and crabs, sometimes a young harbour seal slipping by right beside you like it was nothing at all. Other times, the storms came and battered away at the barn and the house, and a good blow might last three or four days, and you'd see the sun for only an hour before a new storm would come in right at you again until you thought you would crack. It was during those times my father would start to act like he wasn't my father. He'd bang me around for some foolish thing I'd done."

"He beat you? You never told me." I was taken completely by surprise. How could we have lived together all those years without him ever revealing this?

"It wasn't worth telling, I guess. Besides, I was afraid you knew what I knew — kids who grow up getting batted around by an old man with a temper usually grow up to be just like their fathers."

"That's what they say. But why didn't you ever tell me about it?"

"I didn't tell you at first because I thought it might scare you away from marrying me. Then I didn't tell you after because I thought you'd feel like I had somehow lied by holding it back." Jim was about to either laugh or cry. I didn't know which. "Then after about thirty years I figured it didn't matter anyhow because I turned out not to be like him at all, so what's the point in wasting words on it?"

"Then why tell me now?" I asked.

His face softened into a smile. "Guess I figured I didn't have anything to lose and should get it off my chest." His whole body seemed to relax as I shook my head and called him a big goof. "C'mon," he said, "I want to show you something."

"Something" was the cliff where the barn had tumbled right off the edge into the sea. "I would have liked to have been here during the storm where she let go," Jim said. "I've seen it fall in my dreams a thousand times and thought that if I had been here maybe I could have done something to hold it back. It's crazy, I know." Below us there was a scattering of loose boards, bleached greyish-white by the sun, salt and sea. Certainly not enough left to make a body think it had ever been a two-storey barn. And if the rocks were down there that had once been part of a carefully laid foundation, well, they just looked like all the other ones.

"The barn was right there," Jim said, pointing with his finger into some place that was now only air. I could almost see it suspended in space before us, floating on the light breeze. To think that the barn was gone, the foundation and lumber dropped below into the sea and the very land it once stood on evaporated to nothing. I felt small just then, and vulnerable.

We walked around the dent in the ground that was all that was left of Jim's family home and then crossed over the rim of lichen-covered rocks, and stood inside the old house. "Right about here was my room. The ice pellets used to beat against my window like machine-gun fire. Over there was the kitchen with the wood stove. When all the trees were gone here, I had to row softwood in a dory from up the inlet. Hard and slow work, but I liked it. If I didn't get there and back quick enough to my father's liking, he'd call me slow and lazy and sometimes take a belt to me until I bled." I could see the pain in his face as if the beating had just happened. Then he took a big gulp of air. "Doesn't matter now. All turned out okay. I still miss him as much as my old mother, who never did an unkind thing in her entire life. Funny, eh?"

"Not funny at all. Times were different then."

"I guess. Look at this. My father would never have imagined this could happen. He believed in this place and thought he had captured the best of both worlds — the sea and the soil, cod and cabbages. At least it was enough while it lasted."

"Nothing lasts forever." That was all I had to offer up, that sad, tired old phrase, as we poked around in the soil that had once been beneath the wooden floor. I expected to come across some old child's toy or an old shoe, but there was only dirt and stones and bricks shredded into fragments by the weather.

Suddenly, Jim walked from his old bedroom to the kitchen, for I knew the geography of this troubled home now, and across the threshold where the door had been. He walked straight out, turned left, and, with a sudden burst of energy, ran toward the cliff's edge, about twenty yards away. "Jim!" I screamed at him, afraid that the return trip down memory lane had rattled him badly. What was he about to do? My heart jumped up into my throat.

Jim knelt down on the ground and began to scrape away at the weeds, and I wasn't sure if he was looking for something real or imagined, but when I scrambled over toward him, I could see what he had found. I knelt down beside him. He carefully lifted a dilapidated wooden lid. Below was a dark, clear pool of water. "This well never went dry. Ever." He sounded proud and exuberant and that made me feel tingly inside. "We had the best, purest water in the county, my old man said. And it never dropped an inch."

Jim threw off the wooden lid and leaned over. The water was almost flush with the ground. He pushed his face right into it and drank long and hard. When he looked up at me, droplets of water streamed from his face and caught the sunlight as they spilled onto the ground. "You know something, Mary? I feel like it was okay that I had heaven and hell, both of them, right here. I had the best life. And it just got better when I left here. I feel so completely alive."

I held his face in my hands. The cold drops of water collected on my fingers, and I put them to my mouth. The taste, oh my God, the taste of it all.

To the gulls still spiralling above, we must have seemed like a curious pair of humans, kneeling side by side as if in prayer beside a hole in the ground. I looked up at those gulls, catching the updraft of air at the edge of the headland, and wondered at the amazing fact that this well, dug by Jim's temperamental father, was now only eight feet from the very brink of the cliff and a drop off of over a hundred feet.

The well was full to the brim with fresh, life-giving water, impossibly close to the end of the land where soil and stones gave way to empty air. A miracle of nature that could only result from this being the best well in the county, right here in heaven-and-hell land. But the miracle would be transient. In a year or two, five at the most, the land would give up, the rocks would be loosed by the wind, and the cold, fresh water of the Crofter's well would spill out into the air, cascade down the side of the red dirt cliff and wash into the sea.

———

"Tide's sneaking up on us," Jim said, helping me to my feet. "Time to dance you ashore." It was an old expression of his. Walking on rocks was always like a dance. Jim would lead, I would follow. It was as if his feet agreed to the shape of each stone, negotiated a perfect hold, while mine rebelled at every step. A fresh wind had come up off the sea, and it had the sting of winter to it. Halfway back to shore, the dryer rocks had given way to little slapping waves, and we were ankle deep before we had finished the dance of rocks back to the mainland. We walked home with numb toes and warm hearts. Jim fell asleep that afternoon, the first of many daytime naps that lasted frighteningly long — two hours, three. Sometimes I'd have to wake him for dinner.

———

The ice came but no snow. The inlet began to freeze over quicker than any year I had ever seen. While the back yard grass remained green but frozen stiff, the pans of ice heaved and hawed in the inlet, a vast glazed expanse, reshuffled each day as the tides pushed renegade islands of ice right up to the foot of the sandy little beach. On some days Jim would forget to stoke the stove, and the house would go cold. If he caught me carrying in logs or splitting softwood at the chopping block, he would feel terribly bad, beg my forgiveness and say he'd never let it happen again. I told him I didn't mind. I needed the exercise, and besides, this was better than doing like those ladies in the magazines who lifted weights or jogged around city streets to stay healthy. I didn't mind the work at all.

And there were days when Jim was with me and days when he was only half there. He'd lose his shoes or lose his coat or his boots, or wonder where he had left the money in his wallet. He'd try to tell me about a dream he had but lose himself in the middle of a sentence and only in his most desperate moments come right out and say, "I don't even know who I am," or, even more frightening to me, admit, "I don't know where I am."

Once or twice I caught him napping outside on his stick furniture, where he had gone to enjoy the view of all that inlet ice at sunset. I had to keep a close eye on him, all right.

I won't try to tell you these were the best of times, but they were not the worst. I just felt the weight of so much responsibility. At first it didn't bother me at all, but it soon began to wear me down, until one day, feeling exhausted and drained, and secure in the fact that Jim was napping soundly on the chesterfield near a warm wood stove fire, I lay down on the afternoon bed and closed my eyes.

I opened them when a brazen goldish red beam of light from the west window shone straight into my eyes. I had slept to nearly four-thirty. The sun was going down. The house was cold. I shook myself awake and realized I was alone in the room. In the kitchen, the fire had gone out in the stove. The door was open. Jim was nowhere around. Panic shivered in my limbs and a knot of fear twisted into a tourniquet in my gut.

Outside, it was still but cold, bitter cold. I walked quickly to the road and slipped on the ice of a frozen puddle. I fell hard and scraped my shin on a jagged rock. I stood back up, steadied myself and made it to the road.

Not a car, not a soul in sight. I retreated to the back yard and walked slowly across the frozen green lawn. Before me was Jim's high-back home-made chair. Each step was painful to me but not nearly as painful as something stabbing at my heart.

Somebody was in the chair. I advanced toward the dark, silent silhouette of my husband. The red wash of the December sun made the ice of the inlet go blood red, a screaming colour that invaded me with cold and fear that conspired into something hot and awful.

Jim had positioned himself here to watch the sun go down over the inlet he loved. He had even dressed warmly in the only coat he could probably locate — one of mine, a bulky blue winter affair with a hood. As I kneeled down in front of him, I knew that I was not at all prepared for this. His head was slumped over. I was having a hard time getting air into my lungs, and I could hear my blood pounding in my ears.

Fear had scissored big holes in my ability to reason and clamped shackles onto my arms and legs. I could not bring myself to pull the hood back off my husband's head and read the sorry news. Instead, I gave up on everything, my belief in myself, my hopes and my happiness. I put my head upon his knees and wept. No sound could escape from me, but my body quaked with convulsions of despair.

The next thing I knew I felt the lightest pressure of a hand upon my head. I felt a human hand stroking my hair and I looked up. In the dying winter light, I saw the face of my husband and heard the sweet song of my own name, "Mary, Mary, Mary."

I was unable to find a path back to the world of language as he lifted me towards him and wrapped his arms around me, repeating my name again and again, pulling us both back into the realm of the living.

"I was just sitting here," he said, "remembering summer. The sun was warm on my face, and I was enjoying it so much. I guess I fell asleep. It felt so much like summer. Remember what it was like?"

"I remember," I said. "I could never forget."

"Nothing is ever really lost," he said, and continued to stroke my hair as if I was a little child, as if he was the one whose strength allowed me to cope with living.

"I know that," I said, realizing just then that I had come to grips with the eventual loss of my husband. During all our life together he had been building up my own strength, preparing me for the time when the water in the well would be released from the hill, greet the sky, then slip down the cliff of the faltering land and find its way back into the sea. Sooner or later I would be able to accept this absolute fact. But as I led my husband back into the house, I knew that first I would drink deeply from the well and appease the thirst that was in me.

Poems in a Cold Climate

BERNICE MORGAN

A woman stands in a window, smoothing the sleeves of her red wool dress. Through the double glass she watches the first snow of winter swirl into drifts around her car.

A passerby, glancing at the lighted window, would think her young, happy, a woman waiting for her lover, would imagine an open fire, wine glasses on a tray in the room behind her. The passerby would shiver and trudge on, feeling deprived.

Sarah Norris is in fact neither young nor, at the moment, happy. She is the recently deserted (she can think of no other word, although this one seems dramatic, replete with soap opera overtones) wife of Ted Norris, who is, by the grace of God, Sarah's typing ability, and years of summer courses, now a Ph.D., professor of cultural anthropology and author of the just-published book *Patterns of Settlement and Folklore in Newfoundland Outports*.

The room behind Sarah is as comfortable as the passerby would wish. It has soft chairs, soft lighting, many books, and pictures that do not scream for attention. It is, a friend has told Sarah, a civilized room. The idea pleases Sarah, who pretends to be a civilized person. Really, the room gives nothing away. It is a room that could, and does, exist anywhere in the world where American magazines and American furniture can be shipped.

Half a mile from this civilized room the continent of North America ends, slashed-off black cliffs knife into the North Atlantic. Sarah Norris is thinking about these cliffs as she stands looking out at the snow and stroking her wool-covered arms. How easy it would be to gun the car up that last steep hill. To shoot out over the ocean for a second before plunging down into the icy darkness. She shivers. It would be a cold going and Sarah loves her comfort.

Stupid, really, to even think this way. Self-indulgent and pointless, her grandmother would have said. Over the years Sarah has replaced God with a group of women, her grandmother and great-aunts, who gaze down with stern disapproval from some Protestant heaven Sarah refuses to believe in. Having spent their lives fighting the sea, moving slowly inland, these women have no sympathy for thoughts of easy death.

Sarah cannot assess how serious these thoughts of death are. Is it possible that she is really considering such a thing? She thinks no. Yet the picture of that last, minute-long flight fascinates her — the car arching through swirling snow into a frozen sea. She suspects she would change her mind halfway through that final plunge; reverting to type, she would try to climb out, claw her way back onto the cliffs.

It is Sunday, the fourth since Ted left. Having deliberately rejected her parents' Sunday rituals of church, roast beef and afternoon drives, Sarah thought she had no rituals of her own. She now knows better. Memories of late breakfasts, of toasted muffins and marmalade, of the untidy living room strewn with newspapers and coffee cups, of long walks and sometimes, when the boys were gone, of afternoon love-making all depress her.

I'll just have to make new rituals, she tells herself, reviewing a catalogue of ways a single woman can spend Sundays. The muffins and marmalade, newspapers and coffee and even the long walks — she could borrow the neighbours' dog — can all be enjoyed alone. What about sex though?

She thinks about the men she knows: those at the office, all firmly married and totally unattractive; her dentist is half her age, besides he has long limp fingers, quite revolting. The only other man Sarah can think of is Mike. The thought of going to bed with plump, rumpled Mike makes her smile.

Maybe she could go down to the waterfront and shanghai a Spanish or Portuguese seaman — she's always thought they looked sexy and quite harmless, if one of them could be cut off from the pack. Into bed, sex and a few murmured phrases neither could understand, out of bed and back to the waterfront. It would be efficient and quite satisfactory. It's an idea worth thinking about — altogether as fascinating as the car going over the cliffs at Cape Spear.

When the phone rings she is still smiling, adding convincing detail to the scene with the Portuguese. Will she ask him to take a bath first? No, better not, he might be insulted. Maybe she can turn it into a game, they will take a shower together. He might think this is the usual prelude to sex in Canada.

"Well, you certainly sound happy. What have you been up to?" It's Beth, of course, making sure no one has forgotten tonight's poetry reading. " . . . you know the last time we had a reader in — that art gallery reading — there were only twelve of us."

Sarah knows. She often wonders why the Poets' Guild sponsors these readings when so few people seem interested. Well, it puts some badly needed government money into the hands of a few writers, and sometimes the visiting poets are quite nice, willing not just to read their own work but to do workshops with the Guild. And for the poets it's almost irresistible, every author in Canada seems eager to visit Newfoundland at least once. Sarah cannot understand this sudden popularity of the place she has lived in all her life. In the last few years it has become exotic rather than quaint, culturally rich rather than backward, an impressive addition to any writer's curriculum vitae.

She assures Beth she will be at the reading. Yes, she remembers it's been moved to a downtown pub. No, she doesn't need a lift, she can clear the snow off her car in a minute. As she hangs up, Sarah wonders what Ted is doing tonight.

It would be awkward if her husband turned up at the Ship Inn with his girl. But it seems unlikely. Leah (a young anthropology student whom Sarah has not seen but whom she has a very clear picture of, having forced Ted to describe her in detail) would surely prefer a more upscale place. Anyway, if Ted saw the sign Poets' Guild Reading on the door (Sarah knows they are there, having made the signs herself) he would never go in. Now a published author, Ted has no patience with people he refers to as hobby writers, a term that infuriates Sarah. It is so unfair. Useless, of course, to point out that at least three of the group have had books published and that every one of them gets an occasional poem in one of the little magazines that spring up and die continually across Canada. Ted has selective hearing.

Everyone has a special thing, Ted once told her, something that becomes a logo of identity. It can be almost anything, a distinctive eye coloration, a talent for fortune telling, for making good fudge, winning at card games or taking diesel engines apart. Whatever it is, it becomes in each person's mind the thing that defines them, that makes them separate, better than anyone else. Hers, Ted said, was the idea of herself as a poet.

Sarah does not recall what had gone before this conversation. They had never mentioned it again but she thinks of it often. Maybe it is so. Occasionally, Ted said things to remind her of it, like, "The poet at forty . . ." (looking at family pictures taken on her birthday) or, more coldly, "The poet is temperamental" (this when she'd refused to attend a faculty Christmas party). He made these remarks in a charming, teasing way that many women found endearing.

For the first time Sarah wonders what Ted's special thing is. Surprising, really that she hasn't pondered this question before. It might, as the magazines say, have saved their marriage.

Sarah has not told her sons that their father is gone. In a few weeks they will be home for Christmas, Peter from the University of Toronto and Jesse from whatever god-awful job he is now doing in Alberta. She will explain to them then — or maybe it will all be over by then.

She decides to go out to clear snow away and make sure her car will start. It hasn't moved since Friday. Quickly she pulls on an old jacket Ted has left hanging in the back porch. It smells of him. Sarah can remember him wearing it years ago when they'd taken the boys skating on Burton's Pond. The bitter cold had driven the grownups back into the car, where they sipped cocoa from a thermos and listened to CBC music. She remembers cuddling into the furry collar of the coat. He'd put his arm around her and hummed along with the radio all the songs from *Showboat* — "Old Man River" and "Only Make Believe" — as they watched their sons swoop across the blue and white ice.

The Hollywood snow, so different from the real stuff that will come later, sweeps away easily. By the time Sarah stomps back into the house she is feeling cheerful and competent. The living room looks so inviting and tidy that she quickly lays a fire. After the reading she will ask a few people back.

Just as she is about to leave, the phone rings again. This time it is Mike, the token male in the poets' group. He is looking for a lift. Other men come and go (Beth says this is because Ruth and Marcie are feminists and scare them off), but Mike, chaser of dreams, joiner of good causes, sometimes teacher and always bum, remains. He attends all the workshops and even takes his turn at entertaining the women in his grubby basement flat. The Guild has been together for sixteen years. Sarah knows this because it began the year that Peter, her youngest son, started school. After so long no one hesitates about asking small favours, visiting each other during sickness or confiding to each other griefs they cannot write poems about. Once every two or three years a new person comes and gets absorbed into the circle, or someone moves away, often writing to the group for years afterwards.

Ted had all the tribal customs of the Poets' Guild worked out. He once joked that he was going to produce a paper on the subject for some anthropological journal.

On the streets leading downtown the snow has turned to ice. Sarah parks near a church several blocks from the waterfront pub she's never been in. Mike tells them insiders refer to it simply as the Ship. It turns out to be a comfortable place, apparently subjected to a burst of decorator's fever that passed before the project was finished. An artificial log burns happily inside an open Scandinavian wood stove, oak church pews are pushed up to red arborite tables. One corner of the room is raised and covered in orange carpet. This platform holds an untidy collection of sound equipment, cords, loudspeakers and a mike, along with an old-fashioned parlour piano painted shiny black.

Sarah and Mike are half an hour early, but Beth is already there, sitting alone in a pew jammed tight against the orange platform. She waves and they zigzag between the empty chairs to join her. Two regulars, no doubt having read the sign on the door, sit as far away from the platform as possible, drinking steadily and silently.

The only visible employee is a woman of about forty with black curly hair and very red lips. She has a pleasant motherly face but keeps it firm and businesslike. She is getting through a Sunday night shift as painlessly as possible.

Neither Sarah nor Beth is used to pubs; Mike is too poor, so no one offers to buy a round. Instead, awkwardly, they each order and each pay for one drink. The waitress is very conscientious, counting out three piles of change, but she doesn't come back to their table. She has resigned herself to a low-drink, low-tip night. Watching her, Sarah thinks they have already been catalogued. She can see the woman pulling off her tight boots, hear her telling her daughter about the terrible slow night, poetry reading bunch — Newfoundlanders, but not a lively crowd and terrible tippers.

Beth, who is small, dark and nervous, keeps counting the empty chairs, willing them to fill. "We did everything we could, sent out a press release — of course no one printed it — put signs up all over the university, at the health food stores — what about the bookstores? Did anyone put posters in the bookstores?"

Sarah nods. She doesn't share this sense of responsibility and is afraid that any minute Beth is going to insist that the three of them take some action — call Guild members, make a larger sign for the door, go out into the alleyway and force passersby to come in.

Mike will have none of this. He pats Beth's hand in his absent-minded way, tells her to hush, relax, people will turn up. He tells them that a copy of *Pottersfield Portfolio* containing his new poem arrived today. He's pleased — the editors gave it a full page and a nice layout — but he is a bit mystified; for some reason the last verse is missing.

"I don't know if it was an accident or intentional. Maybe the poem is better without the last verse. Look, what do you think?" Mike pulls the magazine and a crumpled notebook from his knapsack, which, like Mike, is a relic of the wonderful sixties, still showing the stains of wine spilled at Woodstock. Mike has written a poem about the knapsack.

They talk, Beth stops counting people. Mike eventually catches the eye of the waitress and they each order another drink.

Slowly the room begins to fill: Mary and her husband Andrew, Ruth and Marcie and, at another table, Pat with her new boyfriend and an unknown couple. A local printer-cum-publisher arrives with two people from the university's English department.

Beth counts twenty-seven people. "Not too bad a showing. Of course some of them are just here to drink. Still, you can never be sure. I think one of those guys in the corner is a *Telegram* reporter; he might be interested in poetry."

Then Cora and Margaret arrive with the poet. He is young, tall, thin, good looking. They've driven around the bay, given him the obligatory view of real Newfoundland that St. John's presumably cannot offer. He's been lucky; Margaret has an aunt in Bareneed and they were invited to dinner.

Margaret brings him over to their table.

His name is Julian Grant. Is this possible, Sarah wonders, or is he one of those writers who make up a name for themselves? He is aglow with spillover from the experience of an outport Sunday dinner complete with fourteen assorted relatives of Aunt Grete's and, he tells them, roast beef, salt meat and cabbage, three other vegetables and Yorkshire pudding, topped off with trifle and strong tea, and a large drink in the living room while the women were in the kitchen cleaning up, and stories — he calls them yarns, and has written several down in his little notebook during the drive back to town.

Sarah nods and smiles and nods, willing herself to flow with the brimming goodwill. But honestly, she is thinking, do people believe these events are real? If he arrives at Aunt Grete's door next Sunday, the relatives may well be in the middle of a bitter argument. And without doubt, unless he is accompanied by Margaret, Aunt Grete, whom he now thinks of as his closest relative, will not remember ever having seen the sky over him.

Sarah is probably being unjust; she often is.

She estimates Julian Grant to be only a little older than Jesse. Jesse would admire him. Admire the soft worn cords, the faded L.L. Bean shirt that sells for $150. Sarah has become an expert at estimating how much the casual look for men costs.

The poet jumps onto the platform, begins arranging material on the piano stool — his file folder, three magazines and his published collection of poems. All have little markers of coloured paper. In a conversational tone he tells them that the coloured markers are his wife's idea. Different colours indicate poems for different moods, so that he can suit his reading to the audience. But, he says, looking up with a happy smile, he will not tell them what the colours indicate. He also has extra copies of his book, which he hopes they will buy later. He takes his time, moving the sound equipment back, tapping the mike with the tips of his fingers. He asks the waitress to please turn off the music and, if possible, dim the lights. The woman, Sarah notes, obliges with the first kindly look of the night.

Eventually he begins to read. He has a confident, pleasant voice. Even the regulars sitting at the bar seem to listen.

The readers are always good looking, either handsome young men or handsome older women. Sarah mulls over this phenomenon. Where are the plain young women, the ugly old men poets?

Julian Grant is good. He gestures a lot. Sarah, who notices hands, likes his. They are tanned and long fingered. Between poems he talks about how he gets ideas, about his place in Nova Scotia — an old farm house

195

overlooking the river — about his wife Teresa and his five-year-old daughter Amanda, about the pets they shelter in the winters and free in the springs. Sarah suspects this easy involvement. He and Teresa do not seem to get stuck with dogs in the early stages of prolonged death or neurotic cats who want to live on top of the fridge. She resents this ability, which she totally lacks, to garner all the blessings of caring without any of the messiness. Is it just very good luck, or are some people more selective in their loving?

Or maybe the secret is Teresa. Sarah imagines a beautiful Irish woman with dark red hair and pale, pale skin that gives her a fragile look. But Teresa is not fragile. She drowns the cats, dogs and birds when Julian is in town talking to his publisher. He doesn't know this, of course, and continues to write poems about them foraging through the summer countryside.

He tells the audience he has just put in a flush toilet, a real sign of success, he says, for an Atlantic Canadian poet. Then he reads a wonderful poem about this acquisition. Leaning back, his hips jut out, the muscles at the back of his legs make a long strong line in the grey cord. He is the only person in the room with hip bones.

"If I had a daughter I would lock her up," Sarah thinks.

She turns her head slightly to study the faces around her. As always, the audience is made up of middle-aged women and a smattering of men, one or two obliging lovers and husbands who have grown to accept the eccentric activities of their partners. Sarah once heard Andrew, Mary's husband, tell Ted, "Well, it's better than Valium . . ."

In the dim, blue light the ageing faces tilt upward, moon-like, adoring, held captive by the beautiful young man, by the words that flow down so neatly, so cleverly contrived, so charmingly delivered.

Sarah thinks she might be ill. She can feel bile rising at the back of her throat. She hates Julian Grant. She hates him more than she has ever hated anyone. She begrudges him his apple tree, his Teresa, his Amanda, his view of the river, even his flush toilet.

There is a lot of applause when he finishes. People get up, mill about looking happy and relieved: happy for the audience that the poet was so good, happy for the poet that the audience was so good. They chat, buy more drinks, buy the poet drinks.

"He was great — even Andrew enjoyed it!" Mary whispers to Sarah.

Beth and Mike go up to talk to him, and Beth buys one of his books, which she brings over to show Sarah. He has written, "To Beth of New-foundland, fellow poet. From your friend Julian."

Sarah decides she will not, after all, ask anyone back to the house tonight.

Mike, Beth and Sarah walk up the hill together. Mike recites a few of the poet's lines. There is a long pause. Then Mike says, "You know, the likelihood of anyone publishing a first book of poetry after the age of forty is one in 600,000."

They are all quiet.

The night has turned clear and still. Snow scrunches underfoot. Inside their clothing their bones are ever so fragile, thin as the shells of sea creatures bleaching on rocks. They move closer together, the heavy cloth of their winter jackets touching, so aware of the cold flesh underneath that, had they been another race, they would have embraced and cried in each others' arms.

from The Bay of Love and Sorrows

DAVID ADAMS RICHARDS

Karrie's father owned the gas bar just above Oyster River, a small gas bar, a hang-out for kids, with a penned-in mass of dark, worn tires in the back yard — tires worn by miles of travel to places going nowhere along the hard-bitten coast — and with the grass unkempt and bordered by a rundown fence. A circular drive led to their gas pumps and small store that sat dead in the heat on summer days.

———

Tommie Donnerel was a neighbour. He was busy renovating his house, building a new room for his brother and restoring the front porch. Sometimes he would come down to the gas bar for a moment. Or he would be seen at the dances at the community centre. Karrie liked him, but he never seemed to pay much attention to her.

He had the run of the farm now that his parents were dead, and people seemed to empathize with him, because his older brother was retarded.

Karrie liked to think of him as heroic and to think that she was willing to invest in him because of his sterling qualities, which were apparent to everyone.

The trouble, if it could be said to be trouble, was that his best friend was Michael Skid. Michael was the person who helped him with the renovating of his house, the one with him after the death and during the funeral of his parents, who were killed in an accident at Arron Brook. Karrie had to weigh this as a serious problem, for, all in all, she wished to be liked and side with the right people on her road. And Michael Skid was well known as wild and unpredictable. Besides this, she didn't like the way he looked at her. And there was that fling he had had with Nora Battersoil. And what became of it no one knew. But Karrie's stepmother said he was awful, and that like most rich people from town he loved to argue about the world and used some kind of drugs.

So Karrie bided her time and waited. And just as she suspected, the summer following Tom's parents' death the two men had a falling-out of some kind. In fact, she heard they had almost had a fistfight. Michael went away, and Tom was left to finish the porch and the room alone.

For a long while, Tom seemed to be unmoved by Karrie or her reddish blonde hair. She had invited him over to the local graduation party at the church centre — as soon as she had heard about the falling-out between him and Michael — but he had not come.

She then sent him an invitation to come to her graduation, which took place a week later. Yet, in the cramped auditorium with so many sweaty people, the gowns of the graduates half-askew, and the outside June evening pale with gusts of heat, she couldn't see him.

She won the prize for Home Economics, but when she received it she felt that no one clapped for her like they did the others.

Then she went to the prom with a boy from her class, who wore an audacious white tuxedo and kept saying he knew where all the parties were. They ended up driving the roads in his father's car until after midnight, finally finding a party at a house of a boy neither of them knew. The boy, whose name was Lyle McNair, saying: "Come — get acquainted — please don't stand back, now."

They spent the evening sitting in the kitchen with Mr. and Mrs. McNair, who tried to make them feel welcome.

But after an hour Karrie insisted that she go home. She let her date kiss her once, smelling stale aftershave on his white chin. Going up to her bedroom she combed the perm out of her hair, and got into bed with a romance novel.

———

Sometimes that summer she would go to the first Mass on Sunday instead of the late Mass, because Tom was known to do so. After Mass one morning she stayed behind to light a candle, just to see if he would stay behind too. But he didn't. And she left the church by the back way and ran home down the narrow path.

Later, in July, she walked the highway when she knew he would be bringing hay up from the lower field. She would pretend to be surprised every time she saw him.

This, in fact, went on for a long while. She was very sad about this, and quite sensitive. And she would write in her diary: "How can he go out into the middle of the bay alone? I went out to the shore — but as always — he came in on the far side of the wharf and didn't even notice me — why is he so cruel?"

It was very strange, but all this made her feel somewhat special. She found her stepmother cruel to her too, and bossy. Especially once when Vincent, Tom's brother, came by the gas bar with a note written on his shirt that Tom had pinned there. There was a great deal of gaiety about this note, and everyone had joined in this gaiety except her. Her stepmother had laughed the loudest, looking around at everyone with her face beet-red and startled.

"Please send home by ten o'clock," the note read. Vincent started laughing also, without knowing why.

And then one night, Karrie invited Vincent into the house for a Coke. The house was very warm, had a miserable quality permeating it, which Karrie herself had understood from early youth. It was not that the house, with its pink shutters and long wainscotting, was a violent house. It was the absence of affection.

Karrie wandered about, as if sleepwalking, got Vincent a Coke and a dish of ice cream, and watched him eat at the kitchen table. It was her stepmother, Dora's, quart of strawberry ice cream, and Dora watched her to see how much she was going to take.

"Do you like that, Vincent?" Karrie said.

He looked up at her, wiped his mouth, and said, "I gotta come home by ten."

"Would you like me to walk you home, Vincent?" she declared suddenly, as she rested her pretty head on her hand in a bored way. There was a fly walking up the wall behind him, and watching it made her eyes brilliant and bright.

"Let him find his own way," her stepmother said, in characteristic mean-ness that Karrie was so familiar with. She looked over at Dora, who was only eleven years older than herself, and said nothing.

Karrie put on a kerchief and lipstick, and she and Vincent started on their way. It was well after ten.

They could hear the waves crashing far beyond them and, beyond the dark immovable trees, they heard the roar of Arron Brook, which always stayed high, and which Vincent was told never to go near.

Thin clouds swept the night sky like crooked hawks, and the moon shone on the old potato field to their right, behind some forlorn hedges. Wrappers and cardboard lay in the ditches that once had many flowers. It made Karrie melancholy and sad to think of this road, and those broken trees, and her mother, who used to come in from work every night at quarter past five all winter long, and who died during a simple appendix operation.

As they approached the halfway mark of their journey Karrie ran out of things to ask Vincent about Tom, and things to say about herself, so she kept talking about the moon, and the clouds, and wasn't it a lovely night — and how many more nights would they have just like this?

They saw a man approaching them along the road. His body looked strong and fit, without ever taking pains to be.

"Tommie — Tommie," Vincent yelled, and ran up to him, patting him all over the chest and shoulders. "Tommie, Tommie."

"Thank God," Tom said. It was at this moment, and with a certain amount of emotion, that Karrie realized how protective Tom was of his brother.

"I brought him home for you," Karrie said, and emotion rang in her voice.

"Thank you," Tommie said. "Thank you, thank you. My God, I thought he had gone up Arron Brook."

"Thank you, thank you," Vincent said, turning around. "But she has to come and see my puppy."

"Oh, the puppy," Tommie said, smiling.

"It doesn't matter," Karrie said.

"Oh no — come on up to the house — come on — have a cup of tea — all right?" Tom said. "Please, I want you to — I wanted to invite you over before now."

"Okay," she said.

And off they went, the three of them together.

The puppy, named Maxwell, stayed in Vincent's part of the house, and Vincent had his own key to the door. He was proud when he was able to open this door, and prouder still that Maxwell ran to him before anyone and began to pee. Karrie did not like puppies very much but she pretended to for Vincent's sake. And she patted its matted fur with her painted fingernails, crouching down on her haunches.

Vincent was very pleased that Karrie could see his pictures of his mom and dad, and even more pleased when she said she liked the room, and found it "just right" for him.

She had a cup of tea. The wind was blowing, and the trees waved in the darkness. Far below them they could see the streetlight over her house, which her father was proud of.

Each time Tom spoke she would nod and look away from him, and then bite at her lower lip, as if afraid that she was going to say something inappropriate. He seemed so strong and self-reliant at this moment that she felt he wouldn't look upon her as anything but a schoolgirl. And as she sat there she felt her legs shaking just slightly.

She finished her tea too quickly, she thought, and then thought she was too abrupt when she said she didn't want another.

"Do you want me to walk you home?" Tom said.

"Well, okay," she said, as if angry with something.

And they started down the road together.

"I didn't come to your graduation party, or your graduation either," he said.

"I know," she said. There was a peculiar emphasis on the word *know* that sounded, in the dark night, longing and sensuous.

"I wanted to — but I don't know what to do at them things — and then I wanted to tell you that in church — but you were busy lighting candles, I think to your mom's memory, and so I couldn't. And then — well, you ran out the back way, while I waited for you. I haven't been able to figure out when I was going to see you at the right time. A long time ago I tried to ask you for a dance — but I couldn't get up the nerve, I s'pose."

"You did — ?" she asked. There was a tiny smile at the corner of her mouth, just visible, which because of the way she was walking, with her arms folded like a country girl, seemed indispensable to her character.

"I don't know 'nough to go up to no graduation," he said. "I shoulda answered ya — and then I thought ya might have been mad at me — or eventually I thought you had a boyfriend — Bobby Taylor is always over there at the store."

She burst out laughing and turned and hugged him. He could feel her warm body press into him, and he was somehow overwhelmed by her. Instinctively he felt he must hold her the right way or lose her to someone else.

"Bobby Taylor," she laughed. "He's already engaged!"

She looked up at him in a very strange way, as if asking a question, and then, without finding an answer, hugged him hard again.

Act of God

JOAN BAXTER

The wind blasted through the louvres like the cold breath of death, waking Jillian up. The red numbers on the radio alarm flashed — 3 a.m. A crack of lightning coincided with the thunder and a gust of wind that shook the house. Sheets of lightning thrashed at the sky.

Then the power went out. No more red flashing lights to tell her what time, no light to remind her what century it was.

She lay awake, suffocating in the dark, listening to the storm recede, disappointed that it had not unleashed its torrential rains on Talon. The harvest would fail if the rains didn't come soon. She had asked the women farmers with whom she worked in the villages what they would do then. "We will suffer," they said. "Sometimes when God has given us too many gifts, He has to take some back, so we will know how to suffer."

The blackness was complete. She dreaded the depth of the night here. It crowded her, brought fears and doubts. What if the people really hated her, the foreigner come to "help" them? What did those smiling market women really think of her? Did her African co-workers on the rural credit project secretly resent her being there, collecting a salary ten, fifty times higher than theirs, money her country was ostensibly giving to theirs? Was this guilt a western medicine, a placebo to replace real suffering?

She wondered what lay behind the smiles of her counterparts on the project. Had all the friendly village women welcomed her to their country with open arms only to shut her out of their lives?

The neighbourhood cocks were silent — even the sounds of the night insects were muted as though the crickets were downcast by the betrayal of the storm that came without rain. The doubts and undefined fear kept her awake until dawn shone its faint grey light through the windows.

In the kitchen she turned on the tap to fill the kettle and nothing happened. Damn it to hell. Another water cut. Water cuts threw her into confusion, disrupted the routine that permitted her to fabricate a sense of belonging here. The power was still off and the refrigerator was already defrosting on its own, leaking water onto the kitchen floor. Power outages soured her mood the way they soured the milk in the silent refrigerator.

She searched for batteries for the radio and found only an empty package. Threw it on the floor in despair. That meant no morning news. Without those short-wave newscasts from world capitals, the isolation grew. Detached, dispassionate voices reading news helped her remember a world where she had once belonged.

She slammed the kettle into the sink. "No power. No water. Do you want me to die in this damn hole?" She was shouting now. She wanted to fill the silence, the loneliness, the vacuum in the house with her rage.

She put a hand over her mouth. What if someone was passing? A watchman perhaps, going home from his night's work? What stories would start to circulate? "White madam be lunatic-o, and proper."

If she complained at the office about the lack of power and water, people would commiserate. Bukari, her driver, would say, as he always did, that the water and sewerage corporation was making some extra money again by shutting off the pipes so that the Talon water mafia — the men who owned tanker trucks — could sell water to people and "grow fat."

He told her that people in Talon could always go out to fetch water at Independence Valley. That was the name they had given to a half-finished two-storey warehouse on the outskirts of town. It had been started under the country's first president after independence. "But then the money was finished like always because the Big Men chop it," he told her. "Underneath that building, there's water. They wanted to store grain there, it was going to be a silo. Now it's just full of water from the rainy season. It is not good water, but the people go down there whenever the water is off. It's not nice, the stairs are steep and the girls fear the place."

Bukari was the one who recommended and then found a water tank for Jillian to keep on her compound for these emergencies. But Bukari was a rebel, someone who, at least in his mind, tackled the criminals who were the authorities. When she asked Mary, who cleaned and washed twice a week for Jillian, about the water shortages, Mary would shrug and smile and say, "It be an act of God, Madam. God no be blind. He see what awful thing people do nowadays-o. So he send the storm, but the rain do not fall."

Jillian picked up the kettle, slipped on her flip-flops and went out into the grey gloom of the early morning. Dark clouds scudded past on the dawn breeze. Above them was the pale blue promise — threat — of another sunny day. She longed for a week of rain, the kind of weather that made people back home complain because it spoiled summer barbecues and days at the beach. She walked around the house to the water tank that was settled unevenly on four bricks behind the garage, mentally thanking Bukari for his foresight and ingenuity. She fiddled with the lock on the faucet, thinking that if things worked here — if the water corporation provided people with water as it was supposed to — she wouldn't have to lock the faucet on the tank to keep all the women in the neighbourhood from helping themselves. In fact, she wouldn't even need the tank.

There were so-called experts out in the villages working on wells and dams; in town, where there was a water system, it didn't work because of corruption and neglect. So why did *she* feel so guilty? She had been fighting the guilt since she came a year earlier. But the only defence she had against guilt was anger, and that didn't help.

She tossed the padlock to the ground and squatted to fill the kettle.

"Morning, morning, Madam."

Aisha, the tomato girl, was standing a few feet from her, smiling. The metal tray of tomatoes on her head dipped as she bowed. Jillian wanted to tell her to go away. Normally she rather liked the visits of the tomato girl, who came most days in search of a few coins in exchange for a few tomatoes. But right now Aisha irritated her, standing there in her rags, cloaked in need.

"I don't want any tomatoes this morning," Jillian said. Aisha grinned. She understood almost no English. She lifted the plate of tomatoes from her head and began to select the best ones, firm as Madam liked, from the little tomato pyramids arranged so neatly on the tray.

"Fifty fifty," said Aisha, holding up four tomatoes.

"Okay," Jillian said finally, kicking the tap closed. "Give me two piles. For one hundred conies." She went inside, put the kettle on the stove, lit the flame, then searched the basket of odds and ends on her table for a hundred-coni note. She tried to make out the face on the bill, but the brown note was caked with grime — she wondered which of the country's leaders it was.

She was studying the note as she came around the garage, looked up in surprise when she heard the sound of water running and saw Aisha squatted beside the tank.

"What do you think you're doing?" Jillian shouted.

Aisha looked up, startled. She leapt away from the water tank and upset the jug she had been holding under the tap. She and Jillian stared at the yellow plastic jug that had once held motor oil. It lay on its side and vomited the water out in glugs that sounded human.

"Watah, Madam," said the girl, timidly.

"No water," Jillian said.

"No watah," said the girl, pointing across the main road to her neighbourhood of mud and thatch huts.

Rage flared inside Jillian. It was not reasonable, but rage never was. It moved away from the small and fragile girl, snarling like a fanged beast as it turned back on itself at its source somewhere deep inside her. There was something new and dark and awful in there, in her gut, more malignant than cancer.

She picked up the padlock and snapped it shut on the faucet. The girl flattened herself on the ground, flinging one arm over her head in self-defence. Jillian's rage evaporated; shame flooded in, nauseating her.

She sighed. "It's not that I don't want to give you water, Aisha," she said, trying to sound gentle. "But I can't give water to everyone. I know you need water, but if I give you water, I have to give everyone water. You should all march to the sewerage corporation and break it down. As long as you can come to me, the real problem will never be solved . . . "

The girl was crawling away from her, trying to get the tray of tomatoes onto her head and to retrieve the water jug at the same time.

"No, don't do that. It's okay. I'm sorry." Jillian moved towards her, wanting to make amends, to stroke the girl's small bony shoulders that poked out through gaping holes in her pink T-shirt. But Aisha lunged out of her reach and started to run. Tomatoes rolled off the tray, and the empty water jug swung from her hand as Aisha ran towards the gate.

"Come back, I'll give you some water," Jillian said, but the girl was already through the gate and across the road, too far away to hear. Jillian picked up the fallen tomatoes, cradling them against her stomach, and wondered what had happened to her, when she had become so hard.

The power came on at dusk, but the water was still off when she got up the next day. She listened vaguely to the morning news from former Yugoslavia. Did she care what happened in Herza-something? What world *did* she belong to?

Then she headed out for a day in the villages, where she would explain, again, the credit system and how the repayment had to be made. The money, even the few dollars the women's groups were allocated, always came with rules attached.

On the way home that evening she engaged Bukari in another discussion about local corruption, asked him how the water corporation could get away with the deliberate water cuts.

"They're just wicked people," he said. "They want to chop our money, that's all."

"But why don't the people do something about it?" she asked. "I mean, demonstrate, or . . . "

He didn't allow her to finish. "The police will shoot us or arrest us. They always do."

She thought that over, wanted to reply but couldn't find anything to say. Instead she stared out the window at the crumbling mud houses, leaning on each other, one after the other, home to thousands. Stones were laid in rows on top of the sheets of tin roofing to keep them from blowing off. The rusted heaps of tractors, the rusted containers and the wrecks of cars made her angry at her own world that foisted machinery, doomed to break down, on the country and turned it into a junkyard. Discarded plastic bags, in which peddlers sold water, were caught up in the dust devil ahead. Mangy dogs loped across the road with its valleys and humps, not a road at all any more. Gangs of boys, bare but for scraps of cloth that were once shorts, chased tires they propelled with sticks. They were laughing, and they waved as she passed.

She noticed that the concrete skeleton they called Independence Valley looked deserted. "There doesn't seem to be anyone fetching water there, Bukari. Does that mean the water came back on?" she asked.

"No," he said. "Three girls fell in yesterday. They were fetching water from below and there was some pushing because the stairway is very narrow and they fell in. One of them couldn't get out. So no one will go there now."

"That's terrible," she said. Jillian turned around to look again at the abandoned half-finished building in that gravel wasteland, but her view was obscured by the cloud of red dust their Land Rover left in its wake.

———

The next morning she was up early to watch the sun splash light and early heat across the compound. She ran from the kitchen when she heard the "Morning. Morning!" She tore outside, barefoot, to catch Aisha and make amends for her behaviour two days earlier.

It wasn't Aisha. This girl was smaller, even thinner. The plate of tomatoes looked as if it could squash her. Aisha's junior sister perhaps. "Tomato," said the girl.

"Where's Aisha?" Jillian asked. "My tomato girl?"

"Fifty fifty," said the girl.

"Aisha *bene?*" Jillian persisted, trying out one of the few Goroni words she had learned over the past year.

The girl cocked her head to one side and answered in Goroni. Jillian held up her hand. "Wait, I'm coming," she said, dashing inside to find her Goroni-English handbook.

"Now," she said, "say that again, *biala, biala.*" Slowly, slowly. The girl repeated herself, slowly. Aisha . . . something. Just one word. Jillian flipped through the dictionary, looking for a word that resembled the one the girl kept repeating: *Ofieme.*

There it was. *Ofieme.* "Drowned?" she whispered.

The girl nodded and the plate of tomatoes tipped dangerously. "Fifty fifty," she said.

The Glace Bay Miner's Museum

SHELDON CURRIE

The first time I ever saw the bugger, I thought to myself, him as big as he is, me as small as I am, if he was astraddle on the road, naked, I could walk under him without a hair touching. That's the thought I had; he was coming down the aisle of the White Rose Café, looking to the right and looking to the left at the people in the booths. The size of him would kill you, so everybody was looking at him. I was looking at him too because I knew all the booths were full except mine. I was sitting in the last one, my back to the kitchen, so I could see everybody coming and going. He had a box in his hand, looked like a tool box, and I was wondering if he'd sit with me and show me what was in his box. I made a dollar keeping house for MacDonalds and came to the Bay to spend it on tea and chips and sit in the restaurant and watch the goings on. The goings on was the same old thing: girls sitting with boys and boys sitting with girls, trying to pair off to suit themselves, and making a cup of tea and chips last as long as they could so they wouldn't have to leave. It was hard to find somebody on the street. You could go to the show and sit in the dark and hope somebody would sit next to you and hold your hand, but that cost money too and hardly ever worked. It worked once for me, this fella sat beside me, and I knew it was a chance because the theatre was almost empty. I figured he saw my hair before the lights went out. I had this lovely long hair. I was lucky enough, I bought a nut bar on the way in and I gave him a piece. He took my hand. He had a huge hand. Pan shovel hands we used to call people with hands like that. We used to think you got them from loading coal with a pan shovel. My hand disappeared in his in the dark. He put his big hand on top of my knees which I was keeping together. It felt like he had taken my hand off at the wrist and moved it up to my knee. I couldn't see it and for a minute I couldn't feel it and I was sitting there looking at his big mitt and wondering if my hand was still in it. Then it started to sweat and I could feel it again. We stayed like that through two shows. We never said a word. When we came out we walked down to Senator's Corner and down Commercial Street to Eaton's where the buses stopped. We never said a word. We stood next to each other and I stared at the Medical Hall and he stared at Thompson and Sutherland. Then the bus came for No. 11 and he got on. He didn't even look out the window at me.

I was sitting alone in the White Rose because none of the boys would sit with me and none of the girls would because the boys wouldn't. For one thing I had a runny nose. They called me names and if a boy went with me they called him names. George McNeill walked home with me from school one day — it was on the way to his house anyway — and I heard in the cloakroom next day — they had a vent between the boys' cloakroom and the girls' — I heard somebody from another class say to him — "I see you're taking out snot-face these days. Don't forget to kiss her on the back of her head."

For another thing I screwed a couple of boys when I was a little girl. I didn't know you weren't supposed to, but I didn't want to anyway, and I wouldn't but this fella offered me a nickel and I never had a nickel. Then he asked if I'd do it with his cousin and I said no. But then he came to me himself, the cousin, and told me he went to the washhouse every Saturday his father was on day shift for five times and waited for him to come up and waited for him to shower and followed him to pay office and asked him for a dime, and had to promise to cut enough sticks for the week. I found out later he sold two quarts of blueberries that he stole, but he wanted to tell me a nice long story. Anyway I felt sorry for him, and he had fifty cents. So he told me to meet him up in the woods by the Scotchtown road between the bootleg pits and Rabbit Town. I didn't know then that he didn't want to walk up there with me. Anyway, I didn't really screw either one of them because they didn't know how to do it and it was too late before I could tell them, although, God knows, I knew little enough myself of the little there is to know. They didn't walk home with me either, neither one. But they told everybody I was a whore. So I was not only a whore but a snot-nosed whore. You could hardly blame the boys and girls for not sitting with me.

So I was sitting alone in the last booth at the White Rose Café when this giant of a man with a box in his hand came bearing down the aisle looking left and right, and he kept on coming until he got to my booth and saw there was nobody there but me. I remember it seemed like it got darker when he stood in front of me, he blacked out so much light with the size of him. He had on a big lumberjack shirt. I thought, when he stood there holding his box, before he said anything, I said to myself, I wish he'd pick me up and put me in his shirt pocket.

"Can I put this here on your table?" he said; he pointed his chin at his box.

"Suit yourself," I said to him awful loud. He was so big, I thought I had to yell for him to hear me.

"Can I sit down, then?" he said.

"Suit yourself again," I said. So he put his box on the table and sat down opposite me, and I could feel his knees about an inch from mine. I could feel the heat coming from his knees. I could have exploded I was so happy. But I kept my lips tight.

The waitress pounced on us right away. "Hi, snooker," she said. She was dying to find out who this fella was. So was everybody in the restaurant. I could see the ones facing me. I could feel the ones not facing me wishing they had sat on the other side of the booth. Nobody knew who he was. I just wanted to know what he had in the box.

"Something?" Kitten said, and looked at me and looked at him.

"I had something," I said.

"Would you have something else?" the man said. "I'd like to buy you a bite to eat if you don't mind." I near died. That was the first polite thing anybody ever said to me since my father got killed.

"I don't mind if I do," I said.

"Well, what is it then?" Kitten said. "What do you want?"

"I'll have a cup tea and an order of chips," I said.

"Will you now?" Kitten said.

"Yes," I said. "I will."

"I'll have the same," the man with the box said.

"Thank you," Kitten said, and wrote it down, saying very slowly to herself like she was talking to a baby: *Two orders of chips and two orders of tea*. "That will be fine," she said, looking at me and looking at him. "I'll go see if we got any."

She went away and I looked at my little hands and I could feel my knees getting warmer and warmer. I couldn't think of anything to say. My back was cold and I thought I might start to shake if I didn't talk, but I couldn't think of anything. I looked up at him and he was looking at his hands. He had a lot to look at. Nobody said a word till Kitten came back. "Here you are," she said, "two teas and two chips. Medium rare."

We ate a few chips and took the bags out of our teas and put them in the ashtray. Then he said, "Well, what do you think?"

"I think you're the biggest son of a bitch I ever saw," I said.

He looked at me then when I said that as if I just came in, and the look of him made me feel as if I just came in. I felt my back get warm, and I leaned back against the back of the booth. He started to laugh. He must of laughed for two minutes but it seemed to me two days, and it sounded like somebody playing some kind of instrument I never heard before. When he stopped, he said, "Know what I think?"

"What?" I said.

"I think you're the smallest son of a bitch I ever saw."

Then we both of us laughed for two minutes. Then we talked about the weather as if nothing happened, but I could feel the heat on my knees. After a while he said, "Well now. What's your name?"

"Margaret MacNeil."

"Well now, Miss MacNeil. It's been a pleasure meeting you. Do you come here often?"

"Every week at this same exact time," I said.

"Very well then," he said. "Perhaps we'll meet again. What do you think?"

"Suit yourself," I said.

"Okay," he said, "I will. My name is Neil Currie." Then he got up and opened the box.

When he got the box open it was full of brown sticks and a plaid bag. Bagpipes! I never seen bagpipes before. Never knew there was any. Never heard them before. God only knows I heard them enough since. He pulled it all out of the box and started putting sticks on sticks till it was together; then he pumped it up. It snarled a couple of times, then when he had it between his arm and his ribs he came down on it with his elbow and it started to squeal, and everybody in the café either leaned out or stood up to look at the God-awful racket.

Then his fingers started jumping and it started playing something I don't know what it was. To me it sounded like a cut cat jumping from

214

table to table and screaming like a tiger. Before you knew it the Chinaman came from the front. He didn't stop, he just slowed down to squeeze by the man and the pipes. When he got through he walked backwards a minute toward the kitchen and yelled, "Get that goddam fiddle out of here." Then two big Chinamen came out of the kitchen; I always thought Chinamen were small until I saw them two. They each had a hand of cards like they were playing cards and kept their hands so nobody could peek at them while they were out. They were just as big as Neil was, maybe bigger, and you never saw how fast two men can put one man and an armload of bagpipes out of a restaurant and into the street.

I went out after him. I took him out his box. I passed the Chinamen coming back in. They didn't do nothing to him, just fired him to the street and went back with their cards. He was sitting on the street. I helped him stuff his bagpipes in his box. Then he stood up and took the box in his hand. He looked down at me and he said, "One thing I thought a Chinaman would never have the nerve to do is criticize another man's music. If I wasn't drunk, I'd give you my pipes to hold and I'd go back in there and get the shit kicked out of me."

"Where do you live?" I said.

"I have a room down on Brookside."

"Want me to walk down?"

"Where do you live?"

"I live in Reserve."

"Let's get the bus, then. I'll see you home. Sober me up. Perhaps you could make us a cup of tea."

"Okay," I said.

"You live with your father an mother?"

"I live with my mother and grandfather. My father got killed in the pit. Come on. It's starting to rain. My brother too."

The rain banged on the roof of the bus all the way to Reserve and when we got off it was pouring and muddy all the way up to the shack where we lived. My father built it himself because, he said, he never would live in a company house. He had to work in the goddam company mine, but he didn't have to live in the goddam company house, with god only knows who in the next half. My mother said he was too mean to pay rent, but only when he wasn't around did she say it. She only said it once to his face. But he got killed. They had a coffin they wouldn't even open it.

It was dark even though it was only after seven. It was October. We had to take off our shoes and wring out our socks from walking in puddles up the lane. We didn't have a real road in. Just a track where they came with groceries and coal. We hung them down the side of the scuttle and our jackets on the oven door. "I'll get you an old pair of daddy's pants soon's mama gets out of the bedroom. You're the first one I ever saw could fit."

"You're right on time, Marg," Mama said. "I think I'll run up the Hall. Who you got here?"

"You'll get soaked."

"I know, but I better go. I might win the thousand."

"This is Neil Currie."

"Where'd you find him?"

"In the Bay."

"Are you from the Bay?"

"No. I just came."

"Where from?"

"St. Andrews Channel."

"Never heard of that. You working in the pit?"

"I was. I started but I got fired."

"You look like you could shovel. Why'd they fire you?"

"I wouldn't talk English to the foreman."

"You an Eyetalian?"

"No."

"Well, I have to run or I'll be late. Don't forget your grandfather, Margie. I hit him about an hour ago so he's about ready."

"Okay Mom. Hope you win it."

"Me too."

That was my mother's joke, about hitting my grandfather. Anytime a stranger was in she said it. He had something wrong with his lungs. Every hour or two he couldn't breathe and we'd have to pound him on the chest. So somebody had to be in the house every minute. When Mama left I got Neil the pants. "You might as well keep them," I said. "They won't fit nobody else ever comes around here." Then I went in to change my dress.

I expected to be a while because I wanted to fix myself up on my mother's makeup. It was her room, though I had to sleep in it and she had a lot of stuff for makeup. My brother slept in the other room with my grandfather. We just had the three. Where you come in was the kitchen and that's where you were if you weren't in the bedroom or in the cellar getting potatoes. But I didn't stay to fix up because I just got my dress half on when he started wailing on his bag and pipes.

I stuck my head out the door. "Are you out of your brain?" I yelled but he couldn't hear with the noise. So I got my dress all on and went out and put my hands over two of the holes the noise came out. They have three holes. He stopped. "My grandfather," I said, "you'll wake him up." I no sooner said it when the knock came. "There he is now," I said. "I'm sorry," he said. "I forgot your grandfather."

"It's okay," I said, "I think it must be time of his hit now anyway." I went in and I got the surprise of my life.

He could talk, my grandfather, but he didn't. It hurt him to talk after he came back from the hospital once with his lungs and he quit. I don't know if it got better or not because he never tried again; same as he quit walking after he got out of breath once from it. He took to writing notes. He had a scribbler and a pencil by him and he wrote what he wanted. thump me chest; dinner; beer; water; piss pot; did she win; did you pay the lite bill, then put on the lites; piece of bread; ask the priest to come; time to go now father; I have to get me thump; no, Ian'll do it. See, that's just one page. He had a whole stack of scribblers after a while. They're all here. We have them numbered.

So I went in, and I was after sitting him up in place to do his thump; you had to put him in a certain way. And he started to bang his long finger on the scribbler he had in his hand.

"Tell him to play."

"Well, Christ in harness," I said, which is what my grandfather used to say when he talked and now I always said it to tease him. "Watch your tong," he wrote me one day. "Somebody got to say it now you're dumb," I said. "If I don't it won't get said."

"Do you want your thump?" I said, and he wrote in his scribbler, "No, tell him to play." So I told Neil to play. "Isn't that lovely?" Neil said and laughed. And he played. It sounded to me like two happy hens fighting over a bean, and when he stopped and asked me if I knew what tune it was I told him what it sounded like to me and he laughed and laughed.

"Do you like the tune?"

"It's not too bad."

"Would you see if your grandfather liked it?" So I went. And he was sound asleep with his scribbler in his hands on his belly. He wrote on it: "When he comes back ask him if he can play these." And he had a list I couldn't read. Here it is here in the scribbler:

Guma slan to na ferriv chy harish achune

Va me nday Ben Doran

Bodichin a Virun

Falte go ferrin ar balech in eysgich

I took the scribbler out and showed it to Neil and he said he would. "I'll have to practice a little."

"Play some more now," I asked him. "Play that one again."

"What one?"

"The one you put him to sleep with."

"Mairi's wedding."

"Yes."

"About the bean and the chickens."

"Yes."

So he played. I was getting interested in it. My foot started tapping and my knees which I had been holding together all night fell apart. As soon as he saw that, I was sitting on a chair against the wall, he came over and came down to kiss me. I put my two feet on his chest and pushed. I was hoping to fire him across the room but nothing happened. It kept him off, but he just stayed there with his chest on my feet looking up my leg and me with a hole in my underwear.

"What's the matter with you?" he said.

I said, "Just because you play that thing don't mean you can jump me." He ran his hand down my leg and nearly drove me nuts.

"Fuck off," I said. I thought that would shock him back but he just stayed there leaning against my sneakers. He tried to take my hand but I just put the two of them behind the chair.

"I won't jump you till we're married," he said.

"Married?" I said. "Who'd marry you? You're nothing but a goddam Currie." Then he started laughing and moved back.

"And why wouldn't you marry a goddam Currie?" he said.

"Because they just come into your house, play a few snarls on their pipes, and they think you'll marry them for that."

"Well, well, well," he said. "I'll tell you what. I'll play for you every night till you're ready. And I'll make you a song of your own."

"What kind of song?"

"I don't know, we'll wait and see what I can make."

"Well, well, well," I said. "I want a song a person can sing so I'll be sure what it's saying."

"Okay, I'll make you two. One to sing and one to guess at."

"Good," I said. "If I like them. Well who knows what may happen."

"What would you like for the singing one?"

"I don't know."

"Well, what's the happiest thing in your life or the saddest?"

"They're both the same," I said. "My brother. Not the one living here now but my older brother, Charlie. We called him Charlie Dave, though Dave was my father's name. That was to tell him from the other Charlie MacNeils. There's quite a few around here. Charlie Pig and Charlie Spider. And a lot more. Charlie Big Dan. I really liked Charlie Dave."

"What happened to him?"

"He got killed in the pit with my father."

"How old was he?"

"He was just sixteen. He used to fight for me. Wouldn't let anybody call me names."

"He mustn't have been in the pit very long?"

"Not even a year. He started working with my grandfather just before he had to quit for his lungs. Then he started with my father. Then he was killed. They were both killed. He was good in school too, but he got married so he had to work. They didn't even have a chance to have their baby."

"What happened to his wife?"

"Oh, she's still around. She's nice. She had her baby. A sweet baby. They live up in the Rows. In a company house. With her mother and her sister." I started to cry then so I made a cup of tea.

———

So after that he came back every night and it was nothing but noise. My mother took to going out every night. When I told her he asked me to get married, she said: "That man will never live in a company house. You'll be moving out of one shack and into another."

"I can stand it," I said.

"You can stand it," she said. "You can stand it. And is he going to work?"

"He's going to look up at No. 10."

"Good," she said. "He can work with Ian. They can die together. And you can stand it. And you can live in your shack alone. Stand it, then."

The first night, after he played one of the songs my grandfather asked him, he played one he said he made for me. I loved it. It made me grin, so I kept my head down and I held my knees together with my arms.

"What's the name of it?" I asked.

"The name of it is *Two Happy Beans Fighting Over A Chicken*."

"Go whan," I said.

"Do you like it?"

"Not bad. What's the real name?"

"*Margaret's Wedding*," he said.

"Christ in harness." I almost let go my knees.

The next night he played it again and he played another one for my grandfather. Then we went up the Haulage Road to No. 10 to get Ian. I always went to walk home with him because when he started he was scared when he was night shift to come home alone in the dark. I kept on ever since. Sometimes he had a girl friend would go. I never asked him if he stopped being scared. He never often had to try it alone. He didn't come home that night, he decided to work a double shift. So we walked back alone that night, but we took to going up together for Ian when he was night shift till Neil got the job there too and they were buddies in the pit so they worked the same shifts and came home together till we got married and moved to the Bay.

They fought like two mongrels. Miners said they never saw two men enjoy their work so much because it kept them close enough so they could fight every minute. Then on Sunday afternoon they came to our home and they sat in the kitchen and drank rum and played forty-five and fought and fought and fought.

What they fought about was politics and religion, or so they said. Ian would tell Neil that the only hope for the miner was to vote CCF and get a labour government.

"How are you going to manage that?"

"By voting. Organizing."

"When is that going to happen?"

"We have to work for it."

"The future?"

"Yes, the future."

"There's no future," Neil would say.

"There has to be a future."

"See in the bedroom, Ian. See your grandfather. That's the future."

"Well he's there. The future is there."

"He's there all right. He can't breathe, he can't talk, he can't walk. You know the only thing he's got? Some old songs in his head, that he can hardly remember, that your father hardly ever knew and you don't know at all. Came here and lost their tongues, their music, their songs. Everything but their shovels."

"Too bad you wouldn't lose yours. Have a drink and shut up."

"I will not shut up. However, I will have a drink."

He seemed so drunk to me I thought it'd spill out his mouth if he took more; but he took it. "Nothing left," he said. "Nothing. Only thing you can do different from a pit pony is drink rum and play forty-five."

Ian pointed to the cat curled up on the wood box. "Look, it's almost seven o'clock," he said. "Why don't you take that tomcat and go to Benediction since you like to sing so much. Then you can sing with him tonight. Out in the bushes. He goes out same time as you leave."

"What are you talking about?"

"You're buddies. You and the cat. You can sing near as good as he can. He's near fond of religion as you are."

"All I can say," Neil said, "is pit ponies can't go to church."

"Is that all you can say?" Ian said. "Well, all I can say is, if a pit pony went to church, that would do him some lot of good."

"Ian, you do not understand what I am talking about."

"That is the God's truth for you, Neil. Now why don't you go on the couch and have a lay down."

And that's the way Sunday afternoon and evening went. We could've been out for a walk, just as easy, and more fun.

But that second night that he came we walked down the Haulage Road, pitch black, and he sang me the song I asked him for about my brother. I sang it over and over till I knew it by heart. He sang it to me. "That's lovely," I told him.

I took him by the arm behind his elbow and slowed him down till he stopped and turned. I was crying but I told him anyway. "I'm going to get married to you." We kissed each other. Salt water was all over our lips. I think he must have been crying too. I wrote the song down in one of my grandfather's scribblers when we got back. Here it is here in this one here.

My brother was a miner
His name was Charlie David
He spent his young life laughing
And digging out his grave.

Charlie Dave was big
Charlie Dave was strong
Charlie Dave was two feet wide
And almost six feet long.

When Charlie David was sixteen
He learned to chew and spit
And went one day with Grandpa
To work down in the pit.

(chorus)

When Charlie David was sixteen
He met his Maggie June
On day shift week they met at eight
On back shift week at noon.

(chorus)

When Charlie David was sixteen
He said to June, "Let's wed"
Maggie June was so surprised
She fell right out of bed.

(chorus)

When Charlie David was sixteen
They had a little boy
Maggie June was not surprised
Charlie danced for joy

(chorus)

When Charlie David was sixteen
The roof fell on his head
His laughing mouth is full of coal
Charlie Dave is dead.

The next night when he came I told him I had to pay him back for his songs. I'd tell him a story.

"Okay," he said. "Tell me a story."

"This is a true story."

"That's the kind I like," he said.

"Okay. There was this fella worked in the pit, his name was George Stepenak, he was a Pole, they eat all kinds of stuff, took garlic in his can, used to stink. His can would stink and his breath would stink. The men used to tease him all the time, which made him cross. One day my father said, "George, what in the name of Jesus have you got in your can?"

"Shit," George said to my father.

"I know that," my father said. "But what you put on it to make it smell so bad?"

When my grandfather found out I told him a story to pay him back for the song, he wanted to tell him one. He wrote it out for him in a scribbler. Here it is here. Well he didn't write it all out, he just wrote it out for me to tell it.

"Tell about Jonny and Angie loading in '24, the roof so low they hadda take pancakes in their cans."

That's the way it went from then. Every night he'd come and play and sing. Me and my grandfather would tell or write stories. My brother even would sing when he was on day shift or back shift. But he worked a lot of night shift. That's the way it went till Neil got work. When he got work we got married as soon as he built this house. Soon as he got the job he said, "I got some land on North Street. I'll build a house before we get married. It's right on the ocean. You can hear the waves." And he did. He did. And you can see, it's no shack. He must have been a carpenter. Soon as the house was finished we got married and moved in. Him and my brother Ian were buddies by then, working the same shifts. They both got killed the same minute. I was up to Reserve keeping house for my mother when I heard the whistle. I heard the dogs howling for two nights before so soon's I heard the whistle I took off for the pit. They both just were taken up when I got there. They had them in a half-ton truck with blankets over them.

"Take them to Mama's," I said.

"We got to take them to hospital."

"You take them to Mama's, Art. I'll wash them and I'll get them to the hospital."

"Listen, snooker, the doctor's got to see them."

"I'll call the doctor."

"I can't."

"Listen, you bastard. Whose are they, yours or mine? You haven't even got an ambulance. I'll wash them, and wherever they go, they'll go clean and in a regular ambulance, not your goddam half-broken-down truck."

So he took them down to Mama's and they carried them in and put one on Mama's bed and one on the couch in the kitchen. I knew what to get. I saw Charlie Dave keep a dead frog for two years when he was going to school. I went to the Medical Hall and got two gallons. Cost me a lot. I got back as fast as I could. I locked the house before I left so's nobody could get in. Mama was visiting her sister in Bras d'Or and I didn't know when she'd be back.

When I got back, there was a bunch around the door. They started to murmur.

"Fuck off," I said. "I'm busy."

To make matters worse, my grandfather was left alone all that time. He died. Choked. I took his lungs. It wasn't so much the lungs themselves, though I think they were a good thing to take, though they don't keep too well, especially the condition he was in, as just something to remind me of the doctor who told him he couldn't get compensation because he was fit to work. Then I took Neil's lungs because I thought of them connected to his pipes and they show, compared to grandfather's, what lungs should look like. I was surprised to find people have two lungs. I didn't know that before. Like Neil used to say, look and ye shall see. I took Neil's tongue since he always said he was the only one around still had one. I took his fingers too because he played his pipes with them. I didn't know what to take from Ian, so I took his dick, since he always said to Neil that was his substitute for religion to keep him from being a pit pony when he wasn't drinking rum or playing forty-five.

Then my mother came in. She went hysterical and out the door. I had each thing in its own pickle jar. I put them all in the tin suitcase with the scribblers and deck of cards wrapped in wax paper and the half empty quart of black death they left after last Sunday's drinking and arguing. I got on the bus and came home to the Bay and put in the pipes and Neil's missal and whatever pictures were around. Then I took the trunk to Marie, my friend, next door and asked her to put it in her attic till I asked for it. Don't tell anybody about it. Don't open it. Forget about it. Then I came back here and sat down and I thought of something my grandmother used to sing, "There's bread in the cupboard and meat on the shelf, and if you don't eat it, I'll eat it myself." I was hungry.

I knew they'd come and haul me off. So I packed my own suitcase, Neil's really but mine now. They came with a police car and I didn't give them a chance to even get out of the car. I jumped right into the back seat like it was a taxi I was waiting for. I just sat right in and said, "Sydney River, please." Sydney River, if you're not from around here, is the cookie jar where they put rotten tomatoes so they won't spoil in the barrel. So they put me in till they forgot about me; then when they remembered me they forgot what they put me in for. So they let me go.

My mother lived in the house all the time I was away. I told her to, to keep it for me and give her a better place to live. When I got back I told her, "You can stay here and live with me, mother, if you like."

"Thanks anyway," she said. "But I'm not feeling too good. I think I'll go back to Reserve."

"So stay. I'll look after you."

"Yes, you'll look after me. You'll look after me. And what if I drop dead during the night?"

"If you drop dead during the night, you're dead. Dead in Glace Bay is the same as dead in Reserve."

"Yes. And you'll look after me dead too, I imagine. You'll look after me. What'll you do? Cut off my tits and put them in bottles?"

I said to her, "Mother, your tits don't mean a thing to me."

By then she had her suitcase packed and she left walking. "Have you got everything?" I called.

"If I left anything," she yelled back, "pickle it."

"Okay," I said. She walked. Then she turned and yelled, "Keep it for a souvenir."

"Okay," I yelled.

I was sorry after that I said what I said. I wouldn't mind having one of her tits. After all, if it wasn't for them, we'd all die of thirst before we had our chance to get killed.

Marie came over then with the suitcase and we had a cup of tea and she helped me set things up. We had to make shelves for the jars. Everything else can go on tables and chairs or hang on the wall or from the ceiling as you can see. Marie is very artistic, she knows how to put things around. I'm the cook. We give tea and scones free to anyone who comes. You're the first. I guess not too many people know about it yet. A lot of things are not keeping as well as we would like, but it's better than nothing. Perhaps you could give us a copy of your tape when you get it done. That might make a nice item. It's hard to get real good things and you hate to fill up with junk just to have something.

Notes on the Authors

JOAN BAXTER (b. 1955) grew up in Dartmouth, Nova Scotia, and now makes her home in Bamako, Mali, West Africa, where she is a correspondent for the BBC. In 2001 she received the Evelyn Richardson Award for her non-fiction book about Africa, *A Serious Pair of Shoes* (Pottersfield, 2000). "Act of God" is from her collection *Strangers Are Like Children* (Pottersfield, 1998).

CAROL BRUNEAU (b. 1956), a resident of Halifax, has published two collections of fiction, including *After the Angel Mill* (Cormorant, 1995) and *Depth Rapture* (Cormorant, 1998), which includes "The Tarot Reader." In 2001 she received the Thomas Raddall Award for Fiction for her novel, *Purple for Sky* (Cormorant, 2000).

LESLEY CHOYCE (b. 1951) is the author of over fifty books of fiction, poetry, non-fiction and children's literature. He is the publisher of Pottersfield Press at Lawrencetown Beach, Nova Scotia, and teaches part-time at Dalhousie University. One of his best-known works of fiction is *The Republic of Nothing* (Goose Lane, 1994). "Dance the Rocks Ashore" is from his collection *Dance the Rocks Ashore* (Goose Lane, 1997).

JOAN CLARK (b. 1934) was born in Liverpool, Nova Scotia, and lived in Sussex, New Brunswick, before making her home in St. John's, Newfoundland. She won the Canadian Authors' Association Award for Fiction for *The Victory of Geraldine Gull* (Macmillan, 1988), and her novel *The Dream Carvers* (Penguin, 1995) won the Geoffrey Bilson Award for historical fiction. "The Train Family" is from *Swimming Towards the Light* (Macmillan, 1990).

LYNN COADY (b. 1970) grew up on Cape Breton Island and lived in New Brunswick before moving to Vancouver. Her first novel, *Strange Heaven* (Goose Lane, 1998), won the Dartmouth Book Award and was a finalist for the Governor General's Award for Fiction. "Batter My Heart" appeared first in *The Fiddlehead* and is included in her second book, the story collection *Play the Monster Blind* (Doubleday Canada, 2000).

SHELDON CURRIE (b. 1934), a native of Reserve, Cape Breton, and a resident of Antigonish, Nova Scotia, taught for many years at St. Francis Xavier University. "The Glace Bay Miner's Museum" first appeared in the collection, *The Glace Bay Miner's Museum* (Deluge, 1979). It was the basis of the feature film, *Margaret's Museum*, which Currie subsequently rewrote as a novella, and it is included in the collection, *The Story So Far* (Breton Books, 1997).

HERB CURTIS (b. 1949) has lived all his life in New Brunswick; he moves between Fredericton and the Miramichi, where he guides visiting salmon fishermen. His masterpiece, *The Brennan Siding Trilogy* (Goose Lane, 1997), is a compilation of his first three novels, *The Americans Are Coming* (1989, 1999), *The Last Tasmanian* (1991, 2001) and *The Lone Angler* (1993). A different version of "The Party" appears in *The Last Tasmanian*.

WAYNE CURTIS (b. 1945) divides his time between Newcastle, New Brunswick, and Fredericton. He is the author of several books of essays about fishing, fishermen and the Miramichi River, two story collections, *Preferred Lies* (Nimbus, 1998) and *River Stories* (Nimbus, 2000), and two novels, *One Indian Summer* (Goose Lane, 1994), the source of "Heavy Ice," and *Last Stand* (Nimbus, 1999).

DAVID HELWIG (b. 1938) grew up in Ontario and lives in Belfast, Prince Edward Island. He founded the *Best Canadian Stories* series, and he is the author of sixteen books of fiction and numerous works of non-fiction, including poetry, memoir, documentary and translation. His most recent fiction is *Close to the Fire* (Goose Lane, 1999), a novella, and the novel, *The Time of Her Life* (Goose Lane, 2000). "Missing Notes" appeared in *Arts-Atlantic* (61) and was selected for *98: Best Canadian Stories*.

MAUREEN HULL (b. 1949) was born on Cape Breton Island and now lives on Pictou Island, Nova Scotia, in the Northumberland Strait, where she fishes lobsters with her husband. "Homarus Americanus" was published in *The Fiddlehead* and is included in her first collection, *Righteous Living* (Turnstone, 1999). Her work also appeared in the anthology, *Water Studies: New Voices in Maritime Fiction* (Pottersfield, 1998).

WAYNE JOHNSTON (b. 1958) grew up in Newfoundland and wrote his first novel, *The Story of Bobby O'Malley* (Oberon, 1985), while studying at the University of New Brunswick. *The Colony of Unrequited Dreams* (Knopf Canada, 1998), the source of "The Boot," won the Thomas Head Raddall Atlantic Fiction Prize and the Canadian Authors' Association Award for Fiction. His memoir, *Baltimore's Mansion* (Random House Canada, 1999), won the Charles Taylor Award for non-fiction. He lives in Toronto.

ALISTAIR MACLEOD (b. 1936) was born in Saskatchewan, grew up on Cape Breton Island, and spent his summers there while teaching creative writing at the University of Windsor. One of the world's foremost story writers, MacLeod has received many awards, including the IMPAC Dublin Literary Award for his first novel, *No Great Mischief* (McClelland & Stewart, 1999). "Clearances" is included in *Island: The Collected Stories of Alistair MacLeod* (McClelland & Stewart, 2000).

BERNICE MORGAN (b. 1935), a life-long Newfoundlander, lives in St. John's. Her stories have been published widely in literary journals, and in 1996, she was named Newfoundland Artist of the Year for her writing. Her novel *Waiting for Time* (Breakwater, 1994) won the Thomas Raddall Award for Fiction, and *Random Passage* (Breakwater, 1992) has been developed as a TV series. "Poems in a Cold Climate," which first appeared in *The Fiddlehead,* is from her collection, *The Topography of Love* (Breakwater, 2000).

DONNA MORRISSEY (b. 1956) grew up in the isolated western Newfoundland community of The Beaches, where, she says, "There were twelve families and we didn't talk to six of them." She studied at Memorial University in St. John's, lived in various other parts of Canada, and makes her home in Halifax. Her first novel, *Kit's Law* (Penguin, 1999), the source of "Grieving Nan," won the National Booksellers Association Libris Award and garnered international praise.

HELEN FOGWILL PORTER (b. 1939) was born in Newfoundland and lives in St. John's. "One Saturday" appeared in *The Pottersfield Portfolio* (1983) and was included in her collection, *A Long and Lonely Ride* (Breakwater, 1991). A memoir, *Below the Bridge*, appeared in 1980 (Breakwater), and she was honoured with the Newfoundland and Labrador Lifetime Achievement Award in 1993.

DAVID ADAMS RICHARDS (b. 1950) grew up in Newcastle, New Brunswick, near the Miramichi River, and lives in Toronto. He has received many honours, including the Governor General's Award and the Canada-Australia Prize, and his novel, *Mercy Among the Children* (Doubleday Canada, 2000), won the Giller Prize for fiction. The story reprinted in *Atlantica* is Chapter One of *The Bay of Love and Sorrows* (McClelland & Stewart, 1998).

ANNE SIMPSON (b. 1956), a native of Ontario, now lives in Antigonish, Nova Scotia, where she teaches writing at St. Francis Xavier University. "Dreaming Snow," originally published in *The Fiddlehead*, shared the Journey Prize in 1999, and her volume of poetry, *Light Falls Through You* (McClelland and Stewart, 2000), won the Atlantic Poetry Award. Her first novel, *Canterbury Beach* (Penguin, 2001), was a finalist for the Chapters/Robertson Davies Award.

JOHN STEFFLER (b. 1947), a Toronto native, lives in Corner Brook, Newfoundland, where he teaches at Sir Wilfred Grenfell College. His novel, *The Afterlife of George Cartwright* (McClelland & Stewart, 1992), won the Smithbooks/Books in Canada First Novel Award and the Thomas Head Raddall Atlantic Fiction Award. It was a finalist for the Governor General's Award and the Commonwealth First Novel Award. The version of Chapter Ten included in *Atlantica* appeared in *The Fiddlehead* (1991).

J.J. STEINFELD (b. 1946) has lived in Charlottetown, Prince Edward Island, since 1980. He has published one novel, *Our Hero in the Cradle of Confederation* (Pottersfield, 1987), and eight story collections, including *Anton Chekhov Was Never in Charlottetown* (Gaspereau, 2000). "The Coinciding of Sosnowiec, Upper Silesia, Poland, 1942, and Banff, Alberta, Canada, 1990" is from his collection, *Dancing at the Club Holocaust: Stories New and Selected* (Ragweed, 1993).

BUDGE WILSON (b. 1927) was born in Halifax, Nova Scotia, and lived in Kingston, Ontario, before moving back to North West Cove, Nova Scotia. A former commercial artist and photographer, she has written more than twenty books, many of them for children and young adults; her awards include the Ann Connor Brimer Award for children's literature. "Mr. Manuel Jenkins" is included in her story collection *The Leaving* (Anansi, 1991).

Acknowledgements

The editor and publisher are grateful for kind permission to reprint the stories in *Atlantica: Stories from the Maritimes and Newfoundland*.

"Act of God" from *Strangers Are Like Children* (Pottersfield Press) copyright © 1998 by Joan Baxter, reprinted by permission of the author. "The Tarot Reader" from *Depth Rapture* by Carol Bruneau, published by Cormorant Books 1998, reprinted by permission of the publisher. "The Train Family" from *Swimming Towards the Light* (Macmillan) copyright © 1990 by Joan Clark, reprinted by permission of the author. "Batter My Heart" extracted from *Play the Monster Blind* by Lynn Coady, copyright © Lynn Coady, 2000, reprinted by permission of Doubleday Canada, a division of Random House of Canada Limited. "Dance the Rocks Ashore" from *Dance the Rocks Ashore* copyright © 1997 by Lesley Choyce, reprinted by permission of Goose Lane Editions. "The Glace Bay Miner's Museum" from *The Story So Far: 11 Short Stories by Cape Breton's Sheldon Currie* copyright © 1997 by Sheldon Currie, reprinted by permission of Breton Books. "The Party" from *The Last Tasmanian* copyright © 1991, 2001 by Herb Curtis, reprinted by permission of Goose Lane Editions. "Heavy Ice" from *One Indian Summer* copyright © 1994 by Wayne Curtis, reprinted by permission of Goose Lane Editions. "Missing Notes" copyright © 1998 by David Helwig, reprinted by permission of the author. "Homarus Americanus" from *Righteous Living* copyright © 1999 by Maureen Hull, reprinted by permission of Turnstone Press. "The Boot" extracted from *The Colony of Unrequited Dreams* by Wayne Johnston, Vintage Canada Edition, 1999, copyright © 1998 by Wayne Johnston, reprinted by permission of Alfred A. Knopf Canada, a division of Random House Canada. "Clearances" from *Island: The Collected Stories of Alistair MacLeod* by Alistair MacLeod, used by permission of McClelland & Stewart Ltd., *The Canadian Publishers*. "Poems in a Cold Climate" from *The Topography of Love* copyright